dancing *in* quicksand

dancing *in* quicksand

LUCILLE N. PAYNE

To Del Martin, for her pioneering leadership against "wife battering."

To Susan Koppelman, for putting domestic violence into historical perspective.

To the Markets, Posses, and Saints everywhere – for being there.

Come, sing a song with me,
come sing a song with me,
come sing a song with me,
that I might know your mind.
And I'll bring you hope
when hope is hard to find.
And I'll bring a song of love
and a rose in the wintertime.

—Carolyn McDade

TABLE OF CONTENTS

PART ONE

PART TWO

PART ONE

CHAPTER 1

Ash Wednesday

Brooklyn, NY, mid-1990s

THE DOOR CREAKED OPEN. By the *swish* and *swosh* of cloth on cloth, she knew two of them approached. She lay still, eyes closed, chest pressing into the bed. There was rustling at the nightstand. *"Pleease Daddy,* can we wake Mom up?"

"I told you, no," he whispered. "Come on, we're already late for school."

She followed their footfalls out the room, through the hall, down the stairs, sitting up in the bed when she heard the front door shut. Morning was rapidly invading the room, the ratio of shadows to objects now favoring the latter. She eyed the tray they had left on the nightstand. It held her breakfast and two birthday gifts. She donned her robe, downed two aspirins and carried the tray to the kitchen.

Jelly was smeared on the counter, a piece of burnt toast had been tossed in the sink, and snippits of wrapping paper were scattered on the floor. She placed the tray on the table. After making sure the front door was locked, she flipped to page 29 in her Mexican cookbook and retrieved the want ad she'd torn from Sunday's Classified. The print was tiny; it hurt to squint. She plopped three ice cubes in her orange juice glass and reread the ad while resting the glass on her cheek:

CAN YOU SPELL "TOMATO?" Active, computer-literate woman seeks active, computer-literate woman to edit half-century of work journals for photojournalist's memoir. Four weeks. Flex hours. Good pay. Must like cats and chili. Call Lydia Wright for the details....

It was the oddest want ad she'd ever added to her Leap Year File – a ragtag collection of job opportunities buried on page 29 and 366 of her rarely used cookbooks. A 'half-century' of photo journals! This women must be her mother's generation...and the job, a perfect birthday gift – escaping the present while divining the past with a lovely old woman for four weeks. She cringed sipping the juice and tongued a tooth on the right side of her mouth. Closing her eyes, she spelled *tomato* out loud then dialed the Wright number, *for the details*.

"Yeah. What's up?"

"I'm calling about the ad in Sunday's paper – is the job still open?"

"Open for discussion. What are ya good for?"

She was taken aback by the question.

If ya good for nothing, why'd ya call?"

"I didn't say I was good for nothing!"

"Well, I don't read minds, Missy, and silence is an empty page. Fill in the blanks, or kindly get off the horn."

"My name is Pinch O'Malley. I have a Masters in English, was a Teaching Assistant in college, and I taught fourth grade…before my daughter was born." She paused, expecting a response, none came. "I'll be available in two weeks, if that's okay."

"What's ya name again?"

"Pinch O'Malley."

"*Pinch?* That's a weird one."

"I've been 'Pinch' for 40 years. Being 'Lydia' would be weird."

She regretted the jibe immediately. Mama was right; she needed to curb her tongue. Before she could apologize, the woman shouted *Touché Libby*, whatever that meant, followed by a raucous laugh that ended in a thunderous coughing fit. "Are you okay, Miss Wright?"

"Just my lungs getting even for too many years on the butts. Ya got wit, Pinch O'Malley. I like that. But dump the title – name's, *Lydia*. Okay, here's the poop. Pay ya $400 bucks a week for 15 hours of time. First five days ya work here. You can pick the days and time. After that ya can work on ya own except on Fridays. Fridays we meet here at 9am, breaking bread, chewing the fat, and getting a read on where we are and where we're going. Two more things…. We're doing *my* memoir, weeding *my* garden, so keep ya personal life, personal, if ya get my drift. Secondly, I demand honesty. Rubs ya wrong to give and take the truth, best go fish in someone else's pond. So *Pinnch* – ready to give it a go?"

Pinch slumped in her chair. She'd hoped to work with a gentle soul not this hacking crone. "I'll have to pass, Lydia. I like to go to church Friday mornings during Lent."

"Then come when ya done."

"It's not just that. I've got a nine-year-old daughter who—"

"*Jeez Louise.* Ain't even started, and we're already in ya garden. What's ya daughter got to do with it? Ain't hiring her."

"Excuse me, but I need to be available wh—"

"Am I talking too fast for ya, Missy? Said I was flex on time and most days." Her voice softened. "So, what's the real problem, Pinch?"

"I can leave my personal life home, and I'd try to be honest, b—"

"What's this *try* stuff? Ya tell the truth, or ya don't!"

Pinch slipped the ad back in the cookbook and slammed the cover shut. "The truth is, the job appeals to me, but you don't. I'd have a hard time disagreeing with you on editorial decisions. And another thing, I find it rude that you keep interrupting me."

"Rude I can work on, but let's be clear. Ain't paying ya to kiss up. Paying for ya honest opinion. What I do with that is none of ya business. Ya business is pulling pertinent facts from my photo diaries and merging them with the person I am today. A woman you'll grow to love in a week!"

"Am I fired if I fail to love you in a week?"

"Week works for most. Anal retentives take longer. Since ya sound like that persuasion, take a laxative tonight and call tomorrow with ya decision."

"Fat chance!" Pinch said. But the line was already dead.

Steve's gift, the smaller of the two on the tray, came in a chic *Tiffany & Co.* box. Inside was an opal ring. Its stone was huge, in a teardrop cut, and shimmered like liquid stardust when moved. She hated that she loved it and clapped the case shut. Katie's gift, a tiny handmade mirror, was awkwardly wrapped and came with a poem. *Roses are red, violets are blue, I hope when I grow up, I look just like you! Happy Birthday, Mom. Love, Katie.* Pinch brought the mirror to her face then shuddered – the eye of an ugly Stranger looking back! It was not the first time she shared a birthday with Ash Wednesday…but it was the first time her face was "marked" before getting ashes at the church.

Three coats of makeup and a pair of wide sunglasses helped keep the ugliness from view.

A dense and glaring fog shrouded the Brooklyn streets, a cool breeze making the seven-block walk to the church a dismal affair. Pinch pulled up the collar on her raincoat. Tightening her scarf, she tucked in her chin, and pinned her arms close to her body. She plowed her hands into her pockets; one clutched her house keys, the other a set of rosary beads belonging to her father when he was a beat cop in Chicago. She fingered the beads and silently prayed, finding comfort in the ritual motion and rote recitation of *Our Fathers* and *Hail Marys*.

All the pews in the church were filled. The air in the sanctuary smelled like lit candles and wet wool. She walked up the side aisle loosening her scarf and unbuttoning her coat. But she quickly retreated, folding in with the adults standing in the back, when Katie's class rose from their pews to approach the altar for their ashes.

Katie's teacher, Sister Cecelia, stayed on to help administer ashes to the long line of adults. Pinch sat in one of the vacated pews studying her father's rosary beads while waiting for the crowd to thin out. The beads had arrived in the mail that morning…a birthday gift from her brother Kevin, a priest. They were dull black, and smaller than most. Were they with her father when he'd fought in Korea? Were they with him when he died on that snowy street in Chicago? Tears seared her cheek. She lowered her head and removed the sunglasses gently blotting her face then putting the glasses back on before joining the dwindlers approaching the altar. *"Remember thou art dust, and unto dust thou shall return,"* the nun said, her knuckles bumping the sunglasses while swiping the gritty, gray cross on Pinch's forehead.

Pinch cringed then quickly walked back down the aisle and stopped to light a red votive candle for each of her parents and another for her Grandma Rose. She lingered on the leather kneeler in the alcove, hypnotized by the flickering candle glow. And she wondered about today's somber ritual – this personal call for humility performed on a public stage.

Before going home, she lit a candle for the ugly Stranger in Katie's mirror.

"What's wrong?" Katie asked coming in from school, seeing Pinch at the kitchen table, an ice bag at her cheek.

"I hit myself in the face last night, opening the freezer to put the leftovers away."

Katie looked surprised.

"My fault," Pinch said. "I got distracted talking with Dad. I love my mirror, Honey! Thanks for such a beautiful birthday gift." Katie nodded and grabbed a snack. Then spreading her books on the dining room table, she quietly dove into her homework.

Steve came home two hours later bearing a smile and a flower bouquet. His only comment about Pinch's face was – "Statistics bear out that most accidents occur in the home." It was said during dinner and directed toward Katie.

Pinch called Lydia early the next morning and set up an interview for the following week…when the shadow beneath her eye faded deeper still.

CHAPTER 2

The Test

O N A SUNNY FRIDAY MORNING, nine days after their first conversation, Pinch took a bus to Lydia's apartment to discuss the memoir job. The location wasn't far from the public library where she researched medieval chivalry for Steve's book-in-progress, *The Horses of Camelot*. A man hosing the apartment sidewalk turned off the spray as she approached; the doorman tipped his brim holding open the lobby door. After verifying her visit at the reception desk, she took a mirrored elevator and eyed her reflection riding up to the 17th floor. She looked calm, but her stomach was in jitters. It'd been years since she'd gone on an interview. What if she said the wrong thing? And wasn't it odd, Lydia calling her anal retentive when Mama used to chide her for *not* holding back!

Lydia's door was dressed with a wreath that housed a nest and shiny blue egg; a feathered robin perched over the egg, its beak open, as if singing joyfully. Her hand hesitated over the bell. She looked down the hall. Both elevators waited, empty and idle, ready to abet a retreat. But something about the nesting bird stilled her fears. She took a deep breath and rang the bell. A heavy-set woman opened the door. "Hi…. Lydia?"

The woman giggled. "I'm her friend, Smith. You must be Pinch. Come in."

The apartment door opened to a long narrow room, a large picture window anchoring the far end. A tall bushy tree flanked one side of the window; hanging baskets of vines framed the other. Beyond this leafy portal stood the Statue of Liberty, gloriously dressed in the morning sun. Pinch stared at the breathtaking image til something jingled in the bushy tree where two cats suddenly dropped to the floor and strutted toward her like peacocks on parade. She bent down to pet them. "Hi there, kitties. And what are your names?"

"The black and white's, Wilbur. Orville's the calico."

Pinch's chin dropped as Lydia approached. "I'm sorry – I didn't know you were in a wheelchair."

"Sorry for what? These wheels are a gift. Ain't tied down with arthritis anymore, right Libby?"

"I think she went into the kitchen," Pinch said.

"*Who?*"

"Libby."

"Smith's in the kitchen. I'm talking to *Libby*." She pointed to the statue in the harbor.

Pinch blushed; Lydia seemed unfazed tossing catnip to the Wright "boys" fencing for a share of the goods. "Hey you guys, take it easy!" Lydia yelled, the frolicking felines jousting too close to a spray of balloons tethered to a laughing Buddha. "Have a seat, Pinch." Lydia pointed to the couch then with the help of two canes, rose from the wheelchair and lumbered toward a wingback chair under the leafy tree. "Ya not as small as I thought," she said settling into the chair.

"And you're not as big as you sound," Pinch said.

"What's size got to do with it!"

Pinch smiled then shrugged. "You're the one who brought it up."

Lydia pursed her lips, eyeing Pinch as if reading a menu. Pinch crossed her arms and looked out the window. When her eyes fell on the steely statue, she straightened up and gave Lydia her own body-scan. She looked to be in her mid-seventies, her face worn but animated, her jaw moving forward and back, as if chewing on a thought. A lone whisker beneath her chin stirred the air in time with the chewing motion. Her eyes were bright brown, their outer corners starred with crow's feet; a dull scar circling one eye extended from her eyebrow to her nose. Fleecy gray curls crowned her head, covering her ears. Bulky shoes visually balanced the mass on top of her head. Her presence exceeded her physical boundaries.

Lydia pointed at the floor and barked, "Ya got small feet, Pinch."

"I left my big ones home so I wouldn't step on yours."

The crow's feet deepened and the swinging jaw stopped. Lydia turned toward the window and shouted, "*Touché Libby! We got us a live one.*" She returned to her wheelchair. "C'mon, Pinchey. Are ya ready for some chili?"

Pinch followed her to the kitchen where Smith was placing three bowls on the table. A crockpot, pitcher of water, glasses, silverware, and napkins were already in place. Despite her physical challenges, Lydia moved with the grace of a cat in the meadow and made sure everything was set "just so" before leaving her wheels and sitting at the table. Smith filled the glasses with water and passed the French bread, while Lydia filled Pinch in on the job.

"Already picked my photos for the memoir. You'll be keying my journal for each into the computer. After that, we'll do a quickie interview on each of the pictures. Then you'll synthesize what I feel today with what I wrote when I took the shots." She uncovered the crockpot and sniffed the steam. Pinch picked up the scent. It didn't smell like chili…. "Damn," Lydia said, recapping the pot. "Forgot to do the test!"

Smith waved her hand in the air. "Do it while we're eating. I'm starving."

"Then eat, but me and Pinch will wait." She clasped her hands on the table, as if she was about to say grace, and explained the 'Tude Test to Pinch – a hiring tool she used to assess the attitude and aptitude of all potential employees. "Okay, Pinch, first question is, "How many *e's* in *tomato*?"

"None, unless there are more than one."

"How many *e's* in *chili*?"

"Ditto," Pinch said.

"Can rubber fly?"

"Excuse me?"

"Rubber. Can it fly?"

"No."

"*Aaank*. Next question. Can food be art?"

"Yes."

Lydia nodded. "Let's review. Ya aced English and Art but

11

failed Science. One more, then we'll eat, if there's anything left what with Smith choosing hunger over hospitality. Okay, Pinch, last question. What's the worst four-letter word in the world?"

Pinch blinked. "You want me to *say* it…while we're eating?"

Lydia peered into Pinch's empty bowl. "*You* ain't eating. Just spit it out."

The *f*-word never fell easy off her lips, and she wasn't about to 'spit it out' even if it cost the job. She turned to Smith. "Did you ever take this test?"

"Yes, back in the 70s, when Lydia was casting her comedy skits. I failed that question." Smith shrugged. "If you hear a word often enough, it tends to lose its sting."

Lydia tapped her fingers on the table. "Well, Pinch, gonna answer the question?"

"No."

"And ya won't spout it when ya feeling stressed?"

"No."

Lydia nodded. "Conversation is our flint. You'll fit in here fine. Ya quick-witted but not mean-spirited. And honest, in a reactive way, like barking back when I bug ya."

"Which will probably be often," Smith said. "But under that crust, Lydia's got a heart of gold that pumps red blood like normal people."

"If I was normal, Smith, I'd be harassing you about ya weight. With Tom traveling night and day, I'll be left teaching ya kid the ropes when ya croak from a heart attack."

"Well, I'm not dead yet," Smith said. "And just because *you* got religion, it doesn't mean I should reform." She looked at Pinch and rolled her eyes. "Last year we made a bet between me losing weight and Lydia quitting cigarettes. She won, but she's still annoyed."

"Damn right. Busted my butt to quit, and you're still padding yours."

"And thanks for not harassing me about it. Pipe down, and eat while it's hot."

Lydia ladled chili into her and Pinch's bowls, and silence filled the room...the other women immersed in the meal, Pinch buoyed by the atmosphere and lost in tomorrow's concerns. She thought of the fear in the eyes of the battered Stranger she'd seen in Katie's mirror on her birthday morn and later, the anger that had fueled the strength to call for the job in spite of Steve. But today's strength was nourished by acceptance, not fear, the steaming bowl of chili lending cover for the moisture in her eyes.

Lydia and Smith lapped up their chili with wads of crusty bread, their diligence allowing Pinch to cherry pick what to eat and what to push aside. She downed the tomatoes, peppers, beans, leaving the bacon untouched. When all else was eaten, she tried one of the pineapple chunks. The taste was surprisingly cordial, and she mumbled a compliment.

"What's that?" Lydia said.

"The pineapple seems out of place, but it works." The seasoning, however, scorched the inside of her mouth. She refilled her water glass noting the clock on the oven said 10:35. "Do you always eat chili at this hour of the morning?"

Lydia shook her head. "We're usually done by now."

Pinch asked Smith how long it took to make the meal.

"Don't look at me. I just got home from work. Lydia is the chili gourmet."

Lydia handed Pinch her cookbook, *Chili Nights, Warm Hearts*. "It's the third edition, Pinchey. Out in nine languages, too."

"Clever title," Pinch said.

Lydia chuckled. "Was doing a live radio gig in Beantown one night, and the deejay spits out, chili nights, warm *farts!* She started rocking in her chair like a kid on a cup and saucer ride, tears of laughter streaming down her cheeks. "Poor guy apologized the rest of night – the local 'Puritans' lighting up the switchboard threatening to kick him off the air. What a gas!" She wiped her tears. The smile remained.

"Why *chili...?*" Pinch said.

"Been around the world. Saw everyone did 'beans.' Played with the idea, ran the research, and drew up a plan. Naysayers pooh-poohed me...but went with my gut and been flying high on chili residuals since." Pinch returned the book. After scanning some of the recipes, she was glad the job was only four weeks. Lydia pointed to Pinch's bowl. "What's wrong with the bacon – got an issue with pork?"

"I don't eat meat on Friday's during Lent. I hope that's not a problem."

Lydia shook her head. "Got plenty of meatless wonders to choose from." Yes, Pinch thought, but at least I'll be spared the Chicken Liver Chili and other selections in the Organs section of the cookbook. She rose to collect the dirty dishes. "What are ya doing?"

"Cleaning up."

"Not ya problem. Sit right down. Got my own routine." Lydia sidled over to the sink filling it with hot soapy water. Smith stacked the dirty stuff on a tray and slid it over to Lydia who plunged them in the water. Pinch could have done it in half the time. But time was not the priority here. Lydia put cups on the table. "Coffee or tea? Pie or pie a la mode?"

"Dessert? You must be kidding!" Pinch said.

"I'll take that to mean a la mode."

Pinch was stuffed, but her mouth was on fire. "Could I just have the ice cream?"

"Sure. Milk or lemon with ya tea?"

"Milk. How did you know I want tea?"

"Revoke ya right to choose, ya get what's given to ya."

"Is this part of the test?"

"Life's a test – multiple choice. Take away the options, ya left with a life sentence."

Smith cleared her throat. "Chill out, Lydia. We're talking about food, not life-and-death situations."

"I'm talking 'bout habits. Good ones breed confidence. If ya practice on food, ya life's choices will be a piece of cake."

Smith shook her head. "I don't know where you come up with this stuff, but for the record put me down as *choosing* ala mode, every Friday." She looked at Pinch wide-eyed. "Wow, I'm feeling confident already!" Lydia ignored the twit, but her face bore the trace of a smile.

Vanilla ice cream was a good antidote to the super spicy Aloha Chili. Pinch would have enjoyed the balm more had Lydia not asked her for a brief biography. "I thought you wanted to stay in your garden."

15

"Hold ya shovel, Missy. Looking for a walking tour not a seminar on ya petunias."

"I was born in Chicago. My mother was a nurse."

"Who watched ya when she worked?"

"Her mother, my Grandma Rose. You'd have like Rose. She was very creative – especially with food. She'd have her silver teapot on the table when I came home from school. Nothing ordinary came out of her spout. Sometimes it was hot sherbet. Once it was applesauce tea. My favorite was a beet and cranberry juice concoction – not for its taste but for making my tongue look like a rose petal."

"Made any pretty red petals, lately?" Pinch shook her head. Blood-stained tongues were pretty.

"What about ya daddy?"

"He died in a car accident a few hours before I was born. It pushed my mother into premature labor. You wondered about my name. She called me 'Pinch' because I was so small and because how tightly I squeezed her finger whenever she touched my hand."

"Hmm…sorry. Do ya miss, Chicago?"

"Not really. My oldest brother, Bryan, is a workaholic who barely has time for his family. My other brother, Kevin, is a priest in a children's shelter. It's just the three of us, and since Mama died last summer, Chicago doesn't feel the same. But New York is nice."

"Clean sheets are 'nice.' How 'bout, alive? Or gritty, soulful or *tough?* Even dirty, smelly, and crime infested says more about a place than *nice.*"

"I haven't experienced your New York negatives. I don't get out too much."

Lydia shot her a curious look. Pinch quickly added, "You know how it is with family. There's more to do than hours in the day, and since my husband and daughter are happy here, living in New York *is* nice." Pinch lowered her eyes and dug into her ice cream.

"A happy family does make a difference," Smith said.

"What does ya husband do?" Lydia continued.

"He's a medieval literature professor."

"How old's ya kid – daughter, right?"

"Yes, she'll be 10 next month."

"Any hobbies?"

"I like to sew and make Katie's costume each Halloween. I was admiring the quilt on your living room sofa. Did you make it?"

"That'd be my mother. She got into sewing after I was born. We always had fabric in the house. Brought the stuff here, after she died. Thought maybe I'd get into it…" Her voice trailed off though her jaw kept moving, a pendulum ticking off her thoughts. "Told her we did the same thing, ya know, her quilting them squares, me making photo stories, both piecing things together to make a big picture. She liked that. Called my projects *photo quilts.*"

"I've seen where photos can be copied onto fabric. Have you thought about using her memorable pictures to make a photo quilt of her life?"

Lydia frowned then asked Pinch if she had any pets. Pinch shook her head. "My husband's a neatnik. Controlling animals is harder than controlling people." Lydia glanced at Smith. Pinch quickly asked about the Wright Brothers' habits.

"Those boys would run the place if I let 'em. But my kitchen's off limits." She pointed to her wheelchair parked in the hall, the two cats sleeping entwined on the seat. "Most times they're happy just nestling in Grace. Visitors and catnip draw them down."

"Grace?" Pinch asked.

"The big tree in the living room," Smith said. "Lydia's got a name for everything. I'm often *Clarissa,* a fetching woman I played in one of her comedy skits."

"Do you have a name for me?" Pinch asked.

"Working on it," Lydia said, looking long and deep at Pinch.

Smith looked at her watch and rose to leave. "Bedtime calls. I'll see you next Friday morning, Pinch, for chili." She tapped Lydia on the shoulder, petted the cats then she saw herself out.

Pinch looked around the kitchen. She felt so content and relaxed. Then her eyes fell on Lydia's face staring at her, still as a stalking cat. "So. Pinch. How'd ya get the shiner?"

The words hung like storm clouds between them. Pinch peered at her face in the chrome water pitcher looking for tarnish beneath the one eye, but the pitcher was freckled with condensation, blurring a clear reflection. She filled her glass and shrugged. "I don't see anything there."

"Maybe ya need a magnifying glass."

"Maybe you need eyeglasses!"

Lydia raised her glass in a touché gesture though her face lacked frivolity. Pinch felt like a kid in blindfolds, spun around then set free to find her way in the dark. She looked around the room. The naked windows, the stark winter sky, the white-bright overhead fluorescent bulb. "Maybe it's the lighting in here."

"Not talking 'bout lights, talking 'bout shadows. Shot enough still lifes to know the difference between them."

Pinch shifted in her chair. "Did you enjoy doing still lifes?"

"Gave me indigestion. Took the gig cause I needed to eat."

"I'd loved to see them. Any going in your memoir?"

"There not my best stuff."

"Sometimes when you're close to a subject, it's hard to see beyond its minor faults."

"And sometimes it's hard to see the truth when ya want to be blind."

Pinch's heart started racing. She pointed at Lydia's face. "Speaking of blind, what happened to your eye? From the looks of that scar, you're lucky you didn't lose it."

Lydia touched the scar. "Was a tussle for the space between my legs." She seemed disturbed by the recollection, brow furrowed, deep in thought, wincing now and again.

"No need to go into it, Lydia. Some memories are painful to revisit."

"I don't rank my memories. Visit with all that visit me. This here one's an old friend."

"Then why the frown?"

"Some turning points are paved in pain. Ask a woman 'bout giving birth, she's bound to slip ya a smile and a frown." She touched her cheek and smiled, then settled back in her seat.

Pinch relaxed. It looked as if they'd be traipsing through Lydia's garden.

"This baby's called *Aurora* and was born in the 40s, when I worked in a mill town for the local rag. Was my first solo gig. Filled in for a guy called sick that day. The mill was on strike. Rumor had it they were bringing in scabs, and the brass called a news conference hoping a spread in the Dailies would pressure the union to give. I got there early, set up my tripod and camera. Pickets were milling everywhere – the brass pacing on a makeshift stage wearing poisedom. Waiting for the press."

"*Poisedom...?*"

She flicked her hand. "Acting calm when ya poised to piss ya pants. So I'm hanging around, waiting for the show, when holy shit, I hear *pop, pop, pop* and everyone hits the deck 'cept me...a lone fool standing in a field of squatters."

"Why didn't you get down?"

"Tripod jammed trying to ease the camera to the ground. Finally said, *screw the camera* and started to drop when I hear some laughter on a hill behind the crowd. I zoom in with the camera. Three guys are up there with metal noisemakers that sound like Gatling guns when you crank the can. Before I can snap a shot, the stooges crank out another barrage, and the cowering crowd starts to stampede - me in the middle riding my tripod like a kid giddy-yapping on a stick horse." She galloped her hand across the table thumping her fingers shouting, *varooom, varooom!* Pinch laughed, glad that they weren't galloping through her life.

Lydia leaned back and closed her eyes, her smile restful, content. Pinch's mother used to strike a similar pose listening to big band music. She reached across the table and squeezed Lydia's hand. The old woman jumped. "Sorry," Pinch said. "You reminded me of someone."

"I *am* someone. Next time just tell me, don't touch me." She took a long drink of water, swiped her mouth with a napkin and continued. "People were screaming...no one taking mind of this young gal pointing up toward the hill. So I start running, and the tripod finally folds. Hit the deck real hard – camera rim cutting a nifty halo round my eye.

"Boss man was bothered more 'bout his banged up hard-ware than my bloody software. Told him I got trampled by a herd of wildebeests. He blew me off. Said he should've known better, sending a girl on a man's job. Said I'd only do animals shoots from now on. Well, my camera was busted, but the film was okay. Tossed him the reel and said, 'Fine with me. How 'bout we do a two-page spread – *Zoo Comes to Mill Town. Photographer Gets Screwed!*'"

"Uh oh. What'd he say?"

"Well, we swapped a few four-letter charmers. He argued my place in the paper. I argued my place in the world. In the end got to choose my own jobs, set my own pay,"

"You got a promotion and a raise?"

"Hell no. Got fired. So I said, *fuck you*, with all the poise-dom I could muster. Walked out, head high. Bruised, but not broken."

"From the look of things, you've conquered all your challenges."

Her face darkened. "Not all of them. But getting free from that fucker opened doors I never knew existed."

Pinch rose abruptly and walked to the front door. She was buttoning her coat when Lydia wheeled up. "Hey! What's bugging you?"

"You keep spouting that four-letter 'charmer' after making me promise not to. What is it, Lydia – don't you mean what you say, or don't you remember what you've said?"

Lydia stuck out her chin. "I did not say the *c*-word!"

"I'm talking about the *f*-word!"

"Fuck the *f*-word, Pinch. *Can't* is the worst four-letter word. Go home and park ya Victorian values in ya parlor with ya chastity belt, and come back next week energized…not paralyzed."

Pinch eyed the wreath on the door when leaving; the nesting robin and shiny egg evoked spring's promise and a life caught in transition. She thought of a crocus she had once seen peeking through a blanket of snow. "How does a flower survive in the snow?"

"Deep roots and a will to live."

"Then why get rid of values born from deep roots and a will to live?"

"Ya gotta deconstruct before ya reconstruct. Forget what you know." She wheeled back into her apartment and turned to Pinch before closing the door. "Throw 'em all out, Pinchey. Then start all over with a clean slate."

CHAPTER 3

Gertie

STEALING TIME TO WORK WITH LYDIA proved easier for Pinch than re-constructing her values. Working on the interesting memoir made up for listening to the old woman's sermons on "people pitifully handcuffed by their cave man mentality." Today was day four of week one on the job; with most of the journal entries keyed in, she hoped to start interviewing Lydia tomorrow if they didn't waste time over chili.

Pinch stopped short near Lydia's apartment, a plaintive cry piercing the air. Seconds later, a flock of pastel balloons flew by...the airborne Easter eggs brightening the gray winter sky. Then a burly man with veiny cheeks knocked into her shouting, "Watch out, bitch!" The *smack, smack, smack* of his feet on the pavement echoed her pounding heart. She leaned on a lamppost, catching her breath, and watched two sanitation men jump from their truck, and trip the man up, before he could get away. She took a deep breath, another, then another, her mind and body torn from its mooring.

Half a block away she found a young person huddling in a patch of plastic garbage bags. She cautiously touched the shoulder. An arm flew out—"No, don't!" The person hunkered lower, coiling its arms around its rumpled hair, wedging deeper between two bags of trash.

"It's okay, I'm not going to hurt you," Pinch said, her eyes watering from the putrid smell and twisted sight of a child clinging to trash. She breathed through her mouth then rummaged her purse for something to cover her nose. "Would you like a tissue?" she said. The head nodded, and a gloved hand extended. But all Pinch could find was a used paper tissue and the white, silk handkerchief from Steve on their wedding day. She paused then relinquished the hanky. A bedraggled girl, who looked to be in her late teens, eked out a smile before burying her face in the hanky. "You're the balloon girl!" Pinch said, the two of them having exchanged nods before as street strangers often do. She helped her to a nearby bench. When the girl stooped down to retie her shoelace, a cheaply engraved bangle peeked from beneath her coat sleeve. "What does it say on your bracelet?"

"*Gertie*, that's my name." She dabbed at her nose then looked at the hanky; red swaths cut across its shiny white plane. They both looked up when a police car, siren blaring, screeched to a stop beside Lydia's apartment. Gertie nodded toward the scene, her mouth tightening. A fresh line of blood emerged above her lip. "He nearly broke my nose, the creep, wanting me to turn tricks, saying we could make us some real good money. 'What's this *we* stuff?' I said. 'You fixing to sell your body, too?' He already stole the slip of cash I was saving at home for to go to school, and now he's ripped off the sorry few bucks in my pocket." Gertie quietly bled into the elegant hanky, talking in fits and starts. "He said, 'just, try it once. If you don't cotton to it, I'll never ask again.' I ain't book smart, mind you, but I know what *never* means." She pulled off her glove and held up her right hand; her tapered fingers were capped in pale pink nail polish, but unlike its siblings, her pinkie refused to fold when she made a fist. Pinch asked what was wrong with it. "Got slammed a couple times past *never*." Gertie gently pulled a knit ski cap over her hair. "Lost a bonnet, once, but I ain't gonna lose myself playing nasty games for a Creep."

Pinch was pondering the idea of 'losing oneself' when a policeman approached Gertie. "We have witnesses who say the man we're holding roughed you up, is that true?"

"Yeah, he's my husband. The Creep stole my money, too!"

The officer turned to Pinch. "Did you see what happened?"

"No, I found her over there crying."

Gertie needed to fill out a report at the police station. Having no local relatives, she asked if Pinch would join her. Pinch looked at her watch. "Sure. Let me call my boss."

She hustled the half-block to Lydia's and dialed her number from the lobby. Smith answered the phone. "What's wrong, Pinch? You sound awful." She relayed what had happened, and why she'd be late. "I'll give Lydia the message," Smith said. "When you're done at the station, take Gertie to The Market — it's the woman's shelter where I work a few nights a week." Pinch took down the address thinking, *what an odd name for a shelter....* "I'll try to get someone to meet you at the station," Smith said. "Call Lydia if you don't get back today. She's fond of Gertie. Buys her balloons. She'll want to know all the details."

A woman from The Market arrived at the station during the women's debriefing. She "spoke" sign language and was easy to read. When they were done, she drove them to a four-story building that housed various mom-and-pop shops anchored by a food store and used-clothing shop. A hard-faced woman, sitting on a stool outside the entrance, was playing a harmonica and wearing the name tag, *Flo.* Gertie traded glances with Pinch and pulled her cap further down. Flo slid off the stool when they passed and gently put her arm around Gertie. "Looks like you're needing a feather in your cap, Honey. C'mon, let me show you what we've got." Flo ushered Gertie through a maze of clothing racks; Pinch tried to keep up but lost sight of the duo near a locked dressing room. She jiggled the knob to no avail and was wondering what to do when the sign-language woman tapped her shoulder and lead her to entrance of the store then bowed and disappeared.

Lydia didn't answer when Pinch phoned from the lobby later that day. She called Smith. "Lydia had a doctor's appointment. I have her key. I'll clear you to come up. Her chili-pepper order arrived. She's left you a bundle of goodies." The care package contained all the ingredients for Aloha Chili. Pinch sighed; it'd taken three days to recover from that meal, and she hoped tomorrow's chili would clear her system before Katie's birthday, on Sunday.

Working without Lydia's prattle, she quickly keyed in the rest of the journals and readied to leave when a *jingle* in the tree drew her to the picture window. She nuzzled each cat on the nape. Then using binoculars sitting on the sill, she zoomed in on the Statue of Liberty. The face on the icon of freedom wasn't friendly with its stern mouth and haunting eyes that peered, laser-like, beneath a deeply furrowed brow. Was she grieving behind those sealed lips? Warning the wayfarer? Repressing a collective pain…?

On the bus ride home, Pinch considered their dinner options, Steve eating out at a college event tonight. She settled on pancakes. Katie would love it. And pancakes would counter eating chili at nine the next morning. She fumbled with her keys at the front door juggling briefcase, purse and Lydia's care package. After turning the lock, she pushed the door with her knee and was greeted with the scent of cherry tobacco. *"Steve?"* she hollered, shutting the door with a swipe of her foot and was craning her neck toward the stairs when he grabbed her from behind with a giggle spilling the groceries onto the floor. The pineapple cans rolled down the hall. Chili peppers hopped across the floor. The bag of dry beans ripped on the umbrella stand spilling it contents across the foyer floor. The tomatoes fell into a bag of soon-to-be-donated clothes, the French bread ending its slide by the laundry room door.

"I guess that answers that question," he said kissing her on the neck.

"What question?" She tried not to sound annoyed.

"Where you've been? But I see that you've been to the market."

She tiptoed through the beans, put her coat and briefcase in the closet, then tiptoed back toward the laundry room cursing him under her breath, vacuum in hand. He'd corralled the rest of the food by the time she started sucking up the beans and was yelling at her to stop, when Katie bounced through the front door. "Whoa…What is this stuff?"

"Beans," Steve said. "Help me save them from your mother."

"What's the big deal? I'll get another bag the next time I go shopping."

"But aren't you making chili tonight?"

"Yeah, chili!" Katie shouted.

Pinch glared at him. "I thought you were eating out tonight?"

"I changed my mind, and it looks like most of us want chili tonight, right Katie girl?"

"Please, Mom. We never, ever have chili."

Steve nodded and pointed to the beans. Katie dropped her book-bag and fell to the floor picking them up one by one. He took the vacuum from Pinch. "Come now, my dear, I know you want chili tonight – you brought the recipe home from the store."

Steve and Katie retreated to the family room after dinner for his weekly review of her vocabulary words – English the only area of her studies he let cut into his leisure. An excellent student, Katie reveled in his attention. Pinch relished the time to reflect on a day fraught with seeming contradictions. She learned many things, but didn't feel smarter; endured many emotions, "joy" eluding the call. The bulk of her decisions had satisfied others – joining Gertie at The Market, making chili instead of pancakes, antacids with dinner instead of wine. What had she done for herself today? Even dinner was a bust, Steve saying she was in a culinary rut, challenging her to fete the family with provocative fare, "like this tangy chili recipe you got at the market." He was a meat and potatoes guy who had scorned her, early on, when she tried new cooking ideas. How was she to know Lydia's Aloha Chili would merit his smile? Her Catch 22 was being married to man – not bad enough to leave.

Later in bed, she asked God... *What price peace?* Was coping a virtue, or a curse? Was freedom a right or a journey?

The frown on the steely faced statue burned hot in her mind. No wonder the face of Liberty was cast in pain.

CHAPTER 4

Lola's Passion

A POWER FAILURE DURING THE NIGHT stilled the radio alarm. The neighbor's barking dog finally roused the O'Malley's. Steve already missed his morning jog and refused breakfast, gulping down his coffee and pushing Katie to get a move on.

"You're never late for class, Steve. You're entitled this once," Pinch said.

"It's not about entitlements. Routine is the staple of civilization. Get your things, Katie. I'm leaving in two minutes."

"But she hasn't finished eating! And I still need to make her lunch."

"It won't kill her to give up a meal during Lent. Think of the all martyrs who gave up their lives."

"That's right, Mom. Sister CeCe said St. Joan was burned alive." Katie left the table and tore upstairs for her books.

"Ah, yes," Steve smirked, "Joan of Arc...the original French fry! Since that nun is so versed in French history, the Monsignor should ship her over there."

"What an awful thing to say about St. Joan, and you know Katie loves Cecelia."

"That woman has too much power at the church. I just found out Katie's class will be putting on the Passion Play. It should be my ninth grade Religion class. I volunteer to teach there and the Monsignor throws her the bone. Where's the respect?" He grabbed his coat and kissed her goodbye. She thrust an apple in Katie's hand as she ran out the door.

Smith was leaving Lydia's when Pinch stepped out of the elevator. "Just call me, Clarissa," Smith said.

"The fetching woman in Lydia's skit?"

"Today I'm fetching chocolate for this morning's meal."

"Sounds good to me!"

"I saw Gertie at The Market last night. She's joining us today. Leave the door open, I'll be right back."

Libby was aglow in the sunlit harbor; the sea was calm, and shiny as glass, creating a land bridge between them. Pinch saw herself gliding across the water, Libby egging her on saying, "Come, I know where you can eat normal food, with normal people, and live a normal life." The kitchen timer blared. The interruption came none too soon – listening to statues was not a sign of sanity, and this place already had a resident loony-toon. Still, she felt a kinship with the silent woman on the pedestal. She turned hearing someone approach. Lydia waltzed in with the help of two canes, no pedestal infringing her movement.

"Howdy, Pinch. Morning Libby."

"I hear Gertie's coming. I'm glad she's feeling better."

"That kid looks like a quick chew, but she's one tough piece of jerky serving up divorce papers and slamming him with assault."

Smith strolled through the door, box of chocolates in her hand. Gertie followed with a bunch of balloons which she tied to the laughing Buddha, clearly familiar with Lydia's place. Gertie gave Pinch a hug. Lydia looked at her watch. "About time you two showed up. Lucky I didn't close the kitchen." Smith shuffled toward the kitchen strumming the candy box and singing, "The Impossible Dream."

Gertie handed Pinch a wrinkled white cloth. "Sorry for the blood on your hanky. I rubbed my fingers red trying to get out the stain, but the scrubbing come fer naught. I'd a thrown it out, but it's a mighty fine piece. Someday I'll be fixed to buy you one you'll be proud to carry again."

Pinch put it in her pocket. "I've carried this hanky for 15 years, and yesterday was the first time it did me proud."

Smith came in from the kitchen telling Lydia the food was ready. Lydia nodded then grunted when Gertie gave her a hug. "Don't take it personally, Honey," Smith said. "The Statue of Liberty is Lydia's favorite companion. She doesn't talk or feel, so Lydia calls all the shots."

"I reckon that works if you live alone. Ever been married, Miss Wright?"

Lydia ignored the question, telling Gertie to call her *Lydia,* and after putting on some music, she head-bobbed and cane-strutted toward the kitchen. Pinch turned to Gertie. The two of them shrugged. "It's the middle of Lent," Pinch said. "Why are you playing 'Jingle Bell Rock'?"

"My ears don't know it's February, and I like it."

Gertie went to the powder room to wash up before eating. Pinch did the same in the master bathroom, her eyes widening at the rainbow row of nail polish on a shelf beside the sink. She immediately grabbed the orange vial and cradled it in her palm. The label said, *Lola's Passion*. She had worn a similar shade years ago but stopped in deference to Steve. He didn't like anything orange…she didn't need the aggravation. But she really liked orange, and really liked nail polish; she brought *Lola* with her to the kitchen table. Lydia and Gertie were extolling the merits of chicken liver omelets. Pinch took her seat and exchanged a doubtful look with Smith. After ladling out the chili, Lydia raised her water glass in a toast.

"Want to welcome, Gertie, as my newest employee. Gave her the 'Tude Test' while waiting for ya, Pinch. She'll be the proofreader. Ya promoted to editorial Supervisor."

"That's great, Gertie! You can start proofing today."

Lydia held up a hand. "Hold on, Pinch. First ya gotta teach her to read."

Pinch would have jumped at the chance to teach if she wasn't bound by time. "I think she'd do better with a personal tutor. I haven't taught reading in years."

"Good point, Pinchey. Scratch the other title. Make it editorial *Tutor*."

Pinch dropped the subject for now and held up the *Lola's Passion*. "Mind if I borrow this til next week?"

"Keep it," Lydia said. "Now tell me what ya think of my Choco-lenta Chili."

The rust-colored mixture brimmed with lentils, tomatoes

and raisins with an aftertaste hinting of cocoa, cinnamon and cloves. Pinch gave a thumbs up, but asked about the chocolate-covered cherry in the mix. "Made my Chicken Liver Chili last night. Then Smith reminds me – ya don't eat meat, Fridays during Lent. Whipped up the Choco-lenta this morning. But some critter took a liking to my chocolate squares. So, Smith donated a box of candy from her private stash."

Pinch looked at Smith. "I thought that was dessert."

"Try not to think too much here." Smith said.

They finished with blueberry pie a la mode. The talk turned to favorite colors. "Since ya cotton to the color, Pinch, got a tube of orange lipstick for ya, too." The tube was in the bathroom drawer; she put it on before returning to the kitchen. "*Ooowhee!*" Lydia shouted, "next you'll be walking on water."

"Gee, Pinch, you look mighty fine. What's it called?" Gertie said.

She turned the tube over. *"Kiss My Sass!"*

"I like it," Smith said. "Everything about you lights up."

"Yeah, Pinchey. From a pussycat to a power look!"

She had seen it in the bathroom mirror, too, how her green eyes shone, how her red hair dazzled, how her skin had a radiant glow. And she'd choked up recalling how over time Steve had weaned her off everything orange.

Gertie left right after eating; she was still getting settled at The Market. Pinch saw her to the door and wondered how to weave this young girl into her life; they agreed to meet the following week to talk about a literacy plan. Pinch wiped off the lipstick before returning to the kitchen. "Why'd ya take off the *Sass?*" Ya back to looking like a mannequin."

"Stuff it, Lydia," Smith said. "It's her face, let it be."

Which Lydia did…til Smith left. "If ya ask my opinion—"

"I know your opinion but I can't wear it. It's too bold, too provocative."

"Too bad. And let's set the record straight, Missy…ya won't, not can't, wear it. It's your choice, so ya can change your mind. A flash of sass could change a person's life."

"Speaking of changes, how could you hire Gertie to proofread? I thought your 'Tude Test' was a joke, but this is ridiculous."

"Ever take a driving test?"

"Of course."

"I rest my case."

"What does that have to do with Gertie making the grade?"

"In the driving, and the 'Tude' test, ya don't need to ace every question. *You* failed the flying rubber question, Gertie got it right. Smith failed the food as art question, you and Gertie got that right."

"But you're testing for a proofreader. Did you eliminate the spelling question?"

"Course not, just changed the word. She'll only be proofing my journals."

"What word did you ask her to spell?"

"*Shit.*"

"And let me guess—"

"She aced it! And you thought I was just a pretty face."

Pinch wasn't sure what she thought of Lydia, but the old woman had found a way to put money in Gertie's pocket and give her a reason to learn how to read. "I'm glad you're helping her, but I only planned to work here a few weeks. There's no way I can finish the work on your memoir and teach her how to read."

"Stay longer."

"I can't"

"Can't? Or won't!"

"I have other responsibilities."

"Change them."

"I can't."

"Can't, or won't?"

"Okay – won't."

"What if I extend my memoir deadline?"

"Is it fair to start with Gertie if I can't stay and finish the job?"

"Can't stay, or won't stay?"

"Shit!"

Lydia raised an eyebrow. "Looks like she can proof your stuff, too."

Pinch twirled the tube of lipstick. Opened it, smelled it, capped it, smiled. She left it on the table but pocketed the polish. "Okay, we'll give it a shot with Gertie. Any thoughts on how to start?"

"Keep it simple and make it fun. Use my photos to make up some word cards."

"I'll start with words like *fish* and *dead* from your Watershed photos and work up to *chemical* and *pollution*. What other photos can I use?"

"Your choice."

She left the apartment with a bounce in her step. Thinking

about *Lola,* she planned a dinner of favorites – mashed potatoes for Katie and fried fish and creamed corn for Steve. To counter his culinary rut accusation, she bought a can of whole cranberry sauce, one of her favorites only served on Thanksgiving. Grandma Rose would be pleased.

She prepped the food, soon as she got home, then poured a cup of tea, sipping the brew while painting her nails. She had two hours to enjoy them before Steve got home. His recliner beckoned, and so did an old Katherine Hepburn movie on TV. But she dozed off watching the film and woke up in a panic running upstairs, raking through cosmetic bags, finally finding that old bottle of polish remover. She twisted off the cap and was greeted by fumes – no liquid.

The sun was about to die in the sky. She needed to fry the fish. Fear followed her down the stairs chanting ominous scenes from, "When Lola Met Steve." The dire depictions waned in the kitchen where the alpenglow rays of the setting sun lit the room in a tangerine splendor. She nestled the floured fish in hot oil then washed her hands and splayed her fingers in the waning light, thinking how Libby's sun-drenched spikes brightened a winter's day. She turned the fish and fried the other side; the hot oil crackled in applause. The neighbor's dog barked. She doffed her apron and puffed her hair. A key turned in the door.

CHAPTER 5

Monet's Petals

THE OIL WAS STILL HOT in the fryer when the family, hands held, thanked God for the food. "Amen," Steve said, then flicked Pinch's hand aside. Katie complimented Pinch on her nails while scooping a mound of mashed potatoes on her plate. "Whore paint," Steve said, "You look like Fanny Fingerhut." He smiled at Katie. "When I was in high school, the boys voted *Fanny-the-Finger*, Best Teacher in the 'hands on' category."

"Must you…?" Pinch whispered.

"Must *you*?" he replied.

"Miss Fingerhut was your teacher, Dad?"

"She was a whore, Kathryn, with orange fingertips like your mother's tonight."

Katie looked toward Pinch's hands and frowned. "What's a whore?"

Steve didn't reply. Pinch couldn't…mashed potatoes clinging to the walls of her mouth. She wanted to stab his hand when he reached for another piece of fish. She put down her fork and sipped from her water glass.

"Sirens, nothing but sirens," he wailed, wagging his finger in her face. "Take note, Kathryn — no self-respecting woman would want to be seen like that."

Katie gave a half-hearted nod and kept her head down burying cranberries in her mashed potatoes.

Pinch cleared her throat. "I disagree."

Katie looked up.

Steve flinched.

"My mother was a self-respecting woman who thought Daddy was a fine man, Katie. She also thought colored polish on fingernails were beautiful. She called them *Monet's Petals*. We used to paint them, together." Pinch raised her arms and fluttered her fingers over the family favorites then let her hands drift down to the table, her orange fingertips melding into the floral tablecloth.

Steve shoved his plate forward. "Monet was nuts! He couldn't paint the real world so he painted illusions."

"Grandma loved his paintings. I'll show you some, Honey. You decide," Pinch said.

"Can I wear his petals for my birthday on Sunday!"

"Not on my watch!" He stood up and glared down at Pinch as if daring her to challenge that decree. But she didn't need results by Sunday having already planted a different seed of womanhood in Katie's fertile mind. She met his gaze evenly and let his anger ride unprovoked.

Katie's hands shot up in the air, as soon as he left the room, her fingers soaring on one woman's vision, another's memory. Pinch recalled a hot summer day when she and her mother had walked through a meadow integrating their "petals" with God's. It scared her how, with the swath of his tongue, Steve had made an innocent act into an immorality. But Katie seemed undaunted, her hands swinging in broad sweeping motions evoking another memory. It was Father's Day. Pinch was finishing first grade. After saying a prayer at her father's grave, she and Mama had stopped at the park. Pinch ran ahead to the swings begging to be pushed so high her feet would touch the sky. "I want to see if God is home."

"And why is that, Pinchey?"

"I want a hug."

"Okay, close your eyes and hold tight." Her mother gave the swing a strong push. "Do you feel anything on your face and your arms?"

"And on my legs, too."

"Wow, it's a whole-body hug!"

"It's just a breeze, Mama, not a *real* hug."

Her mother had eased the swing to a stop and wrapped Pinch in her arms. "Hugs come in many ways. Sometimes a hug comes in what people say; sometimes it's what people do. Some hugs come in person, like this one from me. Some come from far away, like those breeze hugs from God." It was hard, at six, to fathom the myriad hugs to be had in the world. But she never forgot that a push on a swing could call up a heavenly embrace.

"Will I ever get to wear Monet's petals?" Katie asked.

"Of course!" Pinch said, though she doubted it would be soon. Her life had taken a grim turn, and Steve's hard edges were primed to keep bursting through Katie's bubblegum world.

"Who was Monet? Was he really nuts, like Dad said?"

"Claude Monet was an artist from France with the courage to try something new. His paintings made people see things in a different light. Some people don't like *change*. Daddy is one of those people. He probably meant Monet was different…not nuts. I think he's just tired tonight."

"He's was mad driving home from school. He wanted to do the Easter play."

"Has Sister Cecelia assigned the roles?"

Katie frowned. "I'm the lady who tells Simon-Peter she saw him with Jesus even though he says it wasn't him. I'd rather be Mary Magdalene. She has more lines. What's cool is that we're doing it at night this year so people who work on Saturday, like Dad, can see it."

Steve called Pinch to come upstairs. Grabbing her arm as she entered the bedroom, he insisted she strip off the polish before he left to teach his Religion class. She told him she had no remover but would buy some first thing in the morning and tried not to smirk easing out of his grip, tickled that Monet and 'Fanny' would bed with them tonight. He was smiling a few minutes later when he kissed her goodbye on his way out the door.

Pinch and Katie played, "Name that Tune," cleaning the kitchen, Pinch suggesting they only hum Christmas songs, a testament to the staying power of "Jingle Bell Rock." Then later, Katie watched a show on the red-headed gymnast who'd won a gold medal, in Atlanta's Summer Olympics while Pinch folded clean laundry, toting the towels up to the bathrooms. She flipped on the light in the master bath, eyes widening as she approached her sink. *Lola's Passion* lay bleeding in the shiny white basin. Orange pools amid shards of broken glass.

"Damn you, Steve O'Malley!" She sopped up the polish with toilet paper, fishing out the shards with her right hand, cradling them in her left, and jumped when Katie popped her head in the room.

"Mom, Uncle Kevin's on the phone."

She snapped her left hand shut and angled her body to hide the mess. Smiling over her shoulder, she said, "Sorry, Honey. I didn't hear it ring. Tell him I'll be there in a minute."

She locked the bathroom door, shook the shards in her hand onto a paper tissue and turned on the faucet, rinsing the rest of *Lola* down the drain. Her palm pinched. She plucked two embedded slivers with tweezers. Blood puddled in her palm. She wrapped it in a red hand towel and was rushing to the bedroom phone when Katie called up saying Kevin had to go, that he'd be busy on Sunday and didn't want to forget to wish Katie, "Happy Birthday!"

"That was nice. Did he say anything else…?"

"He said to tell you he loves you, and God loves you, too."

More than a loving brother, Kevin was a surrogate father, a role he'd taken on at the tender age of seven, when Pinch was born, forty years ago. She didn't doubt his love, though she wondered about God's. She wound the red towel tightly around her hand. It looked like a boxing mitt. She remembered when Kevin taught her how to box after she'd watched him and Bryan duke it out. He'd guided her hands into his gloves, but her fingers got lost in the cavernous mitts which teetered on her skinny arms, toppling on contact. "Make a fist," he had said, then pulled the gloves up to her elbows, tying them tightly, testing them for stability. "Now keep your hands up and chin down." He pointed to his nose and smiled. "When you see an opening – hit me!" He was sixteen at the time; she was nine. She got good at blocking his blows but could never bring herself to punch him in the face.

"You'll never defend yourself that way, little one," Bryan had said watching them.

"Don't call me that!" she'd shouted and would have popped him in the nose had Kevin's quick hands not deflected the blow.

"Back off, Bro. She'll do just fine," Kevin had said.

But Pinch took off the gloves and threw them at Bryan. "I don't need mitts. Smart people talk, or walk away from trouble. Only jerks, like you, need to fight!"

Pinch rinsed her hand with antiseptic and crossed two Band-Aids in her palm. Then draping the towel over the mess, she closed the bathroom door and joined Katie in her room for their nightly bedtime chat.

Katie was sitting up in bed playing tic-tac-toe and humming, "Frosty the Snowman." Pinch sat at the end of the bed, her left hand obscured by the covers. "Is Frosty your favorite fairy tale character?"

"Frosty's for kids, Sleeping Beauty is my favorite. Someday, my prince will come and take me to his castle, and we'll live happily-ever-after. Frosty can't do that!" Yes, Pinch thought.

But Frosty melts when things get hot. If only the Prince could melt, too.

Once Katie was tucked in for the night, Pinch threw *Lola's* mess in the trashcan in the back porch. The moon was casting a channel of light on the swing hanging from the oak tree. She put on a jacket, meandered to the swing, shimmied aboard. The pain in her palm shot shivers up her arm when she grasped the gnarly rope. She pulled her wrinkled white hanky from her pocket, balled it up and wedged it between her hand and the rope. She walked her toes backward. Her hand still hurt. She stood still as a statue, suspended on her toes, longing for a breeze hug but afraid to let go.

What do you want? The Stranger asked.

She didn't know, but she knew she didn't have it. She thought about Gertie, kicked out of her home and forced into a shelter. I have so much. How I can I ask for more...?

More of what?

She adjusted the hanky; her diamond and opal rings twinkled in the moonlight. Not things, she murmured. I have lots of things, but I feel so poor. Maybe I just want 'different' – is different okay?

Different is neither good, nor bad, it's simply a change.

But change isn't simple. Or easy.

Neither is standing still. If you want to move forward, you've got to let go.

She took a deep breath and picked up her toes. A light breeze kissed her face as her body soared forward. The air was cold but her heart was warmed by a hug in the quiet of the night. After leaving the swing, she stuffed the hanky in the trash, in the creamed corn can, carefully avoiding the tin's ragged rim. She retired early, had curled up on her side of the bed, when the front door slammed, the bedroom door trembling from the blast of rising cold air.

He climbed into the bed, pushed her hair aside and floated a kiss on the back of her neck. His breath was warm on her shoulder. He rubbed her arm, then her thigh and whispered, "I bought you girls a gift tonight." When she didn't respond to his words, or his touch, he turned over.

Girls? She shivered…Katie now a member of his post-traumatic gift list.

CHAPTER 6

The Stills

S TEVE'S GIFTS were on the kitchen counter – two bottles of nail polish remover and five vials of polish in "colors" from clear to ashen. Pinch sat alone in the kitchen wiping *Lola's Passion* from her fingers; she didn't bother erasing the smile on her face. Katie moaned minutes later when Pinch opened her bedroom blinds. "Can I skip gymnastics today, Mom? My brain is stuck in slumber land."

Pinch tossed an old Monet calendar on the bed. "Maybe this will get you going."

Katie flipped through the first three pages which were all snowy scenes in Arles, France. "Keep going," Pinch said, "his petals show up in the warmer months."

Katie sat up in her bed pondering each picture, telling Pinch his snow scenes were as pretty as his gardens. "How come ladies don't wear hats anymore?"

"Hats go in, and out, of fashion. When I was growing up, girls and women had to wear a hat or a scarf on their heads in church. Even after they changed that rule, my mother, and grandmother still wore hats to Mass on Sunday."

"Who made *that* rule?"

"I don't know, Honey. Maybe the Pope or a council of the cardinals."

Steve was washing his hands when Pinch returned to the kitchen. She nodded. He toweled off then kissed her on the cheek. He wore new running shoes that squeaked *ribit, ribit,* on the tiled floor. He hopped back to his post by the sink. "So, my dear, what do you think?" His large frame filled her peripheral vision. She smiled, thinking of fairy-tale reversals where *her* kiss, to *his* cheek, would turn him into a frog she could ship to the kingdom of *Elsewhere.* She cracked six eggs in a bowl. Threw the shells in the sink. Their eyes met. He must have misread her smile, because he flashed a grin then leaped to the colorless collection on the counter. "I think Katie should start with the clear one," he said, "and work her way up to the darkest white." He puffed out his chest. She gave a nod. Having lost face with his wife last night, he sought strokes from his daughter this morning. His eyes bulged with excitement, a bullfrog preening in his pond. He *ribited* about, so full of himself, there was barely space in the kitchen for her. "You can wear any of them when you want." She gave him a 'duly noted' nod. He missed her assent, his eyes locked on her bandaged palm. His back stiffened; he shuffled his *squeakers* toward the stairwell and back. "Shouldn't Katie be coming down soon?"

"Any minute...."

He covered his gifts with a towel and left. When Katie

arrived, she was followed by a *ribiting* hulk who snapped the towel off the bottles saying, "So! What do you think!"

"Oh my gosh! Look Mommy, I *can* wear nail polish on my birthday!" She jumped into his arms. "Thank you, Daddy. Thank you *so* much!"

"Now, your mother's in charge," he said, releasing her embrace, "and we've decided you'll start with the *clear* one and work your way up to dark white." As if to make sure she didn't fast-forward out of sequence, he picked up the darkest hue, peered at its label. "Do we all agree that you'll wear *Ashes* in the end?"

When all heads bobbed, Steve scooped up the bottles, handing them to Katie. She scanned them one by one then spun around laughing. "Who picked these out?"

"*I* did." He flipped her a wink.

She covered her mouth, giggling. "Wait til I tell my friends my father would rather see me *In the Nude* than wearing Monet's petals!"

He snatched the clear polish from her hand and scowled reading the label. Katie tiptoed behind him shrugging at Pinch before sitting down for breakfast. It was a kitten-like gesture though her face bore the look of a cat that swallowed a frog. He came up behind Katie's chair and laid a heavy hand on her shoulder. "You are not to tell anyone, I want you to wear anything. *Do you hear me, Kathryn O'Malley?*"

"Yes, Daddy. I'm sorry, I was kidding. I love my presents."

He stormed from the room slamming the front door on his way out. Pinch wondered if frogs liked leftover scrambled eggs.

Katie set the five vials by her place mat, ogling them as she ate. When she noticed Pinch struggling, buttering her toast, she offered to help and asked about Pinch's hand. "I cut myself last night…on the rim of the creamed corn can."

"Does it hurt?"

"No," she lied, "it's just awkward," and flexed her hand to dispel any notion of pain.

Katie chomped down her eggs then eagerly opened the clear bottle of polish, staring at the transparent fluid, saying, "*Nuuuude*…. In the *Nuuuude*" – the word rolling easily off her lips. She recapped the bottle, eyes twinkling, lips pursed. "When can I do my *nuuuude* thing, mother dear?"

"Watch your tongue, Katie. Didn't that kind of language just rile your father?" She bit into her toast but stopped chewing when her ears picked up what her mouth had just said. Her chest tightened. She ran to the sink and chucked up her eggs and toast.

Katie was crying by the kitchen table. "It's okay, Honey. I shouldn't talk with food in my mouth." But spilling her gut had little to do with food. She should have been immune. Yet somehow she'd acquired the 'watch-your-tongue' disease, and her body recoiled hearing her spray that toxin onto Katie. Pinch slumped in her chair and smiled at Katie. "Why don't we do 'the nude thing' when Dad is at his afternoon class?"

Katie had prepped her room for the event, bed straightened, everything off it but her teddy bear propping up Monet's calendar. "It'll be like having Grandma Duffy with us," she said. She opened her window a crack so the smell wouldn't make

Pinch sick again, then she wrapped an afghan around Pinch's shoulders to keep her from getting a chill. They chatted as they applied *In the Nude*. And while Katie had adapted well to New York, she'd apparently suffered in silence when Pinch's mother died shortly after the move.

"Why didn't you tell me how much you missed Grandma Duffy?"

Katie shrugged. "I thought I wasn't supposed to talk about her."

"I never said that."

"But you never talk about her, Mom. Sometimes, I feel like she was never even here." She looked at Pinch and smiled. "But you talked about her last night, with Monet's petals. "

Pinch pointed to the vials of whitish nail polish. "I think she'd love these too."

"Yeah," Katie said fluttering her fingers. "Let's call them Monet's snowflakes."

"Did I ever tell you about the time she had a snowball fight with Uncle Bryan? I was four or five. Grandma and I were making a snowman, and Uncle Bryan kept whacking me with snowballs from his snow fort. Well, she finally had it with him and lured him out of his fort, but he ducked just in time, and her perfect strike crashed through the window on the front porch."

"Grandma nailed a window!"

"Yup. And Uncle Bryan had to pay for the new one from his allowance."

"I love how she smelled. And when I slept over, she'd let me snuggle with her fox watching TV."

"I hated that thing," Pinch said, "with its beady eyes and

leather snout. I know they were popular with women years ago, but I wouldn't wear that thing."

"She wore it! Like, *out…?* I thought it was a furry toy. It must have been fun growing up with Grandma Duffy."

"She had her moments," Pinch said, wiping the corner of her eye.

"You're fun too, Mom, but not when you're barfing!"

They capped the afternoon making plans for Katie birthday the next day. She'd wanted a party with friends. Steve nixed that idea having 'booked' the house for watching TV then added, "Ten is too old for a child's party, anyway." So Pinch crafted a two-pronged celebration; on Katie's birthday, mother and daughter would visit Manhattan then her best friend, during Spring Break, she'd take Katie and Vanessa to the Statue of Liberty.

Finding a Monet in an uptown museum had been a bonus on their trip to Manhattan.

The cut in Pinch's hand had worsened over the weekend; by Monday morning, the skin was red and tender to the touch. She walked to a drop-in clinic and met with Dr. Isabel Vasquez, a dapper woman with a strong voice and warm brown eyes who looked to be a bit older than Pinch. Cuts in the kitchen were common; rather than explain a smashed bottle of polish in the bathroom sink, she stayed with the lie about cutting herself on the creamed corn can. She left the clinic two hours later with a tetanus shot in her arm, a prescription in her purse, and a curious look from those warm brown eyes. The glass splinter the doctor removed from her hand stayed behind.

Steve was in a great mood when he came home that evening. "Bryan called me at work. He's got great hockey seats for the night we arrive over Easter break. I changed our plane tickets." He held up the envelope. "We'll leave Holy Thursday morning, instead of at night. You girls can spend the extra time with my mother. She'll be thrilled. She wants us to move back." He put the tickets in the desk and handed Pinch an envelope of blank tests. "They're only quizzes, so I won't need your comments." She rubbed her cut palm. He frowned, then smiled. "Good thing you didn't cut your writing hand, midterms are next week, and my students will expect to see comments."

"What's the matter with ya hand?" Lydia said.

Pinch stopped scratching. "It's just a small cut. Healing, but itchy. Do I smell fish?"

"Yep. Nothing like a little sand and sea to cure some cabin fever."

"Winter *is* getting long."

"Hey! Why don't ya join me in Puerto Rico next week?"

"Hey! Why didn't you tell me you were going?"

"Got the call last night – keynoter at a food convention bailed. Flying out Monday, be back Saturday afternoon. Chili, next Friday morning, is cancelled."

Pinch turned down the trip, claiming too short a notice... and settled in Lydia's office, selecting the *Still Lifes*, the *Nursery*, and *Play Time* photo files from which to cull words for Gertie's reading cards, their titles suggesting simple words and everyday objects. Gertie wasn't joining the trio today; Pinch laid the files on her chair in the kitchen. Smith ladled a fishy brew into their bowls. Today's number was most unique with its watery base, limpy lumps, multi-colored beans, shredded greens tasting too tart to be spinach.

"It's kale," Lydia said.

"What about these pale lumps?"

"Smoked eel."

She'd never had eel. Some things were too foreign to put in your mouth. She pricked the fish with her fork. "What does smoked eel taste like?"

"Smoked eel," Lydia barked.

"No bread today?"

Lydia pointed to a bowl of breadcrumbs sitting on the table where the bread usually sat. "Ain't this the scene – fish, river rocks, seaweed and sand! Betcha didn't know St. Pat flushed the eels out of Ireland before he tackled the snakes."

"That's news to me," Pinch said.

"Well, Paddy had taken to playing the pipes sitting by the river at night. But he played so bad, drove the eels clear down to the bay where the locals bagged 'em and smoked 'em on the beach til they weren't any eels any more."

"Sounds fishy to me." Pinch tilted her head. "What are you dishing out today?"

"Just a wee bit of chili con blarney!"

Smith left right after the meal needing to attend dress rehearsal, at her daughter's school, for the St. Paddy's Day parade. "Are you in charge of costumes?" Pinch said.

"No, I'm St. Patrick. I strut around the schoolyard luring snakes with my tambourine." She asked Lydia to save her a big piece of blueberry-rhubarb pie. "I'll have it later when we color the Easter eggs."

"What a different combo for a pie. Where did you buy it?" Pinch said.

"The bakery at The Market. Fresh outta Gertie's head. That kid's got the making of a genius."

"I didn't see a bakery there, though it is a big place. Where do the women live?"

"Building was an old hotel, covers the whole city block. Top floors house the woman and kids. Ground floor's strictly retail. The bakery's one of the mom-and-pop jobs along with the bookstore, deli, craft shop, card store, beauty salon, florist and the like."

"Independent proprietors?"

"Yes and no. The Market owns and manages the physical space, but past and present residents own and manage the businesses. Gives the women a safe place to get on their feet. Chance to earn money, and learn a trade. What did ya think of the place?"

"Truthfully? I thought it was strange. Someone approached us when we walked in, and the next thing, Gertie is gone, and I'm standing there alone. I thought it was kind of rude."

"Not as rude as what happened to Gertie, so get over it, Missy – it ain't about you!" She pointed to the photo files on the empty chair. "Show me what ya picked for Gertie's word cards." Pinch cleared off the table, remembering how Smith had helped get the dishes to the sink.

"I kept it simple, as you suggested," Pinch said, "and skipped the civil rights-, anti war-, and women's lib- movements for the *Still Life's*, *The Nurs*—"

"Not the *Stills!*" Lydia said and crossed her arms defiantly, her eyes boring into Pinch.

"You said I could choose whichever files I wanted."

"I lied. What else have ya got?"

Pinch handed her the other two folders then left, needing to use the bathroom. When she returned, Lydia was bent over the table, peering at baby pictures. "Hey, lookey here, this tyke was a preemie like you were, Pinch."

Pinch looked at the folder and laughed. "I thought your nursery photos were flowers. Why were you taking baby pictures?"

"Worked at a hospital during the lean years. Best was when the weak got strong enough to leave. Wonder where Chuckie is now." She leaned into each child's eyes, nodding, smiling. When she was done, Pinch returned them to their folder; then, casually spilled the *Still Lifes* on the table, confident their photogenic quality would be equal to the others.

"*Hey! Put those away!*" Lydia turned aside.

Pinch did a double take; she picked up the folder and reread the label. "These must be in the wrong file," she said, gaping at a sordid mix of somber-faced women...not the fruit, fish and flowers commonly seen in a still life picture. "What are these – mug shots?"

"They should have been so lucky. My *Stills* are fucking morgue shots."

CHAPTER 7

The Confession

THE FACES OF DEATH bore a similar look to the Stranger on her birthday morn. Pinch wanted to turn away but couldn't, leaning closer, taking in each gory detail like a lookyloo passing an accident. She asked about the dark dots on one woman's neck. "Cigarette burns," Lydia said, slinking into her chair.

"What about the lines on this woman's cheek?"

"Razor cuts."

Pinch didn't linger on the young woman with a crushed skull, but asked about the older one bearing no visible scars. "Drowned herself when her husband won custody of the kids. The bastard claimed she was an unfit mama, running off outta the blue, leaving him to fend with the brood. Never told how he liked taking the belt to her, now and again, that she split so's the kids wouldn't see the bruises. Not that the tykes didn't know. They always know, but what can a kid do...? She had no support. No one countered his claims. When he snatched the kids, he stole her reason to live and then told how her suicide proved she was unfit. Hard to beat the system when ya out there all alone."

Pinch stroked a shadow below one woman's eye and swallowed hard seeing Lydia studying her face. She scratched her palm. "Is this how you knew about my eye?"

"Yeah. And what's with ya hand?"

"I cut it on a tin can."

"Don't tell me – a creamed corn can?"

"Who told you that!"

"Heard 'bout a gal got cut on a can of corn. Damnedest thing – the tin left a piece of glass in her hand!"

Pinch corralled the *Stills* and eased them into their folder. "Whatever happened to doctor/patient confidentiality?"

"Ya fingered yourself. Doc never said *who*. Wanna tell me about it, or should I guess?"

Pinch rubbed her forehead. Anything was better than sitting through one of Lydia's theories. "My husband didn't like the orange nail polish and smashed the bottle in my bathroom sink. I cut my hand hiding the mess from my daughter."

"Hiding the mess. Heard that one before." She grabbed her canes and limped out of the kitchen.

Pinch took a deep breath, the weight of one lie lifted. She joined Lydia in the living room where the old woman sat in the chair beneath Grace, fanning herself with a magazine, her face red and sweaty. She motioned Pinch toward the sofa. "Come sit with me a spell."

Wilbur and Orville dropped out of the tree and rubbed against both women's legs. Pinch sat on the edge of sofa. "Are you okay, Lydia?"

"Don't rightly know. How long ya been abused?"

"I'm not abused!" Lydia stared stoically like a mother awaiting a child's confession. "It's not what you think. He didn't cut me. He wasn't even home!"

"Don't need to be in the room if he's already in ya head. What about the shiner – did ya face fall into his fist?"

"No! It was just a slap."

Lydia raised an eyebrow. Pinch shrugged. "Maybe a hard slap."

"Or maybe a slam? How about a *grand* slam?"

Pinch walked toward the window, Wilbur cutting her off, mewing at her ankles. She bent down to pet him. Her hands shook. She covered her face, wanting to disappear. Lydia asked if she wanted some tea. She shook her head. "I'm sorry to bring my weeds into your garden, but things are not as bad as you think. Honestly. I can deal with it."

"Ain't playing rummy, Pinch, playing with ya life. Look in the mirror – ya ain't Jesus Christ. Nobody's gonna be saved by ya dying. And what about ya kid…should she have to deal with ya dying?"

A gentle fog was settling in the harbor, Libby's face fading in the mist. Pinch wiped her eyes with the back of her hand. Her fingers were cold. She stared at her nails. They were colorlessly dressed in *Transparency* this week. "At least I'm better off than Gertie. My husband would never embarrass me in public."

Lydia smacked the arm of the chair. "Well, there's the answer!" She pointed to a nearby table. "Do me a favor. Fetch me some catnip in that covered candy dish."

Lydia tossed the treats like a trainer flipping fish to a dolphin and chatted with the cats as if Pinch weren't even there. "What answer...?" Pinch said.

"Go public. The pimp won't. If you can learn to be pitiful, you can learn to be powerful."

Pinch straightened her back. "I'm not pitiful, but you're a batty, old woman."

"Rather be batty than battered. Difference is more than two *e's*."

"My marriage isn't perfect, but don't lump me with the *Stills*. It was *one* hit, on a bad night. I should've read him better. I'm not pitiful, I just haven't mastered the game."

"Jeez Louise, Pinchey. Validate yourself. Set yourself free!"

Her shouts drove the cats back up the tree. Both women jumped when a voice from behind loudly cleared her throat. Smith gave them a wide-eyed look and puttered into the room. She wore a kelly green dress and carried two dozen eggs and a tambourine. Her daughter, Sarah Jane, followed behind with an Easter egg coloring kit; she shook hands with Pinch and gave Lydia a high-five. "Do me a favor and bring me my wheelchair, darling," Lydia said.

"You okay?" Smith said

"Feeling a bit blue, and don't want trip on my grief."

"We can color the eggs tomorrow morning," Smith said.

"Put on the water. Be in shortly. Just helping Pinch pull some weeds from her garden."

"My sympathies, Pinch." Smith strolled to the kitchen, smacking her hip with the tambourine, singing "McNamara's Band."

Lydia plodded to the window. "Come, take a look at Libby, Pinch, let her power creep into your pores."

"No, you look at her – she's a statue. She can't love, can't share, can't live, can't care. She can't talk, and can't walk. Can't stop shit from falling on her face and can't wash it off when it does. She's helpless, Lydia, not powerful. Let *that* creep into your pores!"

Lydia's mouth fell. She muttered something about bird shit, wind and rain. "*Jeez,* Pinch, she's no better than the *Stills.* Silent and scarred with nobody tending her needs."

Pinch had never heard her so despondent. "She'll be fine, she's a national monument. Remember how the country came together, chipping in to restore her, back in the 70s?"

"That's right!" Lydia said, looking restored herself. "Makes ya feel proud being part of a caring community. We can all sleep tight knowing everyday folks will lend her a hand before the cracks in her armor bring her down."

Pinch laid her hand on Lydia's shoulder, the two of them looking at the statue. "People do step forward once they see they're needed," Pinch said. "And there's nothing wrong with needing a helping hand."

"Yeah, shit happens to the best. But how they gonna see it if they're left in the dark?"

"See what? I'm missing the point."

Lydia threw her hands in the air. "*Hallelujah! Praise the Lord! She knows she's missing the point!*" She pointed her finger at Pinch. "Listen up, Missy. You're not a cat. Stop burying your shit. Your silence is feeding his power."

Smith shuffled into the room rattling the tambourine,

staring long and hard at Lydia. "Gotta run, Pinchey. We'll chat when I'm back from Puerto Rico." She gave a wave and sashayed off to the kitchen.

Pinch slammed the door on her way out knowing she'd never come back to this place. But the impact jolted the nest in the wreath and sent the robin and her egg flying to the floor. The bird's head landed under her boot; the egg split cleanly in two. She tucked the egg pieces into her purse then twisted the robin back in shape. Its beak was still tweaked, and sitting now, on an empty nest, it looked to be shrieking – not singing. "Sorry," she said, more to the bird than the Wizard of "Odd" on the other side of the door.

CHAPTER 8

Pipe Dreams

"MOM, I'M PLAYING JUDAS FOR REAL!" Katie dropped her book bag and pranced around the kitchen. "The boy who was supposed to be Judas came back to school today. His face is full of chicken pox scabs, and he doesn't want to go on stage, so Sister CeCe gave me the part because I've been reading his lines."

Steve didn't share Katie's excitement hearing the news at dinner. "Too bad you don't have the chicken pox. Judas Escargot is the worst person to be."

"It's Judas *Iscariot,* Daddy. And don't you remember – I already had the chicken pox. Anyways, it's just a play. The best part is getting to kiss Robert Hamilton. He plays Jesus."

"Isn't she too young to be kissing boys?" he asked Pinch.

"*Daaad,* that's how Judas betrayed Jesus." Katie sauntered over to Steve's chair and bowing said, "Hello, Lord," then kissed him on the cheek. "That's how the Romans knew which guy to take – Judas told them to take the one he kissed."

"I know how it goes, Kathryn, but girls should play ladies,

and boys should be the men. Cross-playing and dressing are inappropriate."

"I'll be wearing a sheet, not a suit."

"No matter. That nun has too much power down there. I've a good mind to mention this to the Monsignor at the meeting tonight."

"But Dad, tonight's the dress rehearsal. Nobody knows the lines but me"

"Well, things would never have gotten this bad had I been putting on the play."

Katie drew silent. Minutes later, she asked to be excused from the table.

Steve continued his ranting, stopping only to gnaw on a fried chicken leg. "The seeds of sexuality are planted early in children. I don't like her playing a man, no less, Judas Iscariot!" He pointed the chicken bone at Pinch. "You should have protested when you found out she was the understudy. Now look what's happened – some lucky kid gets the chicken pox, and my daughter gets betrayed!"

His mouth was like an abscess oozing pus, his voice a drill droning in her head. She rubbed her temples; the tension had started in the morning, her follow-up visit to Dr. Vasquez, knowing the doctor had discussed her wound with Lydia – God knows how they knew each other. Then there was the job issue.... She wanted to quit, but the Stranger resisted. Hard enough silencing your internal voice without needing to tune out the nag at your dinner table. He tossed the chicken bone on his plate. "That wench is trying to embarrass me. Katie ought to be playing the Virgin Mary, not the wretch of mankind parading on stage as a man. I volunteer more than anyone at the church. How dare she treat my daughter like the common brood! Just wait. That bitch doesn't know who she's dealing with."

"For God's sake, get a grip, Steve! It's only a play – a play for *God's* sake. I'm sure the Monsignor will be armed with prayers to purge Katie of *wanton desires* to dress like a man!" She crossed her arms in front of her chest, her head about to explode.

He stared at her wide-eyed. A smirk grew on his face. He pulled his pipe from his pocket, struck a match, lit the bowl, all the while stealing glances her way. "It seems I've failed to *purge* your bent for sarcasm, my dear." He leaned back blowing smoke rings in the air. She rose to leave. He bolted forward and grabbed her arm, skimming figure-8s on the inside of her wrist with the stem of his pipe. She jerked her arm free – what used to scintillate now repelled. "Sit!" he said. "I'll only be a minute." He smiled when she took her seat, though she pushed her chair back from the table not to feel trapped.

"College coeds are cute when they disagree, my dear, but you're a wife and a mother, not a coed anymore. Mothers are role models, and make no mistake, I will not tolerate your sarcasm in my house – understood?" He said the last line waving his pipe beneath her nose. She remembered her joy, buying him the piece five years ago when his first book was published – a manuscript, like his current endeavor, fed on her research and polished by her prose. The beautifully carved briarwood had served as a symbol of her role in his success. She looked away, the symbol now reeking oppression. He got up and stood behind her. Her shoulders tightened when he bent and kissed her cheek. He petted the back of her head like a dog, slid his hand down her ponytail twisting a tress around one of his talons, pulling down *ever so slowly* til her eyes stared up at the ceiling. "As I said before, Katie is a girl and should only play females. And you, my sweet, are a lady – act like one." He kissed the top of her nose, gently released his grip on her hair, and planted the pipe in his mouth before sauntering from the room.

She stared at the ceiling, losing herself in its untroubled blandness til a crack in the plaster grabbed her eye. How long had that been there? Was it something to look into? She longed for the days when a crack was a line you avoided on the sidewalk, something you could skip around – not a warning of structural concern....

"Mommy. I need you!"

The call pierced the quiet like a siren at dawn. She ran upstairs. Katie was in tears, wrapped in a twisted sheet looking more like a mummy than a Biblical disciple. Pinch fared no better, crafting a Judas costume, but something triggered visions of the Statue of Liberty. After viewing *Libby's* garb in the encyclopedia, Pinch ripped the sheet in three and easily fashioned a floor-length tunic draped by a separate shoulder-swag, the remaining piece used for a headdress. Katie strolled toward the mirror saying, "Hello, Lord," and was planting a kiss on a phantom Jesus when Steve called up from downstairs announcing it was time to leave. He frowned when he saw her costume. Katie hugged Pinch goodbye. "Great idea about the statue, Mom. She has a sad face and 'thorns' just like Jesus on the cross."

Pinch thought about Katie's connection of the naked embodiment of a sacrificial life and the overdressed, ironclad symbol of liberty. And she thought about her own, so-called inalienable rights. She had *life*. But just like the cross-to-bear credo she was raised to revere, *liberty,* and the *pursuit of happiness,* played better in word than deed. She locked the front door then cleaned off the kitchen table, eager to view the *Stills* in private. One by one, she lay them on the table – a crazy quilt of brutal lives condensed into black and white glossies. Patterns emerged, scanning them *in toto*. She grouped them first by injury, then age, then ethnicity…gently picking them up and setting them down like a neo-natal nurse tending to preemies. Too young, too old, too banged up, too *still*. She looked into their lifeless eyes, lingering long enough to say a prayer for each before slipping the lot into the folder. When they wouldn't slide in, she shook the folder upside down. Tumbling out was a small sepia photo of a woman lying on an altar, draped in white.

Unlike the *Stills,* this image was backlit, a blurred silhouette veiling the woman's features. Eerie yet elegant, the pose appeared staged. If so, why file her in with the *Stills*? She peered at the picture through a magnifying glass seeking details among shadows. Who is she?

Maybe your best friend, the Stranger said.

I don't have a best friend.

Maybe she's your sister?

I don't have a sister. There's only me.

Then maybe it's you...?

She lay the picture face down and grabbed Katie's tiny mirror off the windowsill. She looked at her face. The area between her nose and lip glistened with beads of sweat. She swiped the sweat with her forefinger. *Of course it's not me. I'm sweating – she's not.* She turned the photo over. Something was scrawled. The letters were smudged. She leaned in with the magnifier. *R.I.P. Mother - 1952.*

The neighbor's dog started barking. She looked at the clock. *Shit. They're home.* She dropped the sepia in with the *Stills* and hid the folder in a box of *Tide* detergent, and was leaving the laundry room when Katie burst through the door. "Hi, Honey. How was rehearsal?"

Katie ran to her sobbing. "Dad and Sister CeCe had a fight. He's going to do the play next year, but the Monsignor said I should still be Judas because it's too late to change things around. Oh, Mom...what if Sister CeCe doesn't like me anymore?"

"Of course she'll still like you, Katie. Dealing with parents is part of teaching. I'm sure Dad's not the first parent she's had a disagreement with, and nothing he does will change her feelings about you. C'mon, it's late. Let's get you out of your costume and up to bed while he's parking the car."

Pinch joined Steve in the kitchen after Katie fell asleep. He was brewing his chamomile nightcap and wearing a smile that lit up the room. She busied herself at the sink, scrubbing a pot with a steel-wool pad, over and over again. He slipped up behind her whistling a ditty and wrapped one hand around her waist, the other around her wet wrist. The scouring motion stilled. She eyed their reflection in the window above the sink. They looked in love. He whispered in her ear. "Would you mind if we had sex tonight and resume our routine the following Saturday?"

She loosened her grip on the pad, its steel-wool edges pricking into her fingers. "I'd rather not. I don't feel a hundred percent tonight."

"A brandy will bring up that number. Come now, my dear, don't make me beg. Call it an early birthday present."

She shrugged, then nodded – he was happy now, God knows how he'd feel Saturday night, after the play. She took a quick shower. Brushed her hair and her teeth. Then threw on her gray negligee, the one with the longest sleeves. The brandy he'd left on her nightstand was green. She dumped it down the bathroom sink. She wished he had poured a cherry brandy; the mint gave her indigestion. He'd be sipping his chamomile tea right now, joining her after the news. Sex would be fast. It always was. Years ago, when she suggested some fore play before intercourse, he had added the brandy to their weekly routine, "to help prime your pump, so to speak." Besides priming her pump, it dumbed down her mind and flooded her senses with delectable sweetness and deodorized his chamomile scent.

She puffed up her pillow, settled in the bed and grabbed *Angela's Ashes* – a memoir about growing up poor, and Catholic, in New York and Ireland. She was barely into the story when she heard his footsteps on the stairs. She closed the book and turned off her light. Her stomach tightened as he neared the room. She wished she'd downed the brandy. Indigestion died faster than disgust.

He labored tonight, panting like a train, polluting the place with his chamomile breath. She silently recited the rosary, counting the beads off in her head. *Hail Mary, full of grace, the Lord is with thee. Blessed are thou amongst women, and blessed is the fruit of thy womb, Jesus. Holy Mary, mother of God, pray for us sinners, now and at the hour of our death, amen.* She paused mid-prayer when he entered her...was it wrong to pray during sex? The digits on the clock glowed blue in the dark; they seemed to be stuck in place. Across the room, the radiator hissed. His sweat coated her skin.

She started praying again – random words punctuating each rock of the bed. *Hail. Womb. Sinners. Death.* His body stilled. Fell limp. Felt heavy. He thanked her. She thanked God it was over.

"Pray we conceived a son tonight," he said and receded into the dark. She lay on her back. Still. Stiff. Splayed as if nailed to the mattress.

"Everyone loved my costume last night," Katie told Pinch while setting the breakfast table. "But I still need a headdress." She quickly sat down, Steve entering the room.

"Good morning, girls. Everyone sleep well?" Pinch nodded. Katie followed suit then dropped her eyes and munched on her *Frosted Flakes*. Steve tapped Pinch on the arm. "I'm making you costume director next year. From what I saw at dress rehearsal last night, Katie looked better than the rest."

"Sister CeCe loved how you got the idea from Libby, Mom."

Libby! Pinch couldn't believe her ears.

"Who's Libby?" Steve asked.

"The Statue of Liberty," Katie said.

"Who told you that?"

"Sister Cece."

"Great, now she's teaching them bastardizations."

"What's a 'basta zation?'"

"A distorted explanation of something true," he said. "It comes from the word *bastard* which is a child born to an unmarried couple."

Katie looked confused. "Jesus was a bastard?"

He slammed down his cup, went to slap Katie but missed, sending her cereal spoon flying. Pinch jumped up. "Stop it, Steve. She's asking a question, not passing judgment."

"I'm warning you, my dear, get a handle on what comes out of her mouth." He turned to Katie. "Did that nun tell you Jesus was a bastard?"

"No, Daddy. I just never heard about Mary and Joseph's wedding."

Katie slept at Vanessa's that night and was gone before Steve got home from his school. The lack of tension in the house was sadly evident to Pinch. Still, she enjoyed the breather from running interference between father and daughter. At breakfast the next morning, Steve talked about wanting a son. "He'd be Stephen Patrick O'Malley, III, and I'd finally get to do all the things a man does with his boy. But we'd need to find a bigger place and one with a garage, maybe on Staten Island."

"Don't get your hopes up. I haven't conceived in 10 years."

"I know, my dear. But God works in mysterious ways. Maybe our time has come."

She glanced at the clock anxious to leave for Lydia's place to drop off the photos and repaired egg before meeting with Gertie for her first reading lesson. "I'll be heading out for the library soon. Aren't you going jogging?"

"My last midterm is this afternoon, so I've got some time this morning. Shall I join you at the library? Get a glimpse of what's there for my *The Horses of Camelot?*"

"It'd be counterproductive. I work faster when I'm alone."

He smiled. "I'll have to amuse myself then. When do you expect to get home?"

"Early afternoon. I need to get the girls after gymnastics, at the *Y*."

He walked her to the bus stop, one hand clasping her elbow, the other carrying her briefcase. Her breath was short; the crammed briefcase was poised to pop open, if jarred, and spill out the photos, word cards, and *Tiffany* box cradling the egg. She sighed audibly once she sat on the bus and gave him a wave and a plastic smile as he left for his morning run. She reached Lydia's just before nine and straightened a feather on the robin before placing the egg beneath it. The bird looked to be singing, again! How fragile joy must be when one misstep

71

can steal it away. She rang Lydia's bell then turned, hearing the elevator *bing*. Gertie bounced into the hall sporting a smile and a cluster of balloons. "Hey, Pinch, I see you got the message."

"What message?"

"To meet me here instead of at the library."

"I never got the message, Gertie."

"Then I reckon we lucked out. Must still be on yer answering machine."

"*Oh no.*" Pinch grasped the doorknob and slowly sank to the floor.

"Gosh, Pinch, what's the matter?" Gertie bent down to help her up while rapping on Lydia's door. When no one answered, and Pinch didn't budge, she ran to Smith's, knocking furiously on her door.

Smith answered first. "What happened?" she said, plodding over to Pinch.

"Don't rightly know. We was talking, then she folded."

Lydia's door opened. "What's going on? Someone lose a contact?"

"Looks like Pinch fainted, but her eyes are open...."

Smith took the balloon; Gertie led Pinch to Lydia's sofa. Lydia peeled off her coat and propped a pillow under her head. "Not surprised ya passed out. No meat on ya bones. Got some Chili Piccadilly in the freezer. Hang on, Pinchey, I'll nuke it."

"No chili. I'm not hungry. Gertie! When did you leave the message?"

"I didn't do it. I left real early this morning and asked the front desk at The Market to call." Pinch started shaking. Smith

72

spread the lap quilt over her shoulders. Lydia approached with water and a worried look. Pinch took two sips, then started to rock in place. Gertie looked about to cry. "Did I do something wrong?"

"My husband doesn't know about this job." Pinch looked at Lydia. No tears, just fire in her eyes.

"Why'd ya come by if you didn't get the message?"

"To return the egg in your wreath. It fell and broke when I slammed your door last week. *Who puts a breakable egg on their door – what were you thinking?*" she screamed.

"Listen hear, Missy—"

"Button it, Lydia," Smith said. "It's okay, Pinch. The egg's not important."

"I also came to resign. I can't – no *won't* – do this anymore. But now, I've got to find out what Steve knows." Smith suggested she call home and erase the message if it's still on the machine. "I don't know the answering code. Steve said I'd never need it…"

Lydia pointed to the portable phone on the table with the catnip candy-dish. "Call The Market, Gertie. Find out if they used her name when they called."

Gertie let out a whoop when she hung up the phone. "The gal who called forgot yer name, so's all she said was the reading meeting was here at ten."

There was a collective sigh of relief. Then Pinch sat up abruptly. "Wait a minute! It can't be on my phone, I haven't given my number to anyone in New York."

"Ya gave it to me when ya came on board, after ya passed the 'Tude Test."

"I gave you a wrong number."

"Ya screwed around from the start!"

"I couldn't risk having you call me at home."

"Wouldn't have been a 'risk' if ya told me the truth on day one."

"I used the number on my police report, Pinch," Gertie said, "the one you gave that nice *copper,* Paul, the day the Creep beat me up."

Punch slumped. "I thought I'd be breaking the law if I lied on an eyewitness form...."

The telephone rang; Lydia told Gertie to pick it up. "It's yer front desk. Somebody sent you flowers, but the delivery guy won't let anyone else bring them up." She covered the phone and giggled. "Reckon he don't trust yer security people."

"Tell 'em to put the guy on. And hit the speakerphone."

"Hello? Hell-*lo!*" The voice hinted irritation.

Pinch bolted upright and waved her arms, catching Lydia's eye. She put a finger to her lips and mouthed, That's...my... husband!

"*Hell-lo!*" The irritation was evident now.

"Yeah, Sonny, hang on a sec." Lydia walked to the phone and hit the 'hold' button. "Ya sure it's him?"

"Of course I'm sure! They must have left your address on the message. You can't let him up, Lydia. He's hoping to find me here."

"He has to come up," Smith said. "It's the only way to guarantee you'll get out of the building undetected. Stall him Lydia. We need to figure this out."

"Does he pack a pistol?"

"Good Lord, Lydia! What do you think he is!"

"I know what he is – you're the one who's confused." She took the phone and reconnected the call. "Sorry to keep ya waiting, Sonny. What ya asking is against the rules, but I'll bend them if ya do me a favor. Got a craving for something cool and sweet. Would ya mosey down the street to *McDonalds* and bring up a chocolate shake with ya flowers?" There was a long pause, the room still as a cemetery, then Lydia gave a thumbs-up and thanked him for his kindness. She relayed her request to the security desk. "And make sure he's got the goods before he comes up."

Pinch got up to leave. "Wait!" Smith said. "We don't *know* if he left. He could be watching the elevators."

Gertie grabbed her coat. "I'll go down and scout out the place?"

Lydia waved her hand in the air. "And what if he's wearing a get-up, Gertie? Or standing outside, or down the street hoping to catch her walking by…?" Two pigeons flew onto the windowsill, pecking at each other then backing off. Lydia tapped on the window with her cane. "Beat it, guys – go find somebody to shit on!" She was doing a serious chew when Smith brought up their adjoining closets.

"Pinch could hide in yours til it's safe for her to go then shoot out to the elevators, via *my* closet." She opened a door near the sitting area in Lydia's living room. "My closet's unlocked so you can get to it from here right now."

Lydia grinned. She nodded at Smith. "Are ya game to kick some ass, *Clarissa,* long enough for Pinch to get out of the building and away from this street?"

"Yes, ma'am! We'll need disguises. Do you still have the stuff?"

"In the trunk in my bedroom."

Lydia handed Gertie a flashlight and directed her to clear a path between the two closets, then she hopped on her wheelchair and tore off toward her bedroom. Pinch paced the room, not sure where to go, or what to do. She rubbed her arms; hearing Steve's voice *here* gave her the chills. "I can't believe this is happening. How could I've been so stupid, thinking I could work on the sly without him knowing?"

"Don't be so hard on yourself," Smith said, "time will show he's the off-balance one."

"He's not a bad person. He just wants me to stay home. But I'll go nuts stuck in the house all day.... It's not the house, mind you, it's the stuck part that gets me down, and I'll never get out if he finds I've been working here." She dropped to her knees and wrapped her arms around Smith's solid legs. "Please don't let Lydia tell him. This truth won't set me free. Promise me, Smith. Promise she won't let him know."

Smith pulled Pinch to her feet. "She's strange, not stupid. Don't worry, she won't tell him. Now, let's get you settled in the closet before he comes back."

CHAPTER 9

The Visit

THE CLOSET WAS LINED IN CEDAR and housed a vintage trunk and an antique sewing-machine cabinet. Fabric, hanging straight ahead, was pushed to one side exposing an open door and the innards of Smith's adjoining closet. "I moved this fake Christmas tree far as she wants to go," Gertie said. "You'll be fine, Pinch. Just hug this here wall going through."

Smith stood at the entrance of Lydia's closet. "You'll come out in my bedroom; it's the first room off the entry. The elevators idle on this floor, and hopefully one will be waiting when you leave. But don't go til we've drawn him in and locked Lydia's door – you don't want to meet him in the hall!" She pointed to the air grate high above the trunk. "Listen to what's going on in here from up there."

"I did a walk-through to Smith's front door. It's easy, Pinch." Gertie handed her the flashlight and gave her a hug. "I'll be waiting downstairs to help you git going." She disappeared through Smith's apartment leaving the door ajar between Smith's bedroom and her closet.

"Don't worry about waking up my husband," Smith said. "He flew in from California on the red-eye this morning, and he's already gone to this world. Don't slam any doors when you leave, or the sound might come through." Pinch peered through the closets and grimaced.

Lydia approached in a wiry blond wig carrying a tall pole and a bag of costume props. She handed Smith a bandana and a pair of pointy-framed, tortoise shell eyeglasses. She grinned at Pinch. One of her front teeth was missing. "My old uppers. Only use 'em for special occasions…you okay, Pinchey?"

"Smith's husband is asleep in there. What if I trip on the tree and wake him up?"

"Just tell him ya an angel, and ya looking for Jesus. He'll think he died and went to heaven."

Smith straightened Lydia's wig and tucked in a sprig of her gray hair. Then she stretched the eyeglasses across her chubby face, the ends barely wrapping behind her ears. "Better tie that babushka tight on ya head, *Clarissa,* or those specs will sling-shot off ya face. She'll never forgive us if we kill the *s.o.b.* I think she thinks she still loves him."

Pinch lit the flashlight and closed the closet door. Carefully skirting the Christmas tree, she tiptoed to Smith's front door, left her coat and briefcase on the floor, then tiptoed back, scaled the trunk, killed the flashlight, and peered through the air grate. Smith secured a dishrag to the end of the pole with a pair of rubber bands and bandied it about, as if she was swatting flies. "Do you think this is strong enough, Lydia?"

Pinch jumped off the trunk and opened the door. "You're not going to hit him, are you?"

"*Jeez, Louise* – it's just a prop. Get outta here, will ya?"

"But you look like clowns. And I'm the one carrying the risk if you flop."

Lydia pulled a coin from her pocket and gave Pinch a dead-man's stare. "Ya been carrying the risk for awhile now, and chose not to see it, but we do. The gift of the clown is buying time for the troubled. So what'll it be, Pinch...*heads,* you greet him when he bolts through my door, or *tails,* we help get ya home 'fore he bolts through yours?"

Someone rapped on the door before the coin hit the ground.

Pinch tore into the closet, shut the door, sat on the trunk; the dim light, eerie stillness, scent of old wood evoked a confessional. She remembered her fear that first Confession. Seven years old and frantically looking for sins that were easy enough to remember, bad enough to regret. The dress rehearsals had helped; Grandma Rose pretending to be the priest, sitting on one side of the screen door, Pinch kneeling on the other side, reciting her improprieties. All her sins had related to her brother, Bryan, and she worried what would happen if she forgot to confess them *all.* She could still see the kindness in her grandmother's face gazing at Pinch through the screen door. "Just memorize the sin that makes you feel the worst. It's not about numbers, or being bad – you're making room inside to feed the goodness in your heart."

She squirmed on the trunk, glancing over her shoulder at the air grate above; muddled voices in the distance gave no clue to what was going on. She touched her heart, then made the sign of the cross, saying 'Bless me father for I have si—' Three time she tried. Three times she failed to complete the prerequisite confessional phrase. When her mind gave into the silence, the Stranger spoke up...*Bless me father, I have not sinned.*

Seconds became hours. Sweat rolled down her chest, welling in her bra. All she'd wanted was some time for herself, a small gift...but huge when you're trapped in an eddy of obedience. She sat up straight, raised her hands, let her fingers dance in the cedar-scented air. When a gush of air blew down from the vent, her hands fell limply into her lap. The hair on her neck bristled. The front door was shut. She slid off the trunk, found the button on the flashlight, was about to enter Smith's closet when the voices grew loud and the mumbles became words. Curiosity overcame Fear. She climbed back on the trunk, peered through the vent and settled in for the opening scene of a one-man ruse and a two-woman sting.

Smith was shuffling around the room 'painting' the walls with the rag-pole. Lydia leaned on her canes nearby, randomly sucking on the milk shake. "Who'd ya say sent the flowers, Sonny?"

"I didn't," Steve said looking unfamiliar in an old parka, jeans, and black cowboy hat he'd bought, on an impulse, at a horse show years ago. Pinch felt like an alien. Everything was new...Lydia's getup, Steve's outfit, Smith's unconventional moves. Most jarring was his presence in *her* space, how he was freely walking and talking while she cowered in the dark like a thief.

Lydia slurped the dregs of the milkshake. "Thank ya, kindly, Sonny. Hey, Clarissa, fetch my purse so's I can give this lad a nice tip."

"Excuse me, ma'am, I don't fetch, I just do cobwebs."

"*Excuse me, Clarissa!* We're in a hurry here— What'd ya say ya name was, Sonny?"

"I didn't."

"Lordy, ain't you the cheery one." She walked out of sight and returned with money in her hand. "Hey! Don't get all comfy cozy. Me and Clarissa, we're tidying up for a meeting today. Ain't got time to entertain a Mr. No-name."

"I won't stay long." He spread out on the sofa and picked up a magazine.

"Where's ya manners, *Tex*? Take ya hat off in the presence of ladies."

He gave a cursory glance at the two women. "I'll remove it when I see one."

His embarrassing presence and appalling rudeness dampened Pinch's curiosity. She was getting ready to step down from the trunk when Lydia barked, "Hey! Put that pipe away! Stella don't allow no smoking in her place."

"Who's Stella?" he asked.

"My sister. Me and Clarissa, we're minding the store, while she's away. And Stella said, no smoking, right Clarissa?"

"No smokers or dopers is what she said."

"Too bad," Steve said. "This place smells like a beanery,

and the aromatic scent of cherry tobacco would vastly improve the milieu. Take a smell."

Lydia sniffed the bowl of the pipe then waved it in the air, like a child making bubbles with a plastic wand. "Stella might like this here cherry *mil-loo*. She placed the pipe on the cocktail table atop a stack of magazines. "Not that it's gonna do a hill of beans, seeing as ya'll be on your way once I give ya this nifty tip."

Steve pushed her hand aside. "Give it to a stylist. You look overdue for a haircut."

Lydia glared at him, arms akimbo, canes splaying from her sides like oars on a beached rowboat. "Ain't you the testy one this morning. What happened – forget ya prunes? Clarissa! Fetch me one of them turbo enemas in Stella's bathroom. If ya don't clean ya-self out, Tex, ya'll wish ya only problem was having a bad-hair day."

He looked at his watch. "Stay calm, old woman. My bride should be coming through your door any minute, and when she does, I'll be out of your hair for good."

Smith plodded up to Lydia shaking a rectangular box. "There's only one turbo left."

"We'll make it his tip." Lydia handed him the box. He pushed her arm aside. Then he stood up, opened his parka and scanned the room. "If ya won't take money, or 'Mr. Turbo,' how might we get ya to vamoose?"

"I told you, I'll leave when my sweetheart comes."

"Ain't ya a delivery boy…?"

"Of course not, and stop complaining. I brought you flowers, and a chocolate shake, for letting me wait for my wife."

Lydia scratched her chin. "Ya not a delivery boy, but ya brought me flowers and a shake. And ya never been to Stella's before, but ya meeting ya Honey here."

"That's correct."

"Hey, Clarissa...when did Stella's place become a holding tank for psychos?"

Smith was skimming the baseboards with the pole. "Sorry, ma'am. I ain't wise to what doctors do with the extras."

"Then fetch me the portable phone."

"Sorry, but I'm needing to finish these cobwebs...."

Lydia left for the phone in exaggerated cane-struts looking agitated but harmless. Pinch almost felt sorry for Steve, so full of himself, no doubt believing he had the upper hand. When Lydia swaggered back into view, the phone was tucked in her waistband. She picked his pipe up from the cocktail table, and waved it back and forth saying "*Cherry mil-loo*," then proceeded to the window and leaned on the sill, facing into the room. She flipped the phone open and shut a few times. "Hey Tex! How 'bout I move things along, let Security know that ya bride's coming?"

Steve's foot jerked; he closed the magazine in his lap. "No need to call Security, but thank you. I'm sorry for being rude before. Truth be told, I'm nervous. My wife's birthday is today, and I wanted to surprise her with brunch in Manhattan, but I've been so busy at work this week, I forgot her schedule... something about a reading meeting, here at ten o'clock?"

"Hot dang, Clarissa! We're getting us a new member. A birthday girl to boot. Think we got time to whip up a chocolate cake?"

"That's very gracious, but she won't be staying for the meeting. If you don't mind my asking, what genre are you reading this month? Mystery? Romance? Science Fiction?"

"Webster," Lydia said.

"Ah, American biography. Daniel Webster was a 19th century statesman, a student of classical literature, and an attorney, too."

"Don't think it's Daniel. Clarissa, fetch me the book." Smith sighed loudly then plodded out of view. "Do ya read much, Tex?"

"Yes. I'm a college professor. Are you familiar with the medieval classics?"

Lydia frowned. "Gotta taste of early evil with my first husband, Sam. Bailed before he got to mid-evil."

Steve chuckled. "I'm talking about Olde England. Camelot, and The Knights of the Round Table."

"Spent lots of nights 'round the table sobering up Sam, but that Camelot stuff's a real stumper."

"I'm an expert on that era. What don't you understand?"

"How'd them camels get over to England – those humpers know how to swim?"

Pinch stifled a laugh. Smith reappeared and handed Lydia a book. "No, it ain't Daniel Webster, Tex. Looks like *Merriam*. Son of gun, Clarissa! This book was writ by a lady!"

"You must be pulling my leg. You're reading the dictionary this month?"

"Course not. Everyone knows ya need more than a month to read a jumbo like this. We been working on Webster for— how long, Clarissa?"

"Since 1972, ma'am."

"Been at it near 25 years, now, Tex. This month we're studying *asses.*"

Pinch couldn't see his face, but his upper body stiffened. He looked at his watch. "You people are nuts. I can't get out of here soon enough – when does the meeting start?"

"Most wander in between 10 and 11. What'd ya say, ya gal's name was?"

"I didn't."

"Clarissa. Did Trudi-Crystal say anything 'bout a new member coming this month?"

"Don't think so, ma'am."

Lydia flipped the phone open again. "Ya sure ya misses is in our group, Tex? Ya didn't even know we was studying *asses.* Seems, she'd want to chat-up her findings with a gen-u-ine professor."

"Now that you mention it, she did want to discuss it, but I've been so busy. What protocol do you use for discussing your...words?"

"*Proto* what?" Lydia asked.

"Protocol. What procedure do you use to study *asses?*"

Were the circumstances different, Pinch would have enjoyed watching these two waltz around the other's agenda. She knew she ought to leave, but really – how does a group discuss the word *ass?*

"Well, Tex, first we chew the fat on simple asses – ya basic boob, basic *butt*-tocks, basic beast-of-burden. Then, we mosey on up to the higher-ass words – a*sshole* and *ass kisser.* Then we tackle what's left – *dumb ass, smart ass, wise ass, jackass, tight* *ass, duck's ass, fancy ass, horse's ass, pain-in-the ass, half-ass.* Did I get 'em all, Clarissa?"

"Forgot ass backwards."

Lydia looked over her shoulder and down to her derriere. "That one's more confusing than you, Tex. If something's ass backwards, it's supposed to go the other way. But if something's ass forward, it's gotta be backwards 'cause asses can't do shit if there facing forward. Gotta ask Trudi-Crystal 'bout that. She's our leader. She knows all the stumpers."

Steve looked at his watch. "You're crazy...."

"Least I ain't a dumb ass, acting like a smart ass, waiting for a fancy ass, no-show."

Steve looked toward the front door then scanned another magazine; Lydia strolled up to the sofa and poked at his boots with her canes. "Ya hungry, Tex? Hey, Clarissa. Fetch some mints over there for Tex."

Smith doffed the lid on the catnip dish and extended the nibblets his way. "I don't eat between meals during Lent," he said tersely.

"Surely a mint don't count as food." Lydia took some catnip and walked behind the sofa while Smith proffered the dish again. He hesitated, then plucked a few. When he leaned forward, Lydia slipped some catnip in the well of his cowboy hat. Then she came around and tapped his leg with her cane. "Go sit in the chair. Clarissa needs to check the couch for cobwebs." She poked at his feet til he moved to the chair. It was the first time, since Steve had arrived, that husband and wife faced each other.

Pinch reared back then froze. Had he seen the sudden

86

movement through the grate? When he didn't flinch, she eased in just enough to still see his face.

He mumbled a sneer as he sat in the chair.

Lydia threw her own barb.

He smirked then chuckled and popped a *catmint* in his mouth. That was his first mistake; the second was looking toward the *jingle* and *tingle* in the branches over his head.

Wilbur and Orville descended on his face scrambling for the treats in the well of his hat.

He let out a scream.

Pinch hopped off the trunk.

The last thing she heard was Lydia crowing – "Jeez, Clarissa, maybe mints do count as food."

CHAPTER 10

The Furies

BOTH ELEVATORS WERE THERE to abet her escape. She leaned into one, hit the Basement button then swept her hand upward, lighting all the floor numbers. She dashed into the other elevator and pumped the Close Door button, slumping against the wall when it finally shut. She looked at her watch. The girls would be finished at gymnastics within the hour! She eyed herself in the mirrored doors and saw a ghost of the women in the morgue shots.

The lobby was empty. With no one to delay the elevator's rise, she hit all the floor buttons then hustled toward the street, her mind awhirl with three furies…fleeing before Steve came down, getting to the Y before the girls were done, constructing a plausible story regarding her morning before facing Steve. The doorman was escorting a newborn family into the building and promised to flag her a taxi after settling them into an elevator.

The street was void of cabs. She blindly took off down the street nearly fainting when someone called her name. "Over here, Pinch." Gertie waved from beside a parked police car. "Gee, you took so long up there. What happened – are you okay?"

"I need to get to the Y right away, but there are no cabs, and Steve will be down any minute…." She looked toward Lydia's building. "Help me get one at the next corner."

Gertie said something to the cop then opened the patrol car door. "Git in, Pinch. It's Paul, that *copper* that brung us downtown when the Creep beat me up."

"Hello, again, Mrs. O'Malley. I'm heading in that direction, anyway."

Her eyes filled, part gratitude, part shame. She glanced at the building then slipped in the car. Gertie shut the door. "And don't ferget to call me so's we can hop-to on my lessons."

"Wait…." She quickly gave Gertie the word cards and their corresponding photos. "Have Lydia go over them with you. I'm not sure when I'll be free." She buckled in as the black-and-white eased into the avenue. While her family tree brimmed with policemen, she'd never ridden in a cop car before and sat there in silence, back stiff, eyes glazing over, hands tightly folded in her lap.

Paul broke the quiet. "That kid's court date has been set, has she told you?"

"We haven't talked much today."

"It's a week from next Thursday, 10am. I hope you can make it."

"That's Holy Thursday. I'm flying to Chicago that morning for a family reunion."

"Any chance you can take a later flight?" He spoke in quiet

confidence, his words overriding the myriad sounds spitting from the console radio. She fiddled with her fingers. Crossed her feet. Adjusted the briefcase on her lap. "These spousal abuse cases are hard to pin down, Mrs. O'Malley. Time tends to rob the gal's memory, or fear straps a muzzle to her mouth. Some think that the guy knows better now than to smack her around, but that's more a wish than reality. She thinks you're the greatest for stopping to help her and could use your support going forward – she's just a kid."

"She may be young, but she's pretty strong."

"She's also pretty alone." He pulled up to the Y and cut the engine. She snapped off her seatbelt, anger ripping through her like a raw breeze. "I'm sorry if I'm making you uncomfortable, Mrs. O'Malley, but I'd rather be sorry to you now, than sorry for her later on."

"I'm sorry about her situation, but my flight is booked, and I really can't change it." She jerked the door open. "Thanks for the ride."

The girls were not yet down from their class so she took the time to pull the hidden research from behind her briefcase lining. Since it looked like Steve couldn't tie her to the phone call, she'd used this cache as proof of having worked on his book all morning. She began to relax, her furies contained, and on the way home joked with the girls about their favorite boys.

The foyer was free of pipe smoke. She placed the research on the kitchen table, noting that the message light on the desk phone was blinking. But she didn't need to hear what she already knew and turned to leave the room. That's when she saw the flowers.

The rose bouquet was wrapped in cellophane and cinched with a ribbon, the pouting tips of the blood-red buds clad in velvet innocence. She approached cautiously, as if a coiled cobra sat on her counter, and untied the ribbon freeing the flowers from their cellophane shawl. Once upon a time he had surprised her in a grotto with a kiss and a rose; but now he favored glittery gifts strewing silks and gems upon her like tinsel on a dying tree – their cool texture and money smell no match for a sweet scented rose. She stroked today's petals. A lump formed in her throat. Living with hidden agendas had left her wary of surprise packages. Had she already paid for this long-stemmed gift? Or would the price, like the petals, unfold over time…?

Katie must have turned on the answering machine, the sound of winding tape breaking into Pinch's reverie. She pretended not to hear the message, staying by the sink, staring at the backyard swing. *"Hey, Stevo! Archie, here. Great idea about the tests. Drop by the office after class today. And good news about next week! The boys are open to new blood, so we'll have a chance to talk about your Fellowship over a few beers. You're a prince among men. Thanks a million, Buddy."*

It wasn't what she'd expected. But Steve would be pleased, things moving along on his Fellowship. Two squirrels ran up the oak tree as if playing tag. She smiled. "Is there another message, Katie?"

"No. Hey Dad, do you want me to save your message?"

"No, Kathryn...."

His frame filled the arch between the kitchen and the hall. One arm hovered near his forehead, as if shielding his face from the sun. He moved aside, letting Katie by, then quickly reclosed the entry. Pinch pretended not to notice, filling a vase with water, watching Katie on the swing from the window. He was in stocking feet; no *squeakers* warned when he came and encircled her waist. "Were you expecting a phone call, my dear?"

"No," she said, hoping she hadn't shaken her head too vehemently. "Wait til you see what I got at the library today."

"I didn't see you when I stopped there today."

"I must have been in the Ladies Room. Felt a little queasy this morning. Thanks for the flowers. How was your jog?" Her voice sounded tinny. She slowly exhaled.

He loosened his hold and turned her around. She braced for the worst, remembering the cats and his scream. But his face was scratch free though his cheeks and neck were randomly dotted with plump red spots, as if he had a childhood disease. She acted surprised and offered to tend his wounds, knowing he would expect that.... He glanced out the window toward Katie then took her hand. "Not down here. Up in the bedroom."

He lay on the bed cringing, her dabs of antiseptic scorching each puckering claw-pox. A tear trickled from his eye. She looked away...sad and annoyed...had Lydia mean to hurt him?

Save your sympathy. If he'd found you there, you'd be nursing your wounds, not his.

The Stranger was right. She needed to keep emotional distance, but not indifference. That would raise suspicion. "Sorry for the stinging. I'm almost done." For the second time, she asked him what had happened.

He flicked his hand in a none-of-your-business gesture, which incited an urge to prod his sores, see him squirm like an unearthed worm, under the guise of cleansing. But the cats, in their innocence, had served her revenge, his soon-to-form scars forever reminding them both of his actions today. She brought him aspirins for his "terrible headache," then went downstairs, prepped lunch and de-thorned the roses by the sink.

Katie was sitting in the tree. She waved at Pinch who nodded then kicked the cabinet in frustration. She had ceded her life to a man that charmed and betrayed with identical smiles. And it took a black eye to finally see that his marriage proposal was a ransom note payable on demand "til death do us part." Was it blindness...or stupidity...that she didn't see the truth sooner?

The Stranger suggested a kinder critique. *Maybe it's too depressing to admit the marriage had failed. Maybe you focused too much on your chores than your choices. Maybe it's too hard to take back what you've already ceded. Maybe it's too scary to imagine living on your own.*

She set the roses in the parlor on her mother's old oak table. Crusted in paint and covered with dust, the antique piece had been put out with the trash by Bryan after Mama had died. But the table's claw feet and carved pedestal reflected a craftsmanship of days gone by. Pinch rescued it and had it restored, but it still needed work. She made a mental note to have it fixed before it fell beyond repair. Then she put on an old jacket to tool around the yard with Katie.

The rake felt good in her hands combing matted leaves from sleepy garden beds. It was five days til spring, her first one in New York. The air was crisp, but not biting, perfect for savoring the season. The daffodils were sprouting through blankets of decay, their slender sage tips reclaiming a place in the sun. She bagged the old leaves. They smelled like root vegetables, hearty and organic, like Lydia's chili dishes. She felt more relieved than ashamed now that the truth about Steve was out in the open. Maybe carrying someone else's sins was a burden best left to a Savior. She fingered the bud on a small rhododendron, wondering its color and timing of its bloom. She envied how plants were free to just *be* and not plagued with concerns about tomorrow…like fearing Katie would master the art of sarcastic rebuttal before learning how to read her father's moods.

After jumping a number of times off the swing, Katie invited her mother to try. Pinch grinned like a fool pumping hard, surging high, basking in a flurry of breeze hugs. When she finally let go, she exceeded her expectations and nearly crashed into the sprouting daffodils. "Whoa, Mom! Did you know that you could fly? Go back and do it again."

"Not without a parachute, don't want to break my leg. Let's go in and have lunch. As soon as your father leaves for school, we'll work on your Judas headdress."

They walked arm in arm to the house. "Guess what, Mom,

but don't tell Dad – I think Robert Hamilton likes me!" Pinch raised her eyebrows. Steve would be relieved; their *Judas* was still interested in boys.

The phone rang as they entered the house but stopped mid-ring. Had Steve picked it up, upstairs? What if it was someone from The Market? She sighed in relief when he ignored her upon entering the room putting his envelope of blank midterms on the desk beside her purse. He was dressed in sweat pants and looked at the clock. "How long before lunch?"

"Enough time to change your clothes for school." Instead of leaving, he leaned on the counter and watched her grill the cheese sandwiches.

No words passed between them, but the air was charged. She felt his eyes tracking her every move. She needed to know if her fear was rooted in something real, or imagined. She looked at his face. It was prickled in pink. He winked. She smiled. "Shouldn't you get ready for school?"

He pursed his lips. "I'm not going in today. I've arranged for you to proctor my midterm exam."

CHAPTER 11

The First Mate

"CAN'T SOMEONE ELSE proctor your test? I need to work on Katie's headdress."

"Just throw a sheet on her head," Steve said. "You said it yourself, 'it's only a play.' Now let me tell you some wonderful news – my boss, Archie Noble, chairs the Fellowship Committee, and as you heard on the telephone message, he's invited me fishing next week."

Pinch turned off the griddle, the sandwiches done. "How did that come about?"

"Every year, during Spring Break, Archie and his cronies take a fishing trip upstate. But the new grading deadlines made it hard for him to leave this year. I gave him a time management suggestion, and he was so pleased that he asked me to come along." He rubbed his hands together. "Let's get moving with lunch. We have to give Archie a $700 check, so you'll need to stop at the bank, before class, and transfer the funds to our checking account. I've filled out the bank form. It's in with my midterms, along with the check."

"When are you leaving?"

"Monday. Archie's calling me tomorrow with the time."
His eyes sparkled. You'd think he'd been given an audience
with the Pope. Behind the glow she saw traces of the man she
once loved.

Katie shrieked when she entered the kitchen, Steve not
shielding his face this time. "What's wrong with your face,
Dad?"

"I was knocked into a briar patch by bikers racing on the
jogging path."

Katie didn't let his statement slide and peppered him with
questions regarding the size, color and brand of the bikes. A
cyclist in his younger days, he spit out data the child had no
way of refuting. When she noted the lack of scratches on his
hands, he changed the subject, complimenting Pinch on the
meal.

It was anyone's guess why a bowl of chalky chowder and
a grilled cheese sandwich earned respect today when the same
meal tomorrow might incite culinary rut accusations. Still,
cooking kudos were rare; she thanked him for the compliment. The meal might've ended on that high note had Katie
not suggested her own culinary twist. "I think we should have
matzo on Holy Thursday."

Steve laughed. "Why, in God's name, would we want to
do that?"

"That's what Jewish people eat on Passover."

"And why do we care?"

"Sister CeCe said The Last Supper is a Passover meal."

Steve smiled. "Really? What else did she say?"

Katie took his interest in the nun at face value and undoubtedly hoped to repair CeCe's image in her father's critical eyes. "She said Jesus was Jewish – we didn't know that! And that the Jews were slaves before Jesus was born, but Moses helped them get away, and ever since then, they celebrate their freedom from slavery during Passover by eating matzo…and some other stuff…at a meal that's called a *seder*. That's what they were doing on the very first Holy Thursday. We call it, The Last Supper, but Jesus and his Jewish disciples were having their *seder* meal. And guess what, Dad? Sister CeCe made us a *real* seder!"

"I send my daughter to Catholic school, and that moron teaches them Jewish history."

"She's not a moron, Steve. I think it's enlightening what she's teaching them."

"Sister CeCe said, 'Christian history starts with Jewish history'."

"Enough about Jewish history. And forget about eating matzo on Holy Thursday. We'll be in Chicago, and while I'm at the hockey game, you and your mother will be dining with my parents – I guarantee, you won't find any matzo in my mother's pantry." He lingered at the table after Katie was excused and called Cecelia a heretic for infecting the children with extraneous information that can only be regarded as counter-Catholic. "I never needed the details behind the Last Supper, and neither does my daughter."

He seemed to have forgotten his favorite mantra was 'the devil is in the details.'

Pinch wanted to debate his stance; the subject was rich,

and his reasoning rife with holes. But given this morning's escapade at Lydia's, it made more sense not to tickle a sleeping bear. Still...he *was* incredibly relaxed right now. She couldn't resist and threw out some bait. "I wonder how many Christians realize Jesus was born and raised Jewish."

He rolled his eyes. "It doesn't matter what he was, it's what he became that's important." He crossed his arms behind his head, started whistling "Danny Boy." Her mind rewound to her college days when she joined a group of his students debating their "Professor Lordship" on *The Canterbury Tales*. They'd succeeded in challenging his blanket assertions but failed to penetrate his cocky reserve, the handsome instructor leaning back in his chair, whistling Irish ditties and mouthing *'show me the details'* between the tunes. He was fond of bragging how he'd never lost a literary duel and fond of ending the banter when cracks started sprouting in his medieval reasoning. His absolute stances were still hard to ignore. Given his current demeanor, she opted to try nailing the tail on her arrogant, mule-headed donkey.

She brought the dishes to the sink and watched his reflection in the window as she spoke. "Steeped as you are in history and tradition, I thought you would admire Cecelia's holistic teaching of events leading up to The Passion of our Lord." It was a good opening volley, slowly delivered and loud enough to rise above his whistling.

"Tradition, as the standard-bearer of values, is one thing, my dear, but bringing in irrelevancies dilutes the distinctions between Christianity and Judaism and diminishes the omnipotence of the Catholic paradigm. The significance of The Last

Supper is that it foreshadows what happened *after* the meal, not whom ate what, and why."

"But surely you agree, Cecelia presented The Last Supper for what it truly was – a meal commemorating freedom from oppression, not a random dinner held in secret with friends? Some may focus on what came later, but the actual meal is steeped in a tradition with roots beyond the birth of the Catholic Church."

She felt the donkey tail pin closing in on the ass when he dropped the religious argument and solely rebutted the meal. "It's absurd to carry into the current century such a strong bond between food and tradition. Today, we eat what we want, when we want it. Tradition may suggest alternative menus, but they're merely suggestions, not mandates. We eat in the present. Our 'daily bread' should reflect our current disposition. I, for one, would rather fall to the whims of my palate than be prey to the dictates of centuries past."

She turned from the sink and nodded. "Your point is well taken, and you may be correct about me being in a culinary rut. I've already bought the corned beef for St. Paddy's Day, but why don't we try something new this year – instead of falling prey to tradition?" She turned back to the sink. "How about sushi! It'll bring us into the 20th Century and prime your nose to the smell of raw fish for your upcoming trip with the Dean." She made her point without cracking a smile but needed to cough to suppress her laughter. He'd never buy the sushi idea; corned beef on March 17th was as holy to him as matzo to a practicing Jew on Passover. She wiped the kitchen table avoiding his face. "Having sushi and matzo, in back-to-back weeks, would surely cure a culinary rut."

He sat up in his chair. "You've missed the whole point. It's not our matzo holiday, and why waste my hard-earned money on sushi when you've already bought the corned beef?" He rose to leave. "The bank may be crowded on a Saturday so you'd better get going to transfer those funds – propriety dictates you be in the classroom well before the students on test day. Don't dally after the test. We don't want to keep Archie waiting. By the way, he'll give you some stuff to bring home. And don't worry about dinner. I'll call for a pizza."

He left the room whistling, "When Irish Eyes Are Smiling." She watched his retreat…the point he'd thought she missed sticking in his Lordship's ass, its paper tail seen only by her smiling, Irish eyes.

She changed her clothes and hotfooted to the bank. The transaction went fast; the chatty teller, lauding Steve, was delighted to have met the prestigious professor's wife.

Proctoring his class went off without a glitch. The door to the Dean's office was ajar when Pinch approached. She knocked softly then leaned into the room; a gray-haired, mustachioed man with long sideburns was stacking essay bluebooks in three piles on his desk. "Ah, Steve's wife. Nice to meet you, Rose." He extended his hand. "Archie Noble. Please, have a seat."

He didn't see her frown and commended her for coming through like this. "Stevie's a lucky devil, you doing all the little things for him." He stowed each essay pile into three different colored, plastic envelopes then pushed them to the corner of his desk and smiled broadly at her. She handed him the check. He scanned, then stashed it in his wallet. "So how's the ol' boy doing – damn bikers."

"He'll survive," she said.

"Not bad enough to keep him from a week of male bonding," he said with a wink.

A week! Sweet Jesus. She'd thought it was just overnight. "It's not like it's contagious," she said.

"Contagious prickers? That's a good one!" He checked his watch then came around the desk and placed his three stacks of tests on her lap atop the envelope of midterms from Steve's class. "Here's the stuff. I'll pick them up Friday when we drop Stevie home." He patted her on the back. "Thanks a million, Rose, you're a lifesaver."

She wiggled in her chair. "My name is Pinch. *Rose* is my middle name." He looked confused. "Steve probably thought it'd be easier to call me, Rose."

"Always thinking of someone else, isn't he? Speaking of easier, I've included my grade sheets with the exams so you'll have a heads-up on each student's academic standing. Steve said you're an old pro at this, so I won't waste time elaborating." He escorted her out the office, a portrait of taste in his cashmere blazer, linen shirt, silk tie, polished shoes. All that was missing was a thread of texture in his ethics.

"I take it you never taught Mrs. Noble the fine art of grading essays?"

"I'm afraid grading my papers wouldn't make her a happy camper."

He walked a few paces ahead. She fought to keep up – her arms full and wearing high heels – and dropped one of his folders while scurrying through a hall door he held open. "Sorry, Dr. Noble…." Their heads met, bending to retrieve it. He held his gaze, she didn't. "Call me, Archie," he said, tucking the folder back in her arms, then lowering his voice told her not to mark up the papers. "Write your comments on a separate sheet, and I'll pull something out from your remarks – you write legibly, don't you?"

"Only when I'm a happy camper."

He looked around. The hall was empty. "What'll it take to make you happy?" He pulled out a wad of bills, flipped five twenties off, stuffing them in her coat pocket. She shook her head. He apparently thought she was negotiating the price and peeled off more money. "It's no big deal, Honey. I've paid more for less, and you're an old pro."

"No!" Shook her head. She felt as if she was invisible… and dirty. She pulled the cash from her pockets and shoveled it back to him. His face darkened. A door slammed somewhere down the hall. She glanced at the tests, smiled then shrugged. "It's not about money, *Archie*. Nothing makes me happier than doing these little things."

That it made sense to him made it all the more wrenching. He folded his money away. "I get it, you were pulling my leg! Steve didn't say you were such a card."

"It probably slipped his mind – along with my name." She threw him a deadpan look. The two of them laughed like old friends sharing a joke.

She used to think she was better off than Gertie, that Steve

103

would never ask her to turn tricks for him. She was right. He never asked....

Having a small window of time, she stopped at church, on the way home, to make a quick Confession. She felt slimy, being with the Dean, and was drowning in lies spewed in self-defense to keep from being skewed by the truth. Shedding sins with amiable, Father Jerry, always lightened her mood; if nothing else, she'd go home spiritually clean.

But the line outside Father Jerry's confessional was long, while no one waited outside the Monsignor's booth, a retired navy chaplain and gentle old soul prone to preach, when guidance would suffice. She checked the clock at the back of the church, sighed and plodded to the Monsignor's booth. She lay her belongings on the wooden seat, knelt before the screen gathering her thoughts, and her sins. The Monsignor slid open his side of the screen. She bowed her head, "Bless me father for I have sinned. It's been four weeks since my last confession. I've been deceitful, and angry, and I've had some hateful thoughts. For these and all the sins of my past life, I am sorry, and ask pardon of God, and penance and absolution of you, Father." She closed her eyes waiting to receive her penance.

The Monsignor was a heavyset man who spoke slowly with belabored breathing. He leaned in closer to the screen. "Who have you been deceiving, my child?"

Her shoulders sagged. "My husband."

"About what?"

She opened her eyes and sighed in the dark. "Where I've been, and what I'm doing."

"You've been doing something behind his back?"

"Yes, Father."

"For how long?"

"Since my last Confession."

His breath rose and fell, hypnotically, like waves undulating at sea. "You know that the sacrament of Holy Matrimony is based on trust?"

"Yes, Father."

"Then I trust you will stop your deceit or discuss the issue with him."

She felt boxed in. Alone. Were it not for the sound of his breathing, she'd have thought that he left, wished he had left instead of waiting for her answer, waiting while she wondered how to satisfy her spiritual confessor without sabotaging her safety. She thought about leaving the booth, but her legs were numb, as if nailed to the kneeler. And she thought about lying to stop this line of conversation. But what then? Recite her penance, cross the aisle and confess to Father Jerry that she'd just lied to the Monsignor? "I'd rather not do what you ask, Father."

He cleared his throat. "And why is that?"

"If I tell him what I'm doing, he'll make me stop. I don't think I should have to stop."

His figure shuffled in the shadows. "What exactly are you doing behind his back?"

"Working part-time."

"Is that all?"

"Yes, Father."

"There must be more if he disapproves. Have you kept your family responsibilities?"

"Yes, everything else is the same."

She pulled a tissue from her pocket, wiped the sweat from her forehead then cringed; the stiff "tissue" was one of the Dean's bills, and the smell of her sweat on his money turned her stomach. Her eyes watered. She buried her face in her sleeve. *Why does he doubt my story when Steve is the one drawing blood and hurling threats?*

The Monsignor doesn't know all that.

But exposing Steve here will just be met with disbelief; he's positioned himself a vital member of the church community, the Monsignor being his most ardent supporter.

He doesn't know your Steve's wife. You're just another voice in the darkened booth....

"He gave me a black eye last month, Father, when I suggested taking a part-time job. I have to choose topics of discussion carefully. Then there's our daughter. I worry about what she'll see, and what he might do if he loses control again."

She heard him grunt. "Has he hit the child?"

"No."

"Perhaps he wouldn't want to hurt you if you were more amenable to his needs."

"With all due respect, it's hard to embrace an agenda that limits your voice while expanding your duties. I spend most of my time anticipating his wants and serving his needs. What about *my* life? When can I choose what I want and need?"

"Your life is what you do in service to your family...that was the choice you made when you married, the vow you renew each day. Now, you're feeling distressed by the confines of home, but we all have boundaries. On the ship, I encouraged the men to create an Eden within. Paradise, my child, is only a thought away! As a wife and a mother, you're a valued part of an important team. But he is the captain, and you're the first mate. Try staying the course, not changing it. Can you think more like the first mate?"

"Like, Eve? You bet!"

He started coughing; the confessional trembled as he rocked back and forth in his seat. She hadn't meant to upset him. She just wanted to be heard. After 15 years as a faithful first mate, she was looking for change, not more chains.

The clock in the choir loft struck six times, Confessions technically over. The Monsignor cleared his throat. "Your problems might resolve themselves with a little more respect and less insolence. Call the rectory if things don't improve – especially if he hurts the child. It often helps to discuss these things in the holy confines of God's house. But let's not get ahead of ourselves. If you shower him with your love, the rest may take care of itself."

How dumb she'd been to expect a priest – lacking safety concerns – to understand a wife and mother's fear.

Getting home had now superseded getting his support. When she said she'd do what she could, he meted out her penance "Say fifteen Our Father's and fifteen Hail Mary's." After reciting the Act of Contrition, he blessed her and said, "Go in peace."

He left, his time to hear confessions over. She stayed in the booth, choosing to recite her penance there rather than risk him seeing her praying in the sanctuary. But dueling images of Steve hijacked her call for atonement. He was the pillar of respect in the broad community, but at home he was a pimp in tweed using her skills to cultivate his seeds, her loyalty to satisfy his needs. Today he showed how far he'd go to ensure his will be done. Yet she was told to stay the course – even though the Lord's Prayer begged God's deliverance "from evil." She thought of her mother's faith in priests but was speeding past the need to get sacred permission to pursue a safe and meaningful life. Still, she was disappointed, like Dorothy when she realized there was no wizard in Oz.

She finished her penance more bewildered than spiritually cleansed. How can I "go in peace" when life is so unfair?

Shoot for the going, the Stranger said, *we can work on the peace part later.*

CHAPTER 12

The Passion

THE KITCHEN TABLE was strewn with tomato-stained paper napkins, Pinch's slice of dinner cooling in a cardboard pizza box. She was cleaning the mess when Katie stomped in. "My hair won't stay under my headdress!"

"You can let it show. Men wore their long hair in those days."

"Then everyone will know Judas is a girl."

"I thought you wanted to play Judas."

"I do. But if they know I'm a girl when they watch, they won't see how good a Judas I am."

Pinch followed her up to her bedroom and tried different tactics, but the headdress slipped off each time Katie moved. "We could cut my hair."

"Let's not panic, Honey, I've got one more idea." She braided Katie's hair then coiled and pinned the pigtails on top of her head. After draping the sheeting over the coils, she cinched the mound with a piece of jump rope.

Katie tilted her head side to side clapping when the head-dress didn't shift. "This is great. No one will know I'm a girl."

"Would you really cut your hair for one night on the stage?"

"It's just hair, Mom, it would grow back. Didn't you ever have short hair?"

"In grammar school, before I found out boys...and husbands like it long."

Steve walked in and pointed to his watch. "We'd better get going, ladies."

"Hey Dad, can you tell that I'm a girl?" He shook his head.

Katie almost tripped skipping out the room. "Let's go, Mom. I've got a kiss to give." Steve scowled. Pinch cringed. If he was riled by his 10-year-old kissing a cheek on the stage in a church, how would he be when his teenage daughter was alone on a date in the dark?

Sister Cecelia was standing by the door when the family reached the school's auditorium. Steve towered above the nun who stepped back and scrutinized his face. "What happened to you?" He greeted her question with a glare.

"He fell in a briar patch," Katie said. Cecelia raised an eyebrow. Steve turned away.

"You're looking splendid, Judas," Cecelia said, then shooed Katie down the hall to a classroom where The Passion Play cast awaited their curtain call.

Steve tried to steer Pinch into the auditorium, but she stood pat, wanting to speak with the nun. When he finally left to grab their seats, she told Cecelia how excited Katie was to be playing Judas. "She thinks you're the greatest, Sister."

Cecelia studied her face, as if searching a map to get her bearings. "She thinks you're the greatest, too, Mrs. O'Malley. Quite a cross-to-bear – isn't it?" Their conversation was interrupted by a burst of playful shrieks from the cast room. Cecelia nodded toward the crowds spilling in. "You'd better claim your seat, or Mr. Briar Patch may sell it."

Pinch plowed her way into the auditorium and spotted Steve near the stage with the Monsignor. She sighed in relief when the ceiling lights flashed and the two men parted. She slid in the seat next Steve, third row center, in a section reserved for relatives of the cast.

When the curtains opened, *Jesus* was alone in the Garden of Gethsemane questioning why he had to die. But he stayed the course, carrying his cross, setting a high standard for all Christianity. Sitting there in the dark, Pinch pondered the meaning of death and martyrdom. She'd been taught that sacrifice was an honorable deed, Christ's sacrificial death leaving a legacy of hope. But what legacy would she leave sacrificing life, love, and limb for Steve?

"Hello, Lord!" Katie's voice directed her attention to the stage where *Judas* stumbled planting the infamous kiss on Robert Hamilton's cheek. Steve dropped his head and sighed. Katie seemed unfazed. Her mission accomplished, she picked up her hem and retreated backstage as the Roman soldiers took Jesus into custody. Then the high Jewish priest sent Jesus to Pontius Pilate, Roman governor of the occupied Jewish Territory, Pilate releasing him to a raucous crowd that demanded his crucifixion. But that wasn't what Judas had planned when he took the handful of coins to betray his Lord. Katie returned to the set...*Judas seeking to* return the blood money. When the request was denied, she tossed the coins across the stage crying, "What crime could be worse than killing God?" It was her final line. The knowledgeable audience applauded. One hand on her headdress, the other on her hem, she tore from the stage stealing a peek at the Reserved seating section on the way.

Jesus was paraded through an angry crowd – a crown of thorns upon his head, a heavy cross at his shoulder. *The cross.* What did Cecelia mean saying Katie's admiration was "a cross to bear?" Respect was a gift, not a burden! Was being a mentor so different from being a mother?

The riotous crowds escorted *Jesus* away. The lights dimmed. A translucent curtain was pulled across the stage. *Clank, clank, clank.* The sound of a hammer hitting nails pierced the air, and the voice of Robert Hamilton cried, *"Forgive them father, they know not what they do."* A backlit cross appeared behind the sheer curtain, a body sagging on the timber further insulting the bleak horizon. Pinch stared at the cross. Its edges seemed to merge with the inert body, blurring the line between the bearer and the burden. She fought to find meaning in the odd illusion. Am I my own cross? Must I get through this mess on my own...? But Christ didn't face his crisis alone – someone wiped his brow, another helped when he fell, still another offered a drink when he thirsted.

Maybe crosses weren't meant to be borne alone.

Boom! A drumbeat cracked the air; the audience jumped in their seats. The front of the cross was flooded in light so bright it embraced then erased the crucified silhouette-of-sacrifice. Another drumbeat. The lights dimmed. Another drumbeat. The curtain closed.

When the auditorium lights came on, the cast and crew were assembled on stage awaiting their introductions. Steve jumped up, telling Pinch he'd meet her in the cafeteria; Katie, headdress in hand, was about to be called, front and center, when he rose. She waved in his direction, but her hand went limp watching him walk away. Pinch frantically waved from her seat finally catching Katie's eye. For a brief moment just the two of them existed, touching without touching, speaking without speaking, but she couldn't hold on to Katie's gaze... boring long and deep down the aisle where her father was retreating.

Steve was sipping punch and eating cookies when Pinch joined the post-performance party. Katie was talking to Robert Hamilton, so she slipped out to the restroom meeting Cecelia there. "You put on an incredible performance, Sister."

"It was the children's success. I only provided the facts and forum."

"Speaking of facts, what a creative way to teach The Last Supper – having a seder!"

"Jesus *was* Jewish."

"But most of us forget that. Was it stressed in the convent?"

Cecelia laughed. "It was stressed in my home…my mother was raised Catholic and converted to Judaism when she married Papa. I've always enjoyed the seder. It's about family and history, and freedom and slavery. It reminds us of the things that hold us together in times of trouble. Many suffered in the past. Many still suffer. To me, the seder is a celebration of life. I'm surprised it's not a regular part of Christian instruction, over here."

"Over here?"

"Sorry, I was born in Czechoslovakia. I'm glad Katie liked the seder. She's a delightful child with a lot of spark and not afraid to try new things. I think that's special."

"She is special, thanks. Why'd you leave Czechoslovakia? The pictures are beautiful."

"Pictures don't bleed, and beauty can't buy security." She excused herself leaving Pinch dazed – had she just been scolded, given a history lesson, or both?

Steve was pacing the hall when Pinch returned. "Let's go," he said.

"Give me a minute." She walked passed him into the cafeteria.

Some students were talking with Cecelia, some parents were listening to the Monsignor. Katie ran toward her, braids dangling, face beaming. "Hey Mom! How did I look?"

"Fantastic, Honey. Everyone was impressed."

Katie lowered her voice. "Isn't Robert Hamilton cute?

114

Vanessa dared me to kiss him on the lips, but the real *Judas* didn't do that, so I didn't."

"Good decision. Now if you're finished with your friends, we ought to leave, your father is waiting in the hall."

"Sister CeCe wants me to help her mind daycare kids during school break."

"That's fine," Pinch said.

The Monsignor pulled Pinch aside as she readied to leave the building, Steve and Katie already out the door. Had he seen her spurn Steve just now in the hall? Did he know she was the one who had sassed him at Confession? Her hands began to sweat. She hid them in her pockets and stared at the floor, awaiting a sermon, but his only concern was about Steve's face. "Take care of his wounds. We mustn't let the good man get infected." She nodded, afraid to speak lest he recognize her voice. She hustled out the door. The silence was electric when she joined the family in the car.

Katie flew up to her room as soon as they got home. Steve called her down when he came in from parking the car. Pinch stood in the family room entry, arms folded, a knot growing in her chest. He was easing into his recliner when Katie approached still wearing her toga and chewing on one of her braids. "Daddy...?"

His eyes were on fire. "Your actions tonight were shameful, young lady!"

"What happened?" Pinch said, coming into the room.

Katie shrugged.

"Do you really think Judas would have gazed at Jesus like

a lovebird before he betrayed him? *And what was that kiss?* You practically fell in his lap!"

"I did fall, Daddy. I tripped on my costume when I leaned up to kiss him. *You* try standing on tiptoes in a sheet! Both of us would have bailed, if Robert didn't hold me tight."

She smiled shyly, mentioning the Hamilton boy.

He lunged toward her; his hand darted out like a serpent's tongue grabbing her braid, pulling her head to his face. "Don't sass me, you little slut. And wipe that grin off your face. There's nothing cute about flirting at a sacred performance – you disgraced us in front of the community tonight." He punctuated the last sentence with a yank on her braid.

"Stop it, Steve!" Pinch loosened his grip enough for Katie to pull free. "Go up to bed, Honey, I'll be right there." Katie glared at her father before leaving. He didn't see the look, slithering back into his chair and focusing on the newspaper. "She didn't shame *us* tonight, Steve," Pinch said. *"I* was proud of her performance." He lowered the paper, his face an angry red. "She's ten-years-old, and you're almost 50 – leaving before her curtain call was more disgraceful than anything *she* did."

Katie was in her pajamas, crying in her bed, lying on her stomach when Pinch arrived. She punched her pillow with both of her fists. "I didn't do anything wrong, Mom. I hate him! I hope he never comes back from his stupid trip."

Pinch closed the bedroom door then sat on the bed and pulled Katie near. "I'm sure you'll feel better in a few days, when all of this is behind you."

"I'll feel better in a few days because he'll be gone!"

"Sometimes life isn't fair, Honey, that's where forgiveness

comes in. Remember what was said in the play. *Forgive them, Father, they know not what they do.*"

"Then let's tell him what he's doing. I'd rather tell him, than forgive him. Maybe he'll stop if he knows." But Pinch knew it wasn't that simple. Steve needed perfection, not the truth from his family – without it his dreams were dashed, with it theirs could not exist. She unraveled Katie's braids; Katie grimaced where Steve had pulled on her hair. "He's just a big bully, Mom. I'm glad he got hurt by those bikers today. If he ever hits me like he hit you that time, I'll kick him in the leg til he cries, then I'll run away."

Pinch's hands fell into her lap. "What do you mean, *like he hit me...?*"

Katie slipped under the covers and pulled her teddy bear to her chest. "The night before your birthday you and Dad were in the kitchen, and I came downstairs for an envelope for your birthday card. Then he started to yell and he—" Tears streamed down her face; she wiped them on the teddy bear. "I'm sorry, Mommy, I was scared and didn't know what to do so I ran upstairs." Her mouth tightened. "You said you hurt yourself, but you lied. He did it, and you lied." She turned on her stomach and cried into her toy, shrinking at Pinch's touch, shutting out the liar. Pinch moved to the foot of the bed, rubbing and wringing her hands til the "creamed corn" scar in her palm turned white. It was a small scar, like the white lies crafted to protect Katie's innocence, lies so easy to draw...so hard to erase. She left the room around eleven when Katie finally fell asleep.

Judas was wrong. The greatest crime was losing your child's trust.

The master bedroom radiator was hissing as she entered to get ready for bed. The room smelled like scorched cotton; she opened the front window to stir the air. A gentle fog had descended on the street since the family returned from the play. Up by the bar on the corner of the street, someone was singing an Irish song; St. Paddy's day was two days away but his revelers were already celebrating. Her thoughts ran to Ireland outside a pub on another damp night when Steve's tipsy cousin tried teaching her how to whistle a tune. He'd taught Steve during summer vacations the "young Yank" had spent on the *old Sod* – Kathryn wanting her son to share his childhood with the Cleary clan. Steve had taken Pinch to Ireland on their honeymoon. It was a fun-loving time, with fun-loving people, time bearing out what she had sensed early on…Kathryn the only Cleary without a song in her heart. She closed the window, the outside air suddenly biting.

She threw on a delicate nightgown and wished she'd denied Steve's early marital request to never wear flannel to bed. He was still downstairs having his chamomile nightcap while watching the news. Maybe if she hurried, sleep would arrive before he did. But the sheets were too cool for comfort their chill compounded by the stone-cold grief that her family was dying, the cancer spreading, her silence abetting the disease. She lay in the dark watching digital numbers on the clock drop time from her life. Goosebumps glazed her body. She pulled her knees up to her chest but the chill prevailed. She pulled a turtleneck over her gown adding socks to the mix then slipped back in the bed. Her skin felt better but her soul was numb from coping with what is instead of courting what could be. She didn't feel like she had any choices. But if she *could* magically change "what is," how would she know the right thing to do?

What would you tell Katie to do in your shoes…?

She bolted up in the bed. Oh my God – my cross is to leave him!

She swims through a wall of wavering chamomile. An earthquake shakes the sea. A giant squid secures her in place. The sea calms. He hovers above her. His tentacles probe. She swats; it recedes, belching chamomile. She swims up toward the light, and a young mermaid tosses a braid. She reaches for the tow, but the squid is upon her. They struggle for control of her body. She breaks away but fails to get free. A tentacle shimmies across her legs, plying, probing her body.

She screams for it to stop!! A hairy tentacle brushes her face and covers her mouth. She bites into the flesh. A gut-wrenching scream shakes the sea and the monster retreats.

Her eyes shoot open. Her breath is short. The taste of salt lingers on her lips.

CHAPTER 13

Raggedy Ann Cleans House

"JESUS CHRIST! What's wrong with you?" Steve bolted toward the bathroom. Pinch stiffened in bed, broadly flicking at her flesh as if the squid still trawled her body. She pulled her nightgown tightly around her legs before lying back, arms crossed at her chest. "I can't believe you bit me," he said, climbing back into the bed.

"I had a nightmare."

She curled toward the edge of the bed. He drew her back, his strength and breath triggering another bout of terror. *"Let go!!"* She lit from the bed and grabbed her pillow. "I'm sleeping downstairs."

"So it's another bad dream. What happened this time — the Celibate leave you in the big, bad woods?"

"No, I was about to be raped!"

"Really." He turned on the light and propped up in bed then nodding toward her turtleneck said, "Your attacker must have been blind."

She strode toward the door. He reached out snagging her

nightgown. "Stay with me, my dear. You're upset. You'll feel better not being alone."

"I can't sleep."

He rubbed her thigh. "Well, it *is* Saturday night—"

"—and we already did it this week, so good night."

"Why deny me, when you're getting it in a dream? Was it someone that we know?"

"It wasn't a human."

"Good Lord, *bestiality!*" He pushed her away and ran his hand through his hair. "These perverse adventures of yours must stop! Perhaps a chat with the Monsignor will help, though I'd rather not broadcast your penchant for extramarital romps?"

"Rape is not a *romp!*"

He leaned back on his pillow. "That depends on the point of view. Don't be so naive."

She would have smothered him with her pillow, but he was far too strong to overcome, and prison was not what she had in mind when she pictured living without him.

Fear followed her downstairs, but she shooed it away, fear not as scary as the fiend with the chamomile breath. The air in the living room was colder than upstairs; a distant siren shattered the eerie silence. After putting on a garden smock and candy-cane-colored kneesocks plucked from the laundry room, she nestled on the sofa in a too-small blanket, tossing, resettling, turning then finally getting up to prepare tomorrow's meal. She peeled, seasoned, sliced, diced – her hands on autopilot freeing her mind to brainstorm how to leave Steve. They'd go in the summer. Katie was out of school. Fly back to

Chicago. Her brothers would help. Well, Bryan might not, but Kevin would; he always did and always brought God. She'd need a job. The $1200 cash in the tampon box from Lydia would go toward the plane fare and their first month's rent. She'd need more than that. What assets were lying around the house? She could sell her cookbook collection, unneeded clothes and her jewelry from Steve...though most of the jewelry was in their safe-deposit box, Steve holding both of their keys.

She shivered with excitement. The challenge was taking root. With the food prep done, and an ear on her bedroom and an eye on the stairs, she removed all the "germs of independence" from the cookbooks in her Leap Year File, tearing and tucking the scraps in her smock, briefly reliving two painful memories. The first was Steve demanding she quit her teaching job as soon as they discovered she was pregnant with Katie. The second occurred the following year when she took a Chamber of Commerce position, interviewing merchants, then penning a monthly profile. It was an ideal jaunt for a housebound, nursing mother. But Steve, a man so proud of his punctuality, was suddenly late to baby sit on her interviewing dates. Doing telephone interviews resolved that problem, but she lost the job when her first two mail-in interviews failed to reach their destination. Steve had blamed the U.S. Postal Service claiming he'd dropped her envelope off with the monthly bills. She had given him the benefit of the doubt back then; it would've hurt too much to believe otherwise. Now flushing the "germs" down the powder room toilet, her only question was whether he had used the same trashcan both times.

She restacked the cookbooks on the shelf deciding to keep the *Fanny Farmer,* from Mama, and sell all the rest at the used-book store. It would take three trips, doing it on the sly, and only one if she had the car. But that was another fantasy – he'd never leave town without his keys.

She checked the clock. It was 3:30 am. Too psyched to sleep, and with money on her mind, she rummaged the laundry room for clothing to sell, amassing a large garbage bag of summer clothing. On to the hall where the foyer closet offered up its own trove of seasonal goodies and begged the question, why does a woman with no social life need four warm weather coats and three jackets? She decide to keep the lined raincoat and a down jacket. The rest was history, medieval history considering the full length mink that was crammed, like an afterthought, against the wall. Steve bought it for her one Christmas. He said it was a steal. She wasn't surprised, the nightly news awash with animal-rights activists protesting the sale of natural fur. Like most of his gifts, the mink was more about how she looked than what she liked, and she hated that coat. Wore it only when he insisted. But it needed to stay. Its absence would be obvious, and its bulk provided needed cover for her old suede jacket.

The jacket had been a gift from her mother when Pinch was attending college. She still loved its tawny color, its dew-like texture, and how its fringe gently swayed when she walked. Steve thought it lacked class – too cowboy and too 70s. She stopped wearing it in his presence, too beaten by his critiques. But on a lonely gray morning last November, three months after her mother had passed away, she shyly entered the jacket's embrace, hugging herself in the hall ten minutes before heading outside for a walk. Steve was coming up the front stoop, popping home between classes as he often did. "Good Lord, you're not wearing that monstrosity out!" When she nodded, he called her a child. Told her to act her age. She wore it anyway and was stunned, a week later, to find the jacket buried in a bag of clothes slated for pickup by Goodwill. Tired of confrontation, she slipped the suede under the mink periodically checking that the lush "garment bag" still housed her blue-collar keepsake.

She peeked under the mink and petted the jacket, then sorted the rest of the closet into items to be sold, and items to be saved, the former to be weeded out before summer vacation.

It was now nearly dawn, the automatic coffeemaker dripping its fragrant brew. She poured a cup and brought the Sunday paper in from the stoop. Her head was resting on the comics' section when Steve came downstairs at six.

She straightened in her chair and forced her eyes open. He was dressed for jogging and poured himself some coffee. He looked at her and frowned. "You look like a rag doll."

She shrugged and yawned. "I always liked Raggedy Ann."

"You're a mother, not a clueless moppet. Put on something decent before Katie comes to breakfast." She nodded and laid her head back on the comics, her arm extended beneath her cheek. He sat down beside her and rubbed her hand. "You need a vacation, my dear. I'll make the arrangements when my fellowship comes through. Katie can stay with my parents. We'll make it a second honeymoon." She started to cry. He must have misread her tears of panic for tears of joy, kissing her gently then leaving for his jog wearing an almighty glow.

She propped her face on her hands. What was he thinking? Bruise out of sight, battery out of mind. Let him think what he wants. We both know what happened.

No...all of us know.

And Katie's memory of it, no doubt, more toxic than seeing her mother dressed like a moppet.

Katie barely spoke all morning though she showed genuine pleasure, after church, when Steve gave her a chocolate Easter bunny. The gift, however, was a temporary balm for a sore scalp and wounded heart. When he failed to engage her in a cheery chat, he retreated to the family room reading the Sunday paper, awaiting the dinner bell. Pinch slipped upstairs while the meat was roasting eager to find more salable goods to fatten her going-away dowry. The hair on her neck bristled seeing Steve's empty, open suitcase on their bed. She tried to ignore it, but its large gaping presence seemed to track her every move. She traipsed back downstairs. "Why is your luggage out? You're not leaving til tomorrow night."

He didn't look up. "I thought it'd be better if we packed today."

But *she,* not *we,* always packed his things, and having never gone fishing in the winter, she suggested he pack his own things this time.

"Just throw in a bunch of wool stuff. Archie said that 'the toys' are already up there." He lowered the newspaper. "And don't forget my hiking boots and that waterproof jacket, wherever it is."

Tomorrow was wash day, so he was low on clean underwear. She put his laundry in the wash, then plucked his jacket from its perch next to the mink. One of its buttons was missing, but finding it would have to wait, supper ready to serve. The phone rang as they sat down to eat. Steve took the call violating his own mealtime edict.

"Hey, Archie. *Oh!* Okay. *What?* For how many? Okay. No problem. See you later."

His mouth twisted as he hung up the phone. "We're leaving tonight at five. And since I'm the only Irishman, I'm charged with bringing something for tomorrow's St. Paddy's Day dinner." He paced the kitchen. Threw up his hands. "Etiquette dictates they give a chap more time – do they think I'm a damn magician?"

Katie looked concerned. Pinch was delighted by the early departure, her joy cut short when he told her to cook up their corned beef and pack it to go. "You want that *today!*"

He looked at the clock. "What's the big deal, you've got four hours." He sat down at the table, a smile crossing his face. "Archie is testing me, but I'll show him I'm up to the task. Boil the cabbage and potatoes, too. We'll have a veritable Irish feast in the woods!"

Katie must've seen the protest in Pinch's face. "C'mon, Mom. We can do it."

"That's the way, Katie girl, do your Dad proud!"

They left him eating in the kitchen, Katie seeking his boots and missing jacket button, Pinch upstairs packing his clothes and toiletries. The kitchen floor was strewn with storage containers when she returned, Steve on hands and knees rifling through the cabinets. "Here, this should hold all the food. I don't want to juggle a bunch of small tins. " He handed her a huge Tupperware container and left the room whistling, "How Are Things in Glocca Morra?"

The place looked like a pigsty, food on the table, pots in the sink, containers and rims scattered on the floor. She worked around the obstacles, put the corned beef to boil and was clearing up the floor when Katie came in with a handful of identical buttons. "I can't find the missing one but I found this set in the button jar. Should I try to sew them on?"

"I'll do it, you peel the potatoes." Katie seemed relieved, and they got right to it – one at the sink with a peeler, one at the table with a needle and thread, the only sound in the rumpled room, an occasional sigh from Katie.

When all the buttons were sewn, Pinch asked him if he wanted to wear or pack the jacket. "Pack it. I won't need it in the van. And don't forget my hat, scarf and gloves."

She brought him his hiking boots. They were coated with dust and clumps of dried mud. "Do you want to wear these or carry them, there's no more room in your bag?"

"I'll wear them."

"They need to be cleaned, they're a mess." He shrugged and kept reading the paper.

Katie called from the kitchen, the timer going off. Pinch left the boots by his chair and ran to the kitchen adding the potatoes to the meat, then reset the timer to ring when the cabbage could be added to the pot. Steve was surfing the TV channels when she returned. She nodded toward the boots. "I could use some help with these...."

He hit the mute button on the remote, tilted his head and glared. "Isn't it enough that I bring home the bacon? I don't ask you to help on that front. Don't ask me to help you on yours." She carted his boots to the back porch and stabbed at the dirt with his newest screwdriver; Katie finished the job freeing Pinch to finish the cooking.

Steve was upstairs getting dressed when Archie arrived. "Rosie, how's it going?"

"Not soon enough, I'm afraid."

Steve bounded down the stairs with his suitcase. Pinch handed him the food. "Let me take that," Archie said.

Steve pushed the suitcase forward. "Why don't you wheel this out, I'll be right there."

He ran to the kitchen. Archie gave her a questioning look. She raised her eyebrows and shrugged. "*Clue*...less."

He gave her a once-over look then leaned in and whispered, "Clueless and pretty." His breath smelled like beer. He patted her thigh. "Stay out of trouble while we're gone."

Steve was kicking containers around the kitchen floor. "I can't find my keys in this mess." A horn tooted twice in quick succession. Pinch checked the counters; he searched the desk drawer throwing up his hands when the horn beeped again. He kissed her goodbye on the stoop to a chorus of catcalls from the van. She waved and sighed when his coach sped away with her feudal Lord, his Irish feast and suitcase of fine woolen threads.

Katie was nibbling on the dinner's remains when Pinch returned to the kitchen. "Mom, I called Vanessa. Can we visit the Statue of Liberty tomorrow, instead of during Spring Break?"

"But your class is going to the Paddy's Day parade."

"Not everyone's going. The kids that don't go get out at twelve, so we can do the Statue in the afternoon. But you'll have to write Sister CeCe a note. Please, Mom? Dad will be home during break. What if he wants to come with us?"

"I highly doubt that, Honey."

"But what if he does? Then I'll be stuck." She knelt on the floor. "Mommy *please*."

She ran her hand over Katie's cheek. "Okay, let's do it. Bring Vanessa home with you after school. I'll have lunch ready, and we'll leave right after we eat."

Katie thanked her with a hug. "It must have been cool growing up without a father!"

Pinch stiffened. She kissed Katie on the head then left for the backyard swing staying til the lump in her throat dissolved. Later, after the kitchen was cleaned, they snuggled in front of the TV, both retiring early. Pinch awoke with a start around midnight. She ran down to the laundry room and confirmed the suspicion roiling about in her head. She loaded the dryer trying to put a positive spin on Steve's awkward dilemma – if King Arthur could survive warrior life without any Brooks Brothers' briefs, surely "Lord Bacon" could cope with only two pairs on a five-day fishing trip.

She plucked Steve's keys from the billowing fern in the living room before heading back up to bed. Chalk one up for Raggedy Ann. She may be clueless, but she plays one helluva game of hide-and-seek!

PART TWO

CHAPTER 14

Passing the Torch

KATIE SPRINTED TO THE BUS STOP. She'd be riding to school with Vanessa this week versus being driven by Steve. Pinch trucked the items she was selling to the car jotting down the mileage before leaving home; if Steve asked where she'd driven while he was away, the extra miles had to jive with whatever story she told. The cookbooks and clothing netted $200 cash. It was a glorious start to the morning 'til she brought her mother's table into the hardware store for repairs.

The 30" round table was thigh high with a carved pedestal and a claw-foot base. The storeowner wanted $150 to sand, seal and re-stain the whole piece. "I don't want it rebuilt. I just want the base shored up," she said.

The man rolled his eyes. "I'll get Helga. She does repairs."

Pinch pressed the piece of sagging wood hoping to save money by popping it back in place, but a large splinter snapped off exposing something white inside the pedestal. A stocky middle-aged woman approached. "I'm Helga, let's see what you've got?" She gently ran a callused hand over the table. "My, what a treasure…late 1800s, golden oak."

Pinch pointed to the new gap and item in the base. "Any way we can get that out?"

Helga prodded a pair of rusty levers under the tabletop til the pedestal opened enough to manually pull the base apart. Cradled inside were an orange feather, an envelope and a 1952 Ted Williams baseball card. "Triplets!" Helga cried. "Check out your treasures while I rustle up some wood to reinforce this mama's base." She left without giving a repair estimate, a concern that paled when Pinch picked up the envelope.

It had a military postmark of March 1952, from Capt. James Duffy, to Mrs. J. Duffy in Chicago, Illinois. The envelope was sealed; her eyes filled studying the script, knowing her father had fought in Korea. What does one write to a loved one from war, what does one share from the shadows of hell? She wanted to rip it open, wanted to know him from his own words not her brothers' and mother's memories. But she couldn't bring herself to break the seal and brushed the envelope with the pad of her thumb, content for now to touch what he'd touched, only to be startled when a passing patron picked up the baseball card and yelled to his friend, *"Hey Louie, a '52 Ted Williams baseball card!"*

The ogling duo bombarded Pinch with bids to buy the card. The suddenly affable owner offered to fix her table for free. "Sorry, gentlemen, it's not for sale." When they continued to press, she told them she planned to give it to her husband, "as a birthday gift." They commended her decision, noting that he was a lucky man. She smiled shyly concealing her intent to sell it after asking Kevin what he thought it was worth on the open market – the proceeds added to her going-away dowry. She was slipping the card, the letter and feather into her purse when Helga returned with the scrap wood and a $35.00 repair estimate that included delivery. "Deal!"

Pinch tucked today's "earnings" in the Tampon box then called Lydia hoping to drop off the *Stills* the next morning. "Glad you called, Pinchey. I'm moving to other digs."

"I hope you're not leaving because of Steve. He doesn't suspect anything and blames his bruises on some wild bikers running him into a briar patch."

"What a hoot! Wait'll I tell Smith that we've been upgraded from 'a blimp and a gimp' to bikers on a tear! How's the pretty-boy looking?"

"Not bad considering you set him up to get mauled by the cats."

"Spare the violins, Missy, the boys' previous owner had their front claws removed. Ya gotta own where ya are when the shit comes down. So the Prick got a few pricks.... Lucky I didn't have Security bust him."

"If not because of Steve, why are you moving?"

"Had a power failure in the building yesterday. Felt like a cat trapped up a tree. Smith's been after me to move to a ground floor place. Called last night saying she found one by The Market."

"When are you going?"

"Sooner the better."

"But you love it there. Won't you miss Smith and seeing Libby every day?"

"Smith's got sights on a place in the same building. And given the choice, I'd rather have liberty, than see it, so stop ya hounding."

Pinch laughed. "You've been hounding me since you found out Steve hit me, making me out as his whipping toy, even though it only happened once."

"Never underestimate the power of once. Screwing once won't make ya a whore, but ya sure ain't a virgin anymore! When Jack starts to smack, time to giddy-ap. Don't let the status-quo dogs feed ya fears."

"Are you finished?"

"For now."

"Good. I'm leaving Steve this summer."

"*What!* Why didn't ya tell me last week?"

"I wasn't leaving last week, then things came together."

"Did ya tell Smith?"

"Nobody knows. I decided last night, so keep it to yourself."

"You oughta tell Smith. She'll get the posse right on it."

"And you ought to mind your own business."

"*Touché, Libby! We got us a live one!* This won't be a cakewalk, Pinch. When ya wrestling with shit – let it out."

"Actually, there is something…. I grew up without a father and feel guilty pulling Katie away from hers. How do I tell her that *we* have to leave, because *I* have a problem with her Dad?"

"Ya don't owe her an explanation. Ya owe her a safe place to grow. Let her see him in action. Showing is stronger than telling. Or bring her around for some chili. I'll fill her in on her Daddy's charms."

Pinch laughed. "I'll go with the show-versus-tell approach.

One more thing, then I really have to hang up. We're touring *Libby* this afternoon. Do you have any suggestions?"

"Don't miss the museum. Honor what's written. And lower your sights or you'll miss the message."

"What message?" Pinch said, but phone line was already dead.

They boarded *The Miss New York* for Liberty Island at the Castle Clinton dock in lower Manhattan. The sky was sprinkled with clouds, the water a calm khaki blue. Pinch followed the girls through the boat's main deck, past rows of wooden benches under a ceiling of stowed life preservers. The air smelled of hot dogs. They ascended the stairs to the upper deck where fresh air streamed through the open doors. The view outside was expansive. To the right, a white cabin cruiser skipped up the Hudson River; to the left, a yellow Staten Island Ferry neared its Manhattan dock at the mouth of the East River. Further south, two tugboats pushed a barge toward the Verrazano Bridge, while just ahead, tourists on a passing sightseeing boat waved to tourists on *The Miss New York*. The boat jolted departing the dock, silencing the symphony of dialects on the deck. Someone pointed to *Libby* in the distance. She looked like a toy affixed in the bay. But the toy grew into a tower as they neared – the sound of multi-national tongues replaced by the clicking of multi-national cameras.

Once inside the monument, the crowd was funneled through wide corridors, narrowing into a double helix of single-file steps, spiraling up the Statue's hollow center, to the small observation deck inside *Libby's* spiked crown. Progress was slow on the ascending staircase which stopped each time the next group reached the deck. "Will we ever get there?" Vanessa moaned.

"It's worth the wait," someone on the descending stairs said…and it was.

Everyone huddled by the windows overlooking New York harbor leaving space for Pinch to scan the scripts and scrawls on the ceiling, light fixtures and walls. She was never a fan of graffiti. Yet there was something seductive about being witness to the century-spanning "voices" marking their presence in the head of an icon with sealed lips. She touched her purse after reading a note written by someone from Chicago, her father's letter now quietly dwelling with her license, wallet and keys. She'd almost torn open the envelope outside the hardware store but was gripped with fear his words wouldn't echo the man her heart had desperately drawn. Anxious. Angry. Uncertain. She'd cursed having found it and seriously thought about throwing it away – but not in a city trashcan destined for a rat-filled dump. So the letter went back in her purse. A new plan was devised. She'd burn it, unopened, in the kitchen sink before the girls arrived, saying a prayer over the flame and saving the ashes to be scattered at her parents' graves. But time had run out, the cremation postponed; time had also tempered her emotions and fears leading to the current plan of bringing the letter, not its ashes, to Chicago letting her brothers know of its existence.

The air was heavy in the crowded observation deck. As soon as the girls took their fill of photos, the trio wound down the descending staircase and stopped, as suggested, in the Statue's museum. A scale-size replica of *Libby's* gigantic foot had the girls in giggles and kept them amused giving Pinch time to devour the wall of immigrant's letters, forging kinship with faceless strangers who left home, seeking to live free.

Pinch bought the girls snacks before they all meandered to the plaza behind the Statue. The girls roamed, arm-in-arm, on the grass biting candy bars between animated chats and bursts of laughter. Pinch watched them from a bench beneath a towering American flag, the steady snapping of the cables on the flagpole muffling most neighboring conversations. She thought about her father while watching Katie lick her fingers. Did he also love chocolate? Did he like to explore, or was he rigid like Steve? Steve's father was a kind and generous grandfather. She wished she had something nice to pass to Katie about her *Grandpa Duffy*. But her father was shrouded in fantasy. There was no *there,* there, for her to talk about with Katie. Bryan and Kevin had their flesh-and-blood memories. All she had was his DNA, which couldn't paint a living portrait like the man's own words – or bridge the emotional gap between having a father but wanting a Daddy.

The girls were leaning on the rail at water's edge and looked to be counting the geese on the grass. Pinch removed the letter from her purse. The opaque envelope shook in her hands. She slipped her thumbnail under the flap and shimmied the seal til the brittle glue snapped. She eyed the girls. They hadn't moved. She pulled out the letter. The paper was tissue thin. She pressed open the folds, counted three pages then glanced toward the girls. They still hadn't moved. She laid her forearms on her lap, sighed and began to read:

02 – 29 – '52

Dear Maggie,

I can't think of anything new that will keep the boys out of trouble, but hiding the toolbox was a good idea. Is Pop's back any better?

I wish they'd stop talking about peace and just do it. I'm tired of dragging in prisoners and deserters. Sometimes I feel like we're all just mad dogs fighting for the same bone or a way out of this hell. It's scary, and I don't know what's worse, being scared or being ashamed of my fear. I fight the shame by telling myself that there are no cowards in war just people trying to stay alive. What gets me through is knowing you and the boys are safe and are waiting there for me to come home.

I met up with Rocco Vitale again – the guy whose family owns a funeral parlor in New Jersey. Like me, he was called up in the Reserves. He said he's seen enough dead bodies for a lifetime. If the rumors are true that Truman wants to extend GI benefits to us in Korea, Rocco's leaving the family business and going to Med School when he gets home. He got me thinking, Honey. Between the streets of Chicago and these Korean hills, I've had my fill of locking up people. Being a cop wasn't my choice, Maggie. It was handed to me at birth like the name Duffy and the long line of badges on my family tree. I never did have the fire for it like Pop, and the Captain, but I didn't have the courage to take a stand knowing who I'd have to buck and how I would have let them down.

But I'm living in a freezing foxhole here, surrounded by dead and dying, and I'm tired of feeling trapped. I figure I've paid my dues to tradition, and when I get back, Maggie, I'm going to leave the Force. I want to walk tall down my own path not plod along someone else's. I want to do something that makes people feel good, not cringe, when they see me coming. The GI Bill might give me that chance! It's a big step and I'm now ready to take it. But don't say anything yet. I'll have to check things out on the sly or the pressure from Pop will kill me. I really need to do this, Honey. I know you'll understand.

Love, Duffy

PS: Tell Bryan I'm impressed with his homemade skis, but he shouldn't have removed the slats from Pop's bed. When I get home, we'll go to the lumber-yard and find something safe for him to build. And tell Kevin I agree that God loves them too, but he shouldn't leave food out for the mice in the house. I know they're a handful, Honey, but they sound great to me. In fact, I was wondering, how does a daughter sound to you!

She couldn't stop reading the last line. Having never been a part of his life, it was glorious knowing she'd been part of his dreams. She was wiping her eyes when she heard Katie shout, "Vanessa! Watch out for the poop!"

Katie was aiming her camera at Vanessa who was tiptoeing toward a goose preening on the plaza lawn. Pinch wished James Duffy could see his granddaughter frolicking with her friend on Liberty Island; something about the sun warming her face said he did. She reread the letter marveling how from a continent away, he had placed his doubts and dreams in her mother's care, confident she would not betray him. Was this the kind of man and marital love her mother perceived when imploring Pinch to bite her tongue and treasure Steve…?

She slid the letter away, the girls approaching the bench. With only one picture left in one camera, they wanted to walk to the front of the Statue to get "the best picture ever." But they soon lost interest, amused by the boats and the birds in the bay, and gave the assignment to Pinch. She'd learned a lot about photo-composition working with Lydia these past three weeks and was ready to snap a perfect frontal shot of *Libby* when a tour group walked into the frame, from the right. She moved left. The group encroached again. She crept further left keenly aware, but not sure why, that the picture improved the more she moved left. She pulled back til the tourists were gone then reset her sights but continued to creep left stopping parallel to *Libby's* right side, snapping the girls' last picture.

"Mom! What are you doing?" Katie ran toward her, hands in the air. "We wanted the *best* picture. You can't even see her book from here. It's mostly her leg and big foot!"

"That's why it is the best picture, Katie. When you look at her from the front you see the symbols of liberty – the Declaration of Independence on her arm, the torch in her hand and the crown on her head. But from here you get to see liberty *in action*. Look at her leg. It's bent at the knee, and her heel is raised in the back. She's moving! And even though we can't see it from here, we know from the museum that she has broken shackles next to her feet. This *is* the best picture of *Lady Liberty*. She's not only free, she's moving."

The girls stared up at the Statue then looked at each and smiled. "Too bad her feet are so big," Katie said, "one more step and she'll fall off her pedestal."

"Maybe that's why she looks mad," Vanessa said. "If she falls off, no one will think she's great anymore."

"Or maybe she's frowning because she never *wanted* to be on a pedestal," Pinch said.

Vanessa nodded. "And she's trying to figure out how to get down without getting hurt. I'm never going on a pedestal! Once you're up that high, it's too hard to get back down."

"I'd do it," Katie said. "I liked the view up there."

"But you'd be stuck there forever or die coming down," Vanessa warned.

"Not if I had on a parachute!" Katie grinned, then turned to her mother. "Can Vanessa sleep over tonight since *Daaad* won't be home…?"

Pinch was caught off guard by the request and embarrassed by Katie's scornful reference to Steve. "Not on a school night, Honey."

Katie leaned toward Pinch, whispering, "But he's always there on the weekend."

Pinch stroked Katie's hair. "Not tonight, girls. There's homework to do and school tomorrow. I'm sure Mrs. DeAngelis wouldn't approve, anyway."

"How about Friday?" Vanessa said. "She always lets me do sleepovers on Fridays."

Katie was making circles in the dirt with her foot. "Never mind. My Dad's coming home from his trip on Friday, and we'll probably be busy." She looked up, her eyes vacant. Then she shrugged and turned the other way.

Pinch saw in that look a man in a foxhole eking out life in a deadly clime. "On second thought, ladies... If you promise to do your homework right after dinner and be in bed, lights out, by ten, I'll call Vanessa's mother when we get home and see what I can do."

It took Katie a few seconds for the news to sink in. Vanessa shrieked immediately. They clapped and jumped and bounded off in giggles toward the dock for the trip back home. Then Katie stopped short and dashed back to Pinch. Her eyes glistening, she kissed her mother's cheek and gave her a squeeze that rivaled the love of a breeze hug. "Thanks, Mommy, for giving me the chance."

Katie ran back to Vanessa. Pinch stroked her purse then smiled. *Thanks, Daddy, for giving me the courage.*

CHAPTER 15

Family Jewels

S HE BOUGHT RUEBEN SANDWICHES for dinner, the corned beef and sauerkraut combo on rye an adequate replacement for the spread Steve had stolen for the men. The meal was alive with laughter, Vanessa's parents, with coaxing from Pinch, permitting the Monday sleepover. While the girls tackled their homework, Pinch emptied the dryer of yesterday's wash. She wondered how Steve was faring with only one change of underwear and was pleasantly surprised he hadn't called home given his grip on the marital yoke. She folded and filed his laundry then pulled out her luggage from under the bed. There were only three bags – hardly enough room for her and Katie's capital effects. She slid them away and surveyed the room, smiling at the hope chest at the foot of the bed.

The maple chest was an heirloom from her mother and Grandma Rose. It still exhaled cedar when she opened the lid and held her most precious memorabilia. On top was her green mohair sweater. Woven on two continents and born on

Christmas Day, it was plied with a smattering of mothballs and an herbal sachet. The mothballs and the memory drew her tears.

It was the summer of her junior year at college. Just before leaving, to study abroad, Grandma Rose had been diagnosed with terminal cancer. Pinch didn't want to leave, but her ever creative grandmother found a way to soothe the separation. "Let's make a sweater together! You knit the bodice in Europe. I'll knit the sleeves over here. And our hands will weave our hearts together while we're miles apart." She squeezed Pinch's hands, her grip still firm. "And when you come home at Christmas, Sweetheart, my 'arms' will be waiting for you."

Rose was on life support when Pinch had returned to the States that Christmas Eve. Not having the heart to ask about the sleeves, she was stunned to find the coveted "arms" under the tree with her gifts. Later that day on a rocker in Rose's room, Pinch pieced the sweater together near an IV drip numbing the pain of death…at least for the one who was leaving. The following week, by a frost-bitten grave, she trembled within a mohair embrace. Her Grandma had been her best friend. And there on a cusp of becoming a woman, she was rendered a shivering child.

She buried her face in the sleeves now scented in cedar, camphor, and sage, then laid the sweater aside and removed a white satin box from the hope chest. The jewelry box, now yellowed with age, had been a gift from her mother on Pinch's 13th birthday. She opened the lid. A plastic ballerina did a one-note spin then suddenly stopped; its pirouettes continued once the winder was turned in the back. She scanned the tokens of her teenage years, picking up her high school ring. "There's no money in the Arts," her mother had warned when she mentioned her new boyfriend wanted to be an actor. They were sitting at the kitchen table, Pinch twirling the ring, Mama paying the bills fresh from work and a one-hour stint on a gas station line during the '70s oil-shortage crisis. She wondered if the old ring fit and tried removing her wedding band. But the diamond-studded piece wouldn't move pass her knuckle, as if her skin had grown over the metal, like bark grows over a nail. Hair gel helped wrestle the ring free. After rinsing off the goo, she left it to air dry on a towel by her sink.

The school ring fit and brought back a time when potential, not *poisedom,* had filled her life. She remembered her mother's delight at her marrying, Steve, a college professor; the promise of her daughter having financial security must have felt like holy intervention, to a single mother raising three kids on a nurse's salary. Still, Pinch thought, I've lived my life in contrasting halves. The first as a carefree girl, the second as a careful wife. Yes, money was important. But why aren't *bridles* also mentioned in bridal discussions…or that leaving a marriage is a rite of passage, too. And that saying *I'm done* can be harder than saying *I do?*

She tossed the school ring back in the box and removed her mother's Bulova watch. Its winder was missing. She laid it aside and picked up the pearl hatpin that had secured her veil when she made her First Holy Communion.

She'd felt like a bride that morning dressed in white and draped in lace. Seven-years-old and riding high having successfully made her First Confession! "Fighting with Bryan" had been her most prolific childhood sin. She wondered if Bryan had ever confessed that he hated his little sister.

Her legs began to cramp. She stood up, stretched then went downstairs. The girls were practicing their spelling words at opposite ends of the dining room table, each correct response earning the speller an M&M candy. She kissed the top of Katie's head. "Given the size of your candy piles, the words this week must be easy, or you're rewarding yourselves for being close."

"Sister CeCe said that the more we spell a word, the easier it gets, so we're spelling each word three times, til we run out of candy," Katie said.

Vanessa popped two candies in her mouth. "Or til we eat it all!"

Pinch brought her purse upstairs to slip her father's letter in a secret drawer of the satin jewelry box. A wad of tan tissue paper was tucked in a corner of the drawer. She peeled it open and shrieked in delight when a pair of jade cufflinks fell in her lap.

She had just joined the high school band. When her mother had seen French cuffs on the uniform, she gave Pinch the cufflinks her father had worn on their wedding day saying, "He'd be *so* proud if you wore them when you play." Bryan had scowled the first time he'd seen them on her shirt and demanded that she give them to him.

"*No! They're mine,* Mama gave them to *me!*" she'd said.

He'd been edgy all day having just found out he failed the eye exam needed to become a commercial pilot. Her mother

148

had sighed when she walked into their argument. "What's wrong now, children?"

"I want Dad's cufflinks, and she won't cough them up."

"She doesn't have to, Bryan, they belong to her now."

"But I'm the oldest, Mama!"

"Be grateful then. You have the most memories of your Dad."

But he'd badgered Pinch all weekend, outside of their mother's earshot. When he called her a pervert for wanting men's jewelry, she bumped about the room aping the near-sighted, comic character, Mr. Magoo. Many years older and a foot taller, Bryan had bent down shouting, "Drop dead, you fat mouthed murderer! If it wasn't for you, Dad wouldn't be shopping for a crib the day he died, and I'd be throwing a football with my father right now instead of looking at your ugly face."

He'd never used the word *murder* before when hurling blame for their father's death and made it sound like something she intended. She'd lunged at his chest, punching and crying, saying "Take it back, loser," when Kevin walked in and pulled them apart. She'd cried herself to sleep that night clutching the corner of her pillowcase where she'd stashed the cufflinks afraid he might rummage her room when she wasn't home. He mumbled an apology the next day in front of their mother, but it did not quell the guilt that permeated every pore of her being. It'd been a ridiculous accusation. She'd heard her mother say so. But it did carry a ring of truth – they *were* indeed shopping for her crib.

She heard the girls giggling; they were heading up the stairs. She tucked the letter with the cufflinks in the secret drawer and was placing the jewelry box back in the hope chest when they bounced in the room. "Hey Mom, what are you doing?"

"Getting a head start on spring cleaning."

Katie peeked in an ornate box in the hope chest. "What's with the doll's clothes?"

"It's your baptismal outfit." Pinch smiled holding up the tiny white bonnet, booties and dress. When the girls reached for the clothing, she pushed them away, noting chocolate on their fingers, and sent them to the bathroom to wash their hands. They ran giggling to the sink, racing to see who would finish first. She heard them tussle for the towel, then something skittered across the counter and the laughter died.

"Mommy – it went down the drain!" Katie looked about to cry, her finger probing the drain, when Pinch entered. To allay her concern, Pinch told her it was only a button she'd found in the hope chest.

"It sounded like metal," Vanessa said. "A metal button?"

"It looked kind of big," Katie added.

"What color was it, Mrs. O'Malley?"

"Did you find any other loose buttons in there – what did it go on, Mom?"

"I don't know, Katie! It really doesn't matter. Now please, get out of here!"

The girls froze, then looked at each other and backed out of the room. "I'm sorry, it must be past my bedtime," Pinch said. She laughed, and the girls relaxed. "It probably fell off an old blouse. I was going to put it in the button jar. It's no big deal, don't worry."

She shooed them to bed and tried for 20 minutes to recover

the ring before fleeing downstairs and calling Lydia in panic. "What?" the old woman said, answering the phone.

"Lydia, it's Pinch. You sound funny, are you okay?"

"Ya woke me up."

"My wedding ring went down the drain!"

"Probably looking for ya marriage."

"Seriously, I need a plumber."

Lydia yawned. "Call Big Earl in the morning."

"But this is an emergency!"

"A busted pipe is an emergency."

"But my wedding ring is important."

"So is a good night's sleep. That rock'll stay put if ya don't run the water. When's Tex coming home?"

"Friday night."

"Gives ya time to get it appraised. That baby should fetch a bundle."

"I'm not selling it. I've too many memories."

"Any worth remembering? Any that'll pay ya bills?"

"Don't go there, Lydia. Not tonight."

"Still planning to come over in the morning?"

"Let's see what happens with the plumber."

Lydia gave her Big Earl's phone number. "Come for lunch. Made some Pesto-borscht Chili today. Do ya like beets?"

She did…and wanted to keep it that way.

After getting the girls off to school the next day, Pinch called Big Earl, who showed up within the hour.

"Earleen Honeycutt," the tall woman said and extended

a large hand to Pinch. "How ya'll doing this glorious morning? Chili Mama said you got a problem."

Pinch was glad Lydia had also called the plumber. "You call her, 'Chili Mama?'"

"Among other things."

Earleen looked to be around 60. Other than her height she was the embodiment of stereotypical femininity – soft spoken, pretty face, curves in the usual places. She talked slow but worked fast recovering the ring, reconnecting the pipe, readying to leave in 20 minutes. Pinch offered her a warm drink. She thought about it, then said, "Sure enough."

They chatted at the kitchen table dunking animal crackers in their tea. "You don't sound like a New Yorker," Pinch said.

"I'm not. I hail from West Texas."

"What brought you here?"

"I learned plumbing at my Daddy's side, and when he died, so did the jobs – some don't cotton to a woman tinkering with their pipes if a 'real' plumber is in their sights. When my hubby's plant folded shop, we pulled up stakes and moved up here. Some folk say New York rubs them cold, but it's been good to me and mine. People here have heart." When she got up to leave, Pinch thanked her for coming so quickly. "My pleasure. Take care of yourself."

"Wait—" Pinch ran upstairs to the tampon box returning with a handful of bills. "What do I owe? I hope you take cash."

"Not today, Miss Pinch. This one's between me and Chili Mama."

"But Lydia has nothing to do with it."

"It's not about you, Chile, it's about me. Go on and have yourself a mighty fine day."

She phoned Lydia, as soon as Big Earl left. The old woman rattled off the jewelry appraiser's address before Pinch could get in word. "And how'd things go with Big Earl?"

"I insist on paying for her service."

"What the hell ya talking about?"

"She wouldn't take my money. Aren't you paying for the job?"

"That's news to me, but what's ya bitch – got money to burn?"

"If I'm not paying her, and you're not paying, who is?"

"Let me tell ya something 'bout Big Earl. Got a heart of gold but a strange accounting system. Them folks down there in Texas do things differently."

"But I don't want to get a bill a few months down the road."

"*Jeez, Louise.* First ya bellyache 'cause ya don't get a bill, then ya squawk when ya think ya might get one. Look, Pinchey, I know ya stressed about what's going on in ya life right now, but ya need to pick ya battles. Let this one go. Ya got ya wedding ring back this morning. Now move to what's important, like joining me for lunch."

Pinch pocketed two antacid tablets after hanging up the phone and plucked the *Stills* from the box of detergent in the laundry room, slipping them into her briefcase and leaving it by the door with the Dean's essay folders. Then she re-washed her wedding ring. Between the hair gel residue and gunk in the drain, it still felt slimy when she put it in an envelope with her mother's old watch for the jeweler.

The jewelry appraiser was a few blocks from The Market; she hoped he also did cleanings and watch repairs. The neon light in the window said, *Joseph's Jewelry & Pawnshop.* She'd never been in a pawnshop and paused outside, eyeing the iron bars on the window, and glanced up the street, expecting to see society's dregs when a young woman with a baby carriage asked for help with the door. Pinch followed her in and perused the place while a man at the counter took the young mother's order to engrave the name "Jewel" on her baby's silver cup. Pinch was peering at antique guns through a glass-front, double-locked cabinet when the woman left. The man sidled over to the gun display. "May I show you a pistol?" he said.

She reared back…did she look like she needed a gun? "I'm not here to buy. I have a watch that needs a winder and a ring that needs to be cleaned."

He examined the watch first; an overhead spotlight set his balding head aglow. "You live around here?" His voice seemed to smile.

"No. I was hoping you could fix these while I run some errands at The Market."

He studied her diamond wedding ring under a magnifying glass. "I'd like first crack at this ring if you ever want to sell it."

"I don't…but if I did, what it's worth?"

"Offhand – five grand. I'll give you a better idea when it's clean. Do you go to The Market a lot?"

She felt her face flush. "No – can the watch be fixed? It belonged to my mother. I'd like to use it instead of my other one."

He glanced at the designer watchband peeking from the cuff of her coat. Then he pointed to her opal ring. "That's a looker!"

She covered it with her palm. "Yes, kind of embarrassing."

He gently lifted her hand and smiled. "Never be embarrassed by what you have. It's what you do *with* it that counts."

CHAPTER 16

Just Compensation

I T WAS PINCH'S SECOND TRIP to The Market. She entered the shelter through a door in the Ladies dressing room. A receptionist confirmed her meeting with Gertie then led her up a stairwell and through a maze of halls to the White Room. Its seating, storage and kitchenette reminded her of a faculty lounge, four mismatched chairs skirting a table in the center of the room. She stacked the Dean's essays on the table and pushed aside his grade roster choosing to rank each test on its merit. She was half way through the third essay when a slender woman, in a stylist jumpsuit, burst into the room wheeling a vacuum cleaner. The woman apologized for the intrusion stating she needed to clean the room.

Pinch retreated to a bulletin board, covered in sayings and hand-painted art, on the back wall. Hanging to its right was a lap quilt of an angel with a whimsical grin and holding a heart that read, *Smile. You Are Here!* Tacked on the wall to the left was a copy of the Declaration of Independence – the following passages underscored in red:

When in the Course of human events, it becomes necessary for one people to dissolve the political bands which have connected them with another, and to assume among the powers of the earth, the separate and equal station to which the Laws of Nature and of Nature's God entitle them...

We hold these truths to be self-evident, that all men are created equal, that they are endowed by their Creator with certain unalienable Rights, that among these are Life, Liberty and the pursuit of Happiness...

That whenever any Form of Government becomes destructive... it is the Right of the People to alter or to abolish it, and to institute new Government, laying its foundation on such principles and organizing its powers in such form, as to them shall seem most likely to effect their Safety and Happiness....

She had studied the paper in depth, in a civics class in college, but today it read more personal than political, granting her the right to dissolve a relationship, entitling her to happiness.

It doesn't say you're entitled *to happiness, just the right to* pursue *it,* said the Stranger.

She removed the document from the wall and left it face-down on the table.

When the woman was finished, she asked Pinch to join her for a cup of tea. Her wheat-colored hair framed an easy smile. "Hi, I'm Jody. What brings you here today?"

Not knowing The Market's privacy policy, she simply said she was meeting "a friend" at eleven. "Sorry if I got in your way."

"My fault," Jody said. "My son overslept, and I was running late, but this is my last room so now I can relax."

They talked about the weather, books and favorite foods. Then as often happens, when strangers become comfortable with each other, the conversation went from impersonal to particular, Jody announcing that on April Fool's Day she would begin her fourth month at The Market, having left her husband, January 1st, while he watched the Rose Bowl on TV. "My husband, Doug, and I were in Manhattan at a New Year's Eve party with his brother and wife. Our two kids were staying here in Brooklyn with my sister; we had planned to stay at a hotel overnight and pick them up the next morning. But right before midnight, Doug insisted we leave. *Now!*

"He was drunk. I was scared. We lived in Long Island. He wouldn't let me drive. He told me to shut up, then accused me of having an affair with his brother. His proof was that we were both away from the table too long after dinner! I don't know where his brother was, but I was on line waiting to use the bathroom. You know how it is at these big affairs – it took 20 minutes just to get to the door of the Ladies Room."

"Didn't you tell him that?"

Jody nodded. "He backed up his claim by recalling how his brother insisted on driving me to town for supplies when our families camped together last summer. That's true, but while I shopped and loaded the van, his brother was outside on the pay phone talking to his bookie."

"Did you tell him *that?*"

"I tried but you never win an argument with a drunk."

"Is he an alcoholic?"

"No, a jealous workaholic. He bought me a beeper when we moved to the suburbs. I thought it was sweet til he kept beeping me day and night. Our son, Jake, was an infant. Sometimes I'd be nursing him, or changing his diaper or putting him to bed. Sometimes I'd be helping our daughter, Jenny, with her homework. One night when he was working late, and the kids were both asleep, I treated myself to a bubble bath, and two minutes into my soak, the thing goes off. I ignored it, intending to call him when I was done, but he just wouldn't wait. I finally grabbed a towel and called in, dripping bubbles across the floor. The sad part is that I never saw how bad things were til that night in the car when my life was in danger because *he* was insecure."

Pinch scratched her palm. "How did you end up at The Market?"

"My sister is a local doctor. Her clinic refers woman here. What you lose in privacy, you gain in emotional stability – no more walking on eggshells or lying to keep the peace. I trade services for our room and board here."

Pinch closed the bluebook she'd been working on. Jody pointed to the students' grade roster laying face up on the table. "You're a college professor?"

She pinched a smile, avoiding Jody's eyes, and got up to refill her teacup. The water in the kettle had cooled. She dunked and stirred the bag with her finger, coaxing the tea to brew. *Smile. You Are Here!* The whimsical angel seemed to parrot Grandma Rose. She returned to the table, sighed, and spent the next 15 minutes recapping her last 15 years.

"Did you tell me this because it needs to come out, or are you looking for feedback?" Jody said.

"Maybe both." Pinch laughed. Jody didn't.

"Why wait til summer? The longer you wait, the greater the chance he'll find out."

"I'd planned to tell him anyway, after I've worked out the logistics."

"He's already blackened your eye and hurt your daughter!"

"I know, but I don't want to rush, or scare Katie. I want to keep things civil."

"Why do think he'll be civil?"

"We're two intelligent adults—"

"—with different views of 'appropriate' behavior. If he won't let you work part-time outside the home, what makes you think he'll play nice when you tell him you're leaving?"

Pinch shrugged. "Maybe I'm naïve. This is all new to me."

"It's not new to The Market. Talk to them before you go. To ward off a custody fight, start collecting evidence of his unethical behavior – like copies of the Dean's roster and a few of his students' essays, and I'll write up an affidavit stating what I saw you doing today."

Pinch doubted Steve would fight for custody, but agreed to make the copies.

"Hey, Pinch! *Hey, Jody!*" Gertie walked in with a grin and a shopping bag.

Jody looked at both women then pointed at Pinch. "You're

the one who helped Gertie on the street! We had you as a possible witness, but you're going out of town, correct?"

"How did you know that?"

"I'm Gertie's attorney. Paul, the arresting officer, mentioned it yesterday when we reviewed the case. If you change your mind, The Market, as advocates on Gertie's behalf, will pay any costs you incur by staying." She wheeled the vacuum to the door. Before leaving she suggested Pinch open a safe-deposit box with a nearby, trusted relative.

Pinch sighed inwardly. She had no nearby relatives... trusted or otherwise.

Gertie plopped into a chair. She removed the word cards, their corresponding photos, two yellow pencils and a pad from her shopping bag. "Change of plans," Pinch said. "I'm moving back to Chicago in June, and limited times call for limited goals, so I'm going to teach you how to read this." She handed Gertie the Declaration of Independence.

Gertie looked at her bug-eyed. "Gosh, Pinch. I can't do that."

"Can't – or won't? Look, the title has only four words. I bet you know half of them."

Gertie eyed the title and smiled; she had a great sense of phonics, stumbling only trying to pronounce the "t-i-o-n" in *Declaration* after Pinch broke the title into syllables. But reading words meant nothing without knowing why they were written, and she asked, Gertie, what she knew about the American Revolutionary War.

"We had 13 colonies and fought the Redcoats upstate in New York. I know because my class took a trip to Fort

Ticonderoga. That's where those Green Mountain Boys, from Vermont, helped us send the Redcoats running." She then proceeded to spell "Ticonderoga" from memory and pointed to the green *Dixon Ticonderoga* letters on her yellow pencils when Pinch looked at her in awe. "I been seeing that word ferever. But I don't remember why our boys were fighting to begin with."

"The colonists thought King George III of England was an unfair ruler. They published a protest list called the Declaration of Independence and went to war to get free from his oppressive ways.

"Sounds like the homeboys wanted to divorce the King."

"That's one way of looking at it," Pinch said and ended the session on that note explaining Gertie's homework en route to the copy machine. "Make a copy of the Declaration and starting at the beginning, mark every word you can read with a highlighter pen. Break down the big words, like you did with *Ti-con-der-o-ga*, and find someone here with whom you can practice pronouncing the words you don't know."

Gertie leaned close and whispered. "I'm shy about grown-ups knowing I can't read."

"Ask one of the older children."

"No way! Kids laughed at my reading back when…. And I ain't about to visit that place again." They settled on her reading alone with a grammar school dictionary.

Pinch apologized for missing her court date.

"You were there the day I needed someone most, and now I got an army of angels to help me through the traps. Even Jody's sister, the Doc, is checking fer someone to straighten

162

out my pinkie – reckon everyone's getting tired of hearing them clunker notes when I tinker on the piano after dinner."

"You read music?"

"A tad. Granddaddy played the organ at church but died before I learnt all the notes. I draw tunes from what I remember. Mostly hymns." She smiled. "Granddaddy always said not to fret when I'd go off key, 'Keep playing through, Gertie Mae,' he'd say, 'cause when it comes to music, the Good Lord has a tin ear'."

Gertie got the key to the copy machine from a wisp of a woman sorting papers at a desk, the same silent woman who had met them at the police station, later scooting Gertie away that first day at The Market. "Faith is her given name," Gertie said, "but everyone calls her 'Feather.' She teaches self-defense. Her feet can split air like prairie lightening." Feather greeted Pinch with a smile and a bow, her hands joined together as if in prayer. Pinch tried not to stare at the jagged scar on her neck.

"Is she always so quiet?"

Gertie lowered her voice. "She can't talk. Her hubby slit her throat right through them voice chords in her neck. She raised her boy here. Learnt how to do sign language and how to kickbox, too. Mostly, she just bows. And smiles, if she likes you."

Gertie photocopied the document and agreed to meet Pinch later in the week. She "spoke" with Feather then left for lunch duty in the cafeteria, humming "Amazing Grace" and stopping every few steps to mark her copy with a highlight pen she'd borrowed from Feather.

Pinch was photocopying the Dean's grade roster when Gertie called her from down hall. "I already lit up the first three words!" She pointed toward Feather; her face radiant. "And I got me a reading partner, too. Hey Teach, I think yer underpaid!"

"I think not, Gertie Mae. Sometimes a smile is worth a million dollars."

CHAPTER 17

Rumblings from the Mother Heart

T HE JEWELER HANDED PINCH her cleaned wedding ring and her mother's repaired watch. "I hope you'll see me first if you need some quick cash."

"Why would I need quick cash? I'm not sneaking out of the country!"

The silliness that charmed Archie Noble fell flat on the jeweler's ears. "Sometimes leaving the country is easier than leaving the house. Most things in here represent somebody's crisis. You may be fine today, but time doesn't stop for a runaway life. Appraising your assets now will give you a sense of what you can bank on later." She liked his logic and removed all her jewelry; he immediately began the evaluation.

She wound her mother's watch and held it to her ear. Its familiar *tick-tock* pealed off seconds, peeling back the years. "Come on, Pinchey, it's bedtime," Mama would prod on nights she was scared to go to bed.

"I'm not tired," she'd insist between yawns content to

fall asleep in her mother's arms, this same *tick-tock* serenading in one ear, her mother's heart pulsing in the other. When you're a child, it only takes a hug to be rescued from hell. Then you grow up and the lap of love is replaced with rules, your nightmares converted to "crosses." When life had thrown her mother a curve, she drew on her faith to heal reality's wounds. But where does one turn when the mother heart is silent, and the patron of your faith supports the enemy?

The jeweler whistled when he handed her the appraisal. She did a double take. It was $10,000. "I can understand the watch and rings, but why are my gold chains, and diamond earrings, so high? I like them because they're plain and simple."

"You can like them even more. Your plain gold chains are actually platinum, and your simple, diamond stud earrings are magnificently cut of the highest gem quality." He returned the jewelry and rang up her bill for the ring cleaning and watch repair. On the wall behind the register was a permit to sell firearms and a faded photo titled, "Ex-GI Teaches Women How to Shoot." The name beneath the photo was, Joseph Wright.

"Are you related to Lydia Wright?"

"I like to say we grew up together, and I have a missing toe to prove it. How do you know Lydia?"

"I worked on her photojournalism memoir. I never saw your name, or toe, in her journals. What happened to your foot?"

"I caught up with Lydia in Japan during the Vietnam War. I was on *R & R,* soon to return to the front. She was waiting on a press pass into Vietnam, had just bought a handgun and asked me to teach her how to shoot. She was a quick study and still is. Had a steady hand and a hawk's eye, but she always blew off the safety drills and nailed me in the foot right before she left for Nam. She claims it was an accident."

"Do you think she did it on purpose?"

He smiled like a parent tolerating a cherished child's indiscretions. "She was hitting the gender wall – a woman trying to enter a war zone. I knew the turf and got her a phony I.D. as my brother, Lloyd Wright. The Army sent me home before I laid another foot in the country. I tease her about the toe saying she took me out so I wouldn't blow her cover."

Pinch salivated over this juicy tidbit excluded from Lydia's journals. She wanted to ask him more, but the woman with the baby returned for her engraved cup. "Thanks for your help. I'm having lunch with Lydia today and will chide her for not telling me she has a younger brother."

He peered over his glasses and smiled. "She doesn't, I'm her ex-husband."

Lydia's apartment resembled the shipping room of a mail-order firm. Boxes were stacked five feet high with paths breaking off into cul-de-sacs dead ending in each of her rooms. The sole sanctuary in this cardboard jungle was the kitchen where nothing had been packed. Pinch sat in her usual chair. A bottle of *Lola's Passion* and a fresh tube of *Kiss My Sass* lipstick were next to her chili bowl. "What are these for?"

"Going away presents. Wear 'em when ya give Tex the kiss-off."

Pinch laughed. "It would only inflame him. He hates me in orange."

"Not surprised. It's ya power color. Ya sizzled when ya put on the *Sass,* that day. Not like those pale colors ya favor, where ya look like one of those colorless bugs that live under a rock. Show him lava, not larvae! Talking Mt. Etna, not the Dead Sea!"

Pinch looked at her buff-colored blouse. "I don't expect him to be there when I leave."

"And when was the last time ya got what ya expected? Weasels like Tex feed on hitting ya with surprises. Picture it, Pinch. You're a walking volcano. Tex shows up. *'Beat it or burn, cowboy, 'cause nothing stops hot lava on the move!'* I'd wear an orange lampshade on my head. Shove it in his face. He didn't give a rat's ass about yours when he slammed ya." She ladled chili into their bowls raising her eyebrows in delight. "Enough about Tex, let's eat. Then I'll tell ya about my latest idea." The Pesto-borscht Chili turned out to be delicious, the roasted beets in a garlic/basil sauce a savory foil for the baby lima beans and brown rice.

"Omelets, Pinch, that's my new blockbuster idea. Here's the poop. We take my chili recipes and switch out the beans for a root vegetable. Potatoes, yams, turnips, carrots, rutabagas, parsnips, beets, if ya get my drift. Then we wrap the roots in fluffy egg 'blankets' and garnish the puppies with some wild greens. We can start the taste testing soon as my new place is up and running. Ain't it a dandy? And nobody's done it yet."

Pinch visualized beet juice bleeding through a fluffy yellow "blanket," one possible reason no one had done it yet. "Sounds like a lot of work. Have you given up on the memoir?"

Lydia waved her hand in the air. "We can work on the memoir between tastings."

"You keep saying 'we,' but I quit working here. Why don't you partner with Gertie? She loves eggs. She'd be right up your omelet alley."

"Great idea, Pinchey! Now, about a title. Torn between *Ova Joy*, and *The Ova Bite*."

"I like them both," *ova* my dead body reflecting her thoughts on getting involved in the project. "I met your ex-husband this morning."

Lydia beamed. "G. I. Joe?"

"Is that your pet name for him?"

"No, that'd be, *Joe the Toe*. Nice guy."

"How come he's not mentioned in your Vietnam journals?"

"What's to say? Was a marriage of convenience. Had nothing to do with my job."

"He said you grew up together. I thought he was your kid brother."

"Me and Joe go back a long way, our mothers were best friends, bless their souls. Got hitched after reconnecting in a Tokyo bar during the Vietnam War."

"He said he taught you how to shoot a gun and thought you were a cracker-jack shot."

"He told you that?" She was beaming again.

"But how does one do that? Do you focus on one target... or aim for the nearest foot?"

"It was an accident!"

"Did you do it so they would send him home?"

Lydia started stacking dirty dishes on a tray. "What's this – The Inquisition?"

"Just wondering why you'd cut from your memoir a guy who marries you overseas during a war, who teaches you self-defense so you don't go home in a body bag, and whose foot you 'accidentally' maim, keeping him out of harm's way." Lydia kept clearing the table casting ugly looks at Pinch who relished the rare role-reversal of playing the snoop, putting her on the defense. "Okay, case closed on 'Joe the Toe,'" Pinch said. "But I think he's a sweetheart and despite your disclaimers, I think you loved him, then, you love him still, and I think that he loves you, too."

"Like you're a good judge of love," Lydia muttered, filling the sink with suds.

"It's easier reading someone else's relationship. I'm surprised you tied the knot. I thought you hated men, seeing how you love to bash Steve."

"Tex is a toad passing as a prince. Busting his cover was part of my civic duty – don't mean I hate men."

Pinch shrugged. "You never talk about wanting to be with a man."

"Don't talk up sweets, either, but enjoy a nut cluster now and again." She pointed to Pinch's wedding ring. "Joe give you a price on that rock?"

"Yes, along with some other pieces which should give me a nice deposit on my future."

They cleaned up in the kitchen and moved to Lydia's office. Pinch pulled the *Stills* from her briefcase. Lydia twitched her nose. "Smell's like soap."

"Steve came home early. I had to stash the folder in a box of *Tide* detergent." She handed Lydia the sepia print. "I found this in with the other *Stills,* but it clearly doesn't fit."

Lydia's hands shook eyeing the elegant image. "Thought I'd lost ya again, dear heart," she whispered then lowered her head and cried.

"Is she your mother?"

Lydia wiped her eyes and nodded. "Was a soft-spoken woman. Sang like a swallow. Worked in theater on the stage."

"Did your father act, too?"

"No, a photographer. Took promo shots for traveling shows. They met at a Shakespeare fair. Mother retired and took to sewing when I came on the scene. Things were fine til Daddy lost his job and took to drinking, coming home in a frenzy, tearing up the place then piping down, all humble-like, til another binge beckoned, the circus starting again."

Orville strutted in the room and looked up at Lydia, meowing. She tapped her thigh. He jumped up and curled in her lap. "First time Daddy clocked her, I busted a bottle of gin on his head – damn fool licked himself silly til he passed out on the floor. Grabbed hold of Mother's arm fixing for us to bolt. She pushed me away. Said to stay with Granny til things settled down. Said to stop bad-mouthing Daddy or she'd shut me outta her heart."

"What did you do?"

"There's a time to spit and a time to swallow. Eating his fury sat better than cutting her loose." She frowned. "Wrong decision. Lost her anyways. Fell down a flight of stairs help-ing the bastard up to bed. Coroner called it an accident. *Bull.*

Shit. Was a double homicide. First he killed her spirit. Then he silenced her song."

"Even when you know you should go it's as if an invisible force keeps you there. Maybe your mother thought things would change."

"They did. They got worse." Lydia stared at the photo. "She never cottoned to the coffin scene. Wanted to be laid like Juliet in the final sleep. Seeing her off like that helped to remember the magical woman she used to be." Her jaw started moving in a nervous twitch. She looked at Pinch. "Saw shades of Mother when ya came that first day."

"You saw a magical woman in me…!"

Lydia shook her head. "Saw a shiner peeping through theater-quality makeup, and this time I was coming out *spitting*."

Pinch scratched her neck then cleared her throat. "I'm sorry about your mother, but I'm not her, so keep your precious spit to yourself!" She dropped the *Stills* folder on the desk and stumbled through the maze of boxes toward the front door. The light was on in the closet between the apartments. She pushed the door open. Nothing inside had been packed. She touched the trunk, eyed the grate and stroked the hanging fabrics…reliving her fear, Steve's arrogant visit, and an old lady's unblinking stand. She trudged back to the office. Lydia looked to be in a trance, her mother's photo rising and falling on Orville's purring body. "I'm sorry, Lydia. You're like an itch I can't relieve." Lydia prodded the cat from her lap. She pulled herself up and inched past Pinch toward the bedroom. Pinch walked to the door, no aura of Mt. Etna in her gait.

She banged her fist on one of the boxes. "Someday, Mama. Someday I'll learn to bite my tongue."

Lydia wheeled up behind her. "Silence won't open a locked door, Pinch. Don't be afraid of your voice."

"I never used to be. But these days when I speak my mind, it puts stress on my relationships and handed me a black eye."

"Stress is a test of character. Good relationships hold under pressure. And don't eat crow for that shiner. His hand did that – not ya mouth."

Wilbur started mewing loudly, stuck between two stacks of boxes. Orville scampered over and peered in the gap, pacing the scene til Pinch plucked Wilbur free.

"Silence may have worked for ya Mama, Pinch, but she ain't the one groping for higher ground now. Ya have the right to speak ya mind. What ya don't say could turn against ya in court. Speaking of court—" She wheeled to the kitchen, returning with her chili cookbook. "I'm hosting a lunch for Gertie after her hearing. Pick out a meal for the feast."

"I'm flying to Chicago that morning so I'll miss it, but Aloha Chili would be festive."

Lydia shook her head. "Change it."

"The Rutabaga Ragout sounds interesting—"

"Ya flight, change ya flight."

"Gertie's lawyer said they don't need me."

"Not talking 'bout Gertie's needs. Talking 'bout yours. Call it dress rehearsal, but get ya ass in that courtroom. See the setup. Hear the gavel. Feel the tension. Taste the fear."

Pinch rubbed her forehead, picturing Steve's reaction if she stayed. "I can't, Lydia."

"Can't, or won't?"

"Won't."

Lydia grabbed the cookbook. "It's Aloha Chili, then. Rutabagas are outta season. Looks like courage is, too."

Pinch ran into Smith in the lobby. "You look like you need a hug. And what's with all the folders – are you working on Lydia's memoir again?"

She explained the situation with the Dean's essays, her decision to leave Steve, and meeting Jody at The Market. "I made the copies Jody suggested even though I'm sure there'll be no custody fight – Steve only finds fault with Katie."

"I've been at The Market since it opened in '82. From what I've seen, custody battles are more about the power struggle between warring parents than they are about the kids. So collect what you can and pray you won't need it. What happened with Lydia?"

"She thinks I'm a coward for not changing my flight to attend Gertie's hearing. You met Steve. Do you really think he'd go for that? It's not just me. I've got Katie to consider."

"Things are more complex when a child is involved. Do you feel like a coward?"

"*No!* I'm juggling lies, responsibilities and secrets. Tiptoeing around Steve and being 'happy face' with Katie. It's the hardest thing I've ever done, and it hurt to hear Lydia say that."

"I don't blame you for feeling bad. Just know that The Market is here for you, even if you're not at her hearing. It'd help if I had your flight data, in advance, in case you change your mind." She handed Pinch a business card. "Marlena is a banker. She's on our Advisory Board and well aware of our issues. Talk to her about getting your own safe-deposit box."

Pinch scanned the card. The bank was the same one they used.

CHAPTER 18

Soul Practitioners

THE MESSAGE LIGHT on the kitchen phone was flashing when Pinch got home. She guessed it was Steve. He'd ask where she'd been. Narrowing her options to the library and the food store, she opted for the latter – lying about groceries easier than fabricating facts about her research for his book. The call, however, was from Helga who wanted to know when to drop off the table. Pinch called her back. Anytime that afternoon would be fine.

She sorted through the mail. Mostly bills, solicitations, and a *Tiffany & Co.* catalog addressed to Steve. In an effort to keep their debts in check, she usually buried the jewelry brochures in the trash, but this morning's séance with Joseph Wright had piqued her interest in such things. She combed the catalog comparing the glitz on its pages to the glitter in the safe-deposit box. She had the box's key. It was on Steve's key ring. But clearing it out now would only work if she left before he got home. And that was a non-starter. She needed more time…physically, mentally and emotionally to finally cut that cord. She dropped the

Tiffany catalog by the front door and would ask Helga to take it when she leaves.

The envelope addressed to *Mr. & Mrs. O'Malley* was another invitation to a financial planning seminar. Despite her desire to attend one, Steve always threw them away saying he didn't need a plan to buy what he wanted, dismissing her point that the focus here was on saving, not spending, one's money. It was a marital mockery, strangers inviting her to discuss the couple's financial health and Steve only permitting her to "prep" their bills for payment. She tore open the phone bill, slapped a stamp and *O'Malley* address sticker on the remittance envelope. After circling the due date and amount to be remitted, she clipped the bill to it's now prepped envelope. A call on her birth date caught her eye, drew a questioning frown, then a memory and a gasp. Most people buy a phone plan that incorporates local calls in one fee. But Steve wanted to see *every* call. And standing out, like a fire at midnight, was the 17-minute call to Lydia, the morning she'd awakened with a battered eye!

She wiped her brow and paced the hall. Her hands were wet. She felt dizzy. She was sitting on the hall tree bench, holding her head in her hands, when the doorbell rang. Helga took one look and set the table down on the stoop. She felt Pinch's forehead. "You're whiter than a snowman and hotter than a griddle. Sit. I'll get some ice." She found her way to the kitchen and returned with ice cubes wrapped in a dishtowel. "Put this on your face," she said and brought the table inside, slipping on the *Tiffany* catalog while closing the front door.

"Would you throw that away when you leave? I want to get it out of the house."

"Have you thought about buying a trash can? We have plenty at the hardware store!"

Pinch ignored the joke. She'd rather have Helga think she was weird than explain the situation. The ice helped. She dropped the towel in the sink then had Helga put the table in its usual haunt. The new, spring-locked hinges made opening the base a breeze. Inside was a roll of plastic bubble wrap. Pinch looked up quizzically. Helga chuckled. "I come from a family of nine, and private space was always hard to find. Given the rusty hinges and what you found inside the base, it's clear no one knows this baby opens up – making it a perfect hiding place. Guess you can tell I still get a kick out of finding a place to park secrets. I threw in the plastic to muffle any sounds. But if you don't want it…."

Pinch smiled. The bubble wrap stayed.

Helga gave her a card with her home phone number, "in case you have a problem or want something else fixed when I'm not at the store." Pinch nodded, noting the size of her van when she left.

She closed the front door, leaned against its back, and slowly sliding to the floor. Even if she could con Steve about the call on her birthday, she'd need to sell him more lies, next month, when her calls to Lydia and Big Earl came through. She rested her head on her knees gathering "what if" scenarios and viable defenses to use against an unpredictable foe. A fire engine roared down the street. Its siren cut off the movies in her mind giving space for the Stranger to speak.

Take a deep breath. Focus on now. First things first. Keep it simple.

She wrapped her newly minted photocopies up in the bubble wrap, closed the pedestal base, and moved the table around making sure its contents didn't "speak." Then she cut a small slit in the lining of her purse and slipped in the phone bill, and Marlena and Helga's contact information, sealing the slit with double-sided tape from Katie's arts and craft box. It'd been a full day, the second of five with Steve gone. Her eyes were heavy when Katie came in from school. "What's wrong, Mom?" she whispered. "Is Daddy home?"

"I'm just tired," she said through a yawn. "Sit down and tell me about school."

"Sister CeCe wants us to think about Confirmation names. For homework over Easter break, we have to write about a saint we *like* and read it to the class when we come back." Pinch remembered the excitement of selecting a saint whose name would be taken during her Confirmation – the ceremonial rite *confirming* one's devotion to the church. "Sister showed us some slides, and I really like, St. Joan of Arc. Did you pick St. Rose?"

"Rose is my middle name. It's on my birth certificate. Anne is my Confirmation name. St. Anne was the Virgin Mary's mother, her first teacher. What do you like about St. Joan?"

"She was a soldier in France, and rode a horse, and went to war when she was 14. Grandpa has a cool book of the saints. I'll read about St. Joan when we go there next week."

Pinch graded papers into the night finally putting that job to bed. The next morning she organized her thoughts for a phone call to Kevin. She wanted him to hold an extra copy of the papers hidden in the table but struggled with how to explain the call to Steve when it showed up on the bill. She could say she was returning his call. But why would he call? What couldn't wait til he saw her the following week? She let out a scream. *Calling my brother shouldn't be so much trouble!* It was sobering – the encompassing and insidious ways Steve monitored her life. She'd call Kevin from a pay phone and was collecting some coins when the telephone rang, a woman with a muffled voice asking to speak with Steve.

"He's not here. Can I take a message?"

"Pinch…?"

"Jody?"

"Sorry to sound so strange, but I had to make sure you were alone. I'm off to my daughter's school and wanted to tell you that my affidavit is done. And if you're interested in a teaching job, you can interview with The Market's hiring guru this Thursday at 11:30."

"I can only commit to three months, at most. I don't think that would be fair."

"A lot can happen between now and June, and looking into a job doesn't mean you have to take it, Pinch. Can you drop off a resume before the interview?"

"I haven't worked for so many years that I don't even know what to put on a resume."

"Anything related to teaching English. Attitude is more important here than Ivy League credentials. How are things going?"

"Good, I guess. I'm going to see what's in our safe-deposit box today."

"Take out what belongs to you and your daughter, and make copies of everything else. Deeds, liens, insurance policies, ownership titles, tax papers, you name it."

"I'll need a good excuse for going into the box when he's gone. If I take things out to be copied, I'll have to go back *again* to return them."

"Then bring a small camera and photograph everything relevant. Once a partner suspects you're leaving, documents tend to disappear. When are you taking off?"

"I was planning to go this summer, but something came up, and now I may leave sooner. Problem is, I'll only have the key til Friday"

"You could empty the box tomorrow, and split before he gets home!"

"Too soon, Jody. I'll be lucky to get out before the next phone bill exposes my lies."

"Goals are good, but timelines should to be flexible. Let safety guide your decision."

She hung up still pondering how to explain to Steve why she *had* to go into the safe-deposit box while he was away. Besides the O'Malley items, the box also contained some personal papers Kevin asked her to hold when their mother had died. Retrieving something of his would legitimize entry to the box. She called him from the phone booth at the YMCA. The shelter operator said he was out on the street making rounds and suggested Pinch leave a message on his portable phone. He called her right back. "Hey, Sweetheart! I have a small window, what's up?"

"I need to get into my safe-deposit box without raising

Steve's suspicion. Can you give me a reason to look over those papers you asked me to hold last August?"

"Why would he be suspicious? Can't you access the box when you want to?"

"He has both of the keys. But he's away this week, and I have the key ring. I want to make copies of some personal papers, and going in for your stuff gives me the cover I need."

His breath got heavy. "Send me a copy of my discharge paper."

"I need a degree of urgency."

"What the—"

"Please, Kev, no questions."

"I've got to verify my discharge date regarding…my veteran's benefits."

"*Perfect!* I'll make a copy and mail it right out. One more thing. Are you allowed to have your own, personal, safe-deposit box?"

"Let's say that I can. Do you want me to take my stuff off your hands?"

"It's not that. I need a safe place to store some things, and you're the only one I really trust."

"What the heck's going on, Pinch? Want me to see about flying to New York?"

She longed for the safety his presence bought; seconds passed as she fought off her emotions. "No. You've already helped a lot by working out the box issue."

"Okay *Sparkle!* But you'd better *splain* what's going on when you're here next week."

"I will. Love you, Kev."

Marlena was at lunch when Pinch arrived at the bank. Getting her own safe-deposit box could wait. Right now she wanted to access the joint one. According to the signature card, Steve had last entered the box in late December when he would have deposited the sapphire pendant he gave her on Christmas Day. The box was heavy. The teller nearly dropped it. Pinch settled in a private cubicle, pulled Kevin's folder aside, then stuffed her briefcase with pertinent documents; she'd cull through the jewelry when the papers were returned.

She handed the box back to the attendant who easily hoisted it into its slip. "Feels like you dropped 20 pounds in 30 minutes." Pinch pretended to enjoy the joke and casually asked how long it would take to acquire another box. "We usually have the bigger boxes available which may work better for you than having two of the smaller ones. I can check right now if you don't mind waiting." Pinch claimed she had another appointment. "No problem," the teller said, "I'll call you at home."

"No need for that. I'll come back later." The woman pointed to the bloated briefcase. "Don't hurt yourself carrying that! Regards, to the Professor."

"You know him?" Pinch said, avoiding eye contact.

"Everyone knows Professor O'Malley. Great smile. Nice guy. My cousin was in one of his classes!"

Pinch left the bank feeling naked and invisible – how was she suppose to reclaim her *self* when Steve and his name had a lien on her life? A short time later, under the name, *P. Duffy*, she purchased a card at a printing store for 100 prepaid photocopies, many of which were used that afternoon. Before heading home, she caught up with Marlena. The banker had already spoken with Smith and was making arrangements for Pinch to obtain her own box at a bank across town, to avoid meeting Steve at this location.

That night before bed, Katie talked about the movie she'd seen at school on settlers and the American West. "It'd be so cool, Mom, going to California in a covered wagon!"

"It'd be very cramped, Honey. What would you bring if you only had one trunk?"

"How long would it take to get there?"

"I don't know. Let's say, six months."

"Would there be any stores on the way?"

"Maybe some General stores, but I think they'd only sell food and traveling supplies."

Katie looked around her bedroom and grabbed her favorite toy. "I'd take my teddy bear and the music box from Grandma Duffy; my boom box and headphones, and the nail polishes from Dad; my slippers, and bathrobe for snuggling; crafts box for drawing and making stuff – how big is the trunk?"

"I think it's filled!"

"But I still haven't packed any clothes…and I'd want my lamp and my nightstand."

"There wouldn't be room for much furniture, and since there'd be no electricity, you wouldn't have a boom box, head-phones, or a lamp."

Katie knelt on the floor and ran her hand under her night-stand. "If these legs come off, I'd put them in the drawer with my clothes. We could use them as weapons or for making a campfire. And we could use the top of the nightstand as a seat in the back of the wagon."

"What clothes would you bring?"

Katie frowned. "Do they sell clothes in a General store?"

"Probably cloth, maybe some hats, but I don't think they'd carry ready-made clothes, especially clothing for children."

"Then I'd *definitely* take all my underwear. And my pillow and quilt." Her eyes suddenly widened. "Dad would need a gun, wouldn't he?"

Pinch shuddered at the thought. "Protection is important. There's safety in numbers which is why pioneers usually traveled in groups – when you're alone in a new place, strangers become your family."

"Yeah, like Vanessa. I'd want to take her, too!"

Pinch ran her fingers through Katie's hair. "Good friends find ways to stay in touch."

"We'd need writing paper. And oh…the Christmas ornaments."

"We'd have to leave something behind, Honey."

She kissed Katie goodnight and was closing the door when she heard Katie whisper, "How about *Dad?*"

CHAPTER 19

The Heirloom

THE INTERVIEW WAS HELD in the Lima Room. A good omen; St. Rose was from Lima, Peru. Pinch took a deep breath, walked in and froze seeing Lydia in her wheelchair at the desk, an unlit pipe in her mouth. "What are you doing in here?"

"The hiring diva caught the flu last night. C'mon, have a seat." Pinch didn't sit. "Impressive credentials, Ms. O'Malley. Especially ya stint with the cookbook queen." Lydia pulled the pipe from her mouth and grinned. "Must've been a prize position!"

"Yes, a booby prize."

"Ya resume says ya been tutoring one of our residents – how's that going?"

"Gertie's doing great. Can I see that pipe? It looks like Steve's. His initials are under the bowl."

Lydia turned the pipe over. "There's an *S* and an *O*. Don't see no *B*."

"May I have the pipe?"

Lydia tucked it her pocket. "No, let's move along. Time for the *Daily Living & Living Daily, Wright Employment Test.*"

"I'm not taking one of your crazy tests. You're only a temp here. I'll come back when the hiring 'diva' returns. After calling me a coward, yesterday, I have little respect for you."

"Sorry 'bout yesterday. Just afraid you'll change ya mind, stay with the toad, like so many women do. Smith lit into me after ya left. Wrote my name, under *ass,* in the dictionary."

Pinch couldn't hold back a smile. "Big letters, I hope."

"With a permanent marker so's I couldn't erase it when she left."

She took the test, getting one wrong, saying "no" to the question, *Can roots fly?*

"Okay, here's the poop. Ya good with impersonals, but weak on knowing yourself."

Pinch tilted her head. "And where might I find my flying roots?"

"In ya garden."

"The one I left in Chicago, or the one here in New York?"

Lydia's eyes softened. "Ya only got one garden, Pinchey." She touched her chest. "Here in ya soul. Yours was so choked with weeds when we met, was no room for sowing new seeds. So I grabbed my hoe and plowed into ya plot. Some call it butting in. I call it caring. It's why The Market works. Can you handle that attitude, 24/7?"

Pinch dropped her eyes. "What's the pay?"

"Live here rent free in return for ya teaching. After three months, ya on the payroll."

"I can't commit to living here."

"Can't or won't?"

"Won't."

"And where might ya live while ya working here?"

"At home…til I find a place that works."

"And if ya don't find a place that works?"

She shrugged.

"And what are ya going to do if Tex finds out ya working before ya move out – call and cancel ya classes? Assuming he don't put a fist to ya mouth before ya make it to the phone, and assuming ya still have a phone once he's wise to what ya been doing. Phones have been ripped off the wall for less, Missy."

"The phone!" Pinch removed the phone bill from behind the lining of her purse and started to explain, but Lydia held up her hand.

"First things first. If ya want the job, ya gotta live here. Our families need stability. Not run-ins with cowboys and toads."

Pinch chewed her lip. "When do you need to know?"

"Sooner's better than later if ya want to nail down the spot." She pointed to the phone bill. "What's that about?" Pinch showed her the call about the memoir job. "Are you keeping the same phone number when you move?"

"Yeah, only moving cross town."

"When Steve sees your number here, I'm sure he'll call it and recognize your voice. But if you changed it with no request to forward the calls, he'd get a recording saying that the number is no longer in service."

Lydia scanned the bill. Then she tore it up and swept the

pieces into the wastebasket next to her feet. "There ya go. No statement, no problem."

Pinch smacked the desk. "And what do I do next month when my calls to you and Big Earl show up? Hope I get the bill before Steve, and rip that one up, too!"

Lydia toyed with the hair on her chin. "Or ya can bolt before the next one comes."

Pinch rose to leave. "Don't be a stranger, Pinchey. Hate to think I'll never see ya again."

"You're assuming I won't accept the offer?"

"Assuming ya won't in time."

Cecelia was washing her hands when Pinch entered the bathroom. They joked about meeting in the Ladies Room again. Then Pinch looked at her watch. It was half-past twelve. "Sister, what are you doing at The Market? Please don't tell me that school was let out early."

"Lunch time was extended today so the children could watch a film. They're short-staffed here, and when I'm not needed there, I help at the daycare. Why are *you* here?"

"I interviewed for a teaching job."

"His royal *my*-ness gave his blessing?"

"He doesn't know about it," she said and immediately wished she hadn't told the nun.

"Have you thought about leaving him?"

"Good Lord – can't anyone mind their own business here? It'd be funny if it wasn't so intrusive."

"Children are my business, and nothing is funny about

being abused. Katie's bothered by what's going on at home. He messed up your face awhile back, didn't he?"

Pinch glanced around the bathroom. "Katie told you that?"

"She didn't have to, Mrs. O'Malley. I've been reading wounds all my life, and I see your husband at Church all the time. Narrow minded. Arrogant. Needs to be in control. He's a classic abuser flying under the radar because he looks good – as if ugly had the market on being cruel. Seeing you in those sunglasses, Ash Wednesday, confirmed my suspicions."

"The sun was breaking through the fog. A lot of people wore them for the glare."

"But you kept yours on inside the sanctuary and flinched when I bumped the rim."

Pinch covered her face, crying softly in her hands. "I am leaving him. But Katie doesn't know."

Cecelia touched her arm. "When are you going?"

"I don't know. There's so much to do." She went into one of empty stalls, blew her nose and waited...hoping Cecelia would leave, but she didn't.

"Come back with me to the daycare, Mrs. O'Malley. I'd like to explain why I volunteer here, and how I can help you with Katie."

The daycare was in the Garbanzo Room. "It is an odd name," Cecelia agreed, "but it makes the children giggle."

Gertie waved when they came in. She was sitting with a table of cherubs singing them nursery rhymes while they ate. The women sat at a table in the back, close enough to watch the children, far enough to talk privately. "My parents were

Czechoslovakian Jews," Cecelia began, "and when I was four, Papa was shipped to a death camp and never came back." She gently wrung her hands while speaking, her voice almost a whisper, her eyes peeled on the toddlers. "Mama left me on the steps of a Catholic orphanage the night she fled via the Czech underground. I was close to Katie's age when she came back for me after the war. We moved to this country with her new husband, Rupert, a rabbinical scholar who'd barely escaped my father's fate. But he was deeply scarred by the local extinction of all he held dear – his family, his culture, his religion. Rupert wanted to rebuild the past in America. In contrast, my mother was open to a future that included a daughter with Catholic leanings. He could never see I had the right to be what I wanted to be. To him, my choice was another betrayal. The day I entered the convent, he drove off a pier near the Brooklyn Bridge. Mama was in the car.

"Religion and violence have been integral parts of my life since I was a child. The Market is to these children what that orphanage was for me – a temporary refuge when a lunatic seizes your world. I've lived their fears and their hopes. I know the internal bleeding behind plastic smiles and vacant eyes… a look I see, every so often, on Katie. I'm glad you're leaving him, Mrs. O'Malley. Let me help you help Katie make the move."

"How?"

"I sense she's unhappy with her father right now, but that doesn't mean she'll be glad to leave home when you actually go. History is filled with people leaving their oppressors. I can frame class discussions around how and why they must go. By tuning Katie into a broad, historical context of oppression, she may feel less alone, and ashamed, when it's time for her to go. I'll need to be selective and discreet. Your husband monitors everything I do."

"Does he know you volunteer at a shelter for battered women?"

"He knows I spend time at a daycare center. Very few people know that The Market is a shelter."

"Does the Monsignor know?"

"Of course! The Church refers women here all the time, although we haven't since he ordered family counseling, with a priest, before issuing new referrals."

"*What!* When I told him about my black eye in Confession, he suggested things might improve were I more submissive. Can you imagine sitting through couples' counseling with this man? After taking the hits, you're told by the Church that your wounds are *your* fault – confirming what your husband said each time you *made him* hurt you. It's outrageous!"

Cecelia paled. "He's only one person. He doesn't represent the whole Church."

"Excuse me, Sister, but he does when giving guidance to a parishioner in times of stress." Cecelia seemed to look through her...unblinking and intense. Pinch grabbed her shoulders. "Are you obliged to tell him I plan to leave Steve?"

"No. And I'd still like to help. It's crucial that Katie not go home after school on the day you move out."

"Or be left at the rectory...." Pinch said."

"If you'll trust me with the date, I will personally get her to your new location. Will you be moving here?"

"I'll have to if I accept the job that was offered. Is there someone I can speak with here to clarify The Market's relationship with the Monsignor and members of St. Patrick's church?"

"I'd go to the top." Cecelia wrote down the contact. *Lydia Wright.*

"You're joking! Lydia's just a temp here."

Cecelia let out a hoot. "Would a temp get away with naming the rooms after beans? The Wright Foundation owns The Market."

Pinch cringed. "Is there someone else I could speak with who's less—"

"Yes. Her ex-husband, Joe Wright."

Pinch stopped at the bank before seeing Joe and returned the papers she'd removed from the box yesterday. Then she wrapped her jewelry in a scarf she was wearing and tucked the floppy bundle in her briefcase.

Joe smiled when she walked in. "Is this the tall, thin redhead Cecelia told me about?" He thanked her for sharing her concerns and had already convened a Board Meeting to review The Market's procedures regarding client referrals from religious institutions. "And Cecelia's following up with families that were, or are currently being, counseled at St. Pat's since they changed their referral policy. We need to make sure no one's suffering in silence."

Pinch nodded, impressed by his rapid response. She laid her jewelry on the counter and sorted it into two piles. "These are gifts...and these are the pieces that were passed down by my relatives. I'm not selling any of the heirlooms, so just *add: @ blushed,*

dele

appraise the gifts – not that I need any money right now." He looked at her over his bifocals, a pointed but gentle gaze. She felt her face flush. "What else did Cecelia say about me...?"

"Cecelia was all business. But others were *ova*-joyed by your presence today."

"Doesn't confidentiality mean anything to Lydia?"

"She cares a lot about you."

"I know, but sometimes she has an odd way of showing it."

"At least you have all your toes."

He wrote her a receipt and put the jewelry in his safe saying he'd get word to her when he finished the appraisals. She gave him Kevin's number when he asked for a contact, "in case you forget to come back."

"I'd never forget my heirlooms, Joe. They're my daughter's link to the past."

He took her hand. "*You* are your daughter's heirloom, the rest is just metal and stone. Take care of yourself, Pinch O'Malley. She needs a link to the future more than the past."

CHAPTER 20

The Tin Man

ALTHOUGH JOE HAD ALLAYED her concerns about the Monsignor and The Market, Pinch preferred to live on her own before moving back to Chicago. That night, she scanned the paper for jobs and apartments. Tutors were in demand this time of year, and while the pay was poor, her cache of cash and jewelry would cover the salary shortfall. The apartment search, however, was a bust. With rentals geared to the school year, nothing was available til the summer. She closed the paper when Katie approached and put on a winning smile. Steve would be home tomorrow; it was time to gear up for his return. "It's nice to come home to freshly baked goods, so why don't we make, Dad, a blueberry pie. We can do it now, and I'll bake it tomorrow. The house will smell great when he walks in the door."

Katie was less than enthused but took pains weaving strips of dough into a lattice crust. She brightened licking the blueberry bowl and enlightened Pinch on The Lord's Prayer assignment the class had gotten that day. "Sister CeCe's right, Mom.

We say it everyday, but do we know what the words really mean? I looked up *hallowed* and *trespass* in case she asks me about those lines."

Pinch would have enjoyed hearing Cecelia led the discussion on *deliver us from evil.*

They painted their nails before bed, in *Winter White,* the fourth of the five colorless hues Steve had bought following his Fanny-the-Finger debacle; the last bottle, *Ashes,* would debut Easter weekend, in Chicago. Katie pulled off her socks when her fingernails dried and proceeded to polish her toenails. *"Katie!* Dad didn't say we could do our feet!"

"He didn't say we couldn't. Don't worry, Mom, I'll keep on my socks til I go to bed. You should do your toes, too."

"I don't sleep alone, Honey."

"Dad checks your toes before bed!"

"No. But he does see my feet each morning and night. I'd rather you didn't, Katie."

"I've had it on since Vanessa slept over on Monday, and *you* never saw it."

Pinch relented and retired early to get the most of her last night in the bed without Steve.

~

The castle museum is getting ready to close, but a torch-lit staircase beckons. They descend to a stone cavern. Iron cuffs line the ancient rock walls; ankle-chains litter the floor. A docent in rusting armor tells of medieval torture techniques. His face is masked in metal. His voice soft but strained. A torch fades in the chamber. They turn to leave. "Please oil my hinges, first," the docent says.

There's a shrieking of metal in the rotunda. Katie runs up the stairs. "C'mon, Mom. They're locking the gate!"

The docent nods to a key ring on the wall. "Don't worry, my lady, I have a key."

She oils his arm and leg joints. He thanks her and kisses her hand. There is rust from his mouth on her skin. She wipes it off, and another torch dies.

"Hurry, Mom!" Katie sounds far away.

"I'M COMING!" she yells and starts for the stairs, but the tin man blocks her way. "Please, my mask needs oiling…." The third torch expires.

She does as he wishes then rushes up the stairs. The gate has shut. The drawbridge is rising. "You waited too long," Katie cries from the other side of the moat.

She runs downstairs, reaches for the key. The docent grabs her wrist and pulls her toward the ancient wall. "LET ME GO! MY DAUGHTER NEEDS ME!"

"I need you more. Relax, my dear. Let's see if the bracelets fit."

~

She stopped trying to break free when the bedroom door creaked and a shaft of light pierced the dark room. A figure approached the bed. She bowled it down running full bore into Katie's room where she locked and barred the door wishing the room had a phone to call police.

The door rattled violently. "Mommy, *Mom*-my. Let. Me. In!"

"Katie? *Oh my God—*"

She ripped down the barrier, tore open the door and

tripped over Katie crying in a ball on the floor in the hall. "Honey, I'm so sorry, I had a bad dream."

"You were talking so loud, Mom. I came to see what's wrong."

"I must have woke up when you opened my door. I'm sorry, Katie, so sorry...."

Pinch held her close til they both calmed down then iced Katie's elbow which had taken the brunt of her fall.

Katie snuggled under the covers, holding her teddy bear close and suggested that Pinch take one of her cuddlies back to bed with her, too." Pinch selected a tiger from the stuffed menagerie – a facsimile of the striped toy that had comforted her when she was a girl. She tiptoed away after Katie fell asleep and finally nodded off in a fully-lit room, clutching the tiger to her chest.

She made the call first thing in morning. "I'll take the job, Lydia, and we'll move to The Market on the Tuesday after Easter. Tell Smith that I'll stay for Gertie's hearing. Here's the data she needs to change my flight...." The old woman cried.

After years of putting Steve's needs first, 11 more days would feel like a catnap. Energized by her decision to go, she cleaned the house, baked the pie and when that was done, donned a leotard, stretch woolen leggings, and a large flannel shirt – an outfit providing the warmth and freedom needed to spruce up the stoop. The air was cool but the sun was warm. She washed down the door, the railing and wrought-iron light, careful not to dislodge the spare key Steve had taped behind the fixture. Before going in, she showered the steps with what was left in the bucket sweeping away a season of dust, grit and grime. She paused at the bottom step, pinning sweaty ring-lets back from her face. Seduced by a tease of a breeze, she removed the shirt and flipped up her hair letting the cool air caress her nape. When she started to shiver, she headed up the stoop turning at the sound of a screeching van that pulled to a stop at the curb.

Someone whistled. "Knock it off, guys—" Steve playfully scolded his ogling pals while retrieving his belongings.

Archie approached, beer in hand, his eyes glued to Pinch's nipples, standing at attention, beneath the leotard. She put on the shirt and walked up the steps, her face suddenly hot. Archie put down his beer and grabbed her bucket. "Here, let me help," he said aloud then whispered that he was coming in to pick up his essay tests. He looked disheveled and reeked of lust. He leaned close to her face in the foyer. "Hmm. What's that scent, Rosie?"

She wiped her forehead and sniffed her hand. "Smells like sweat, Dr. Noble."

But the kitchen smelled divine.

Steve was sniffing at the pie and let out a sigh. "What's that, Stevie?"

"A treat from my sweet!" Steve kissed the top of her head then reared back. "Too bad you don't smell like dessert."

She wanted to smash the pie in his face. "I'll freshen up soon as the Dean leaves."

"Guess what, little lady? Next week I'm signing that grant for your man – the start of a reciprocal arrangement, right Stevo?"

"You bet," Steve said looking away then carrying his luggage upstairs.

She gave Archie his tests; he asked her to put them in a brown paper bag so the guys wouldn't know and want in on the action. He was sniffing the pie when Steve returned wearing a change of clothing. "Take the pie with you, Archie. Wrap it for transport, my dear."

"Katie worked hard on that crust for you, Steve."

He waved her off. "Take it, Arch. The girls can make me another."

Pinch looked at Archie. "Why don't I make you one after Easter?"

He nodded and kissed her cheek. "*I* think you smell great, Honey, wild and lusty like a filly in heat. You're a lucky sucker, O'Malley. See you next week."

Steve found his key ring in the desk. After checking the car, he asked her where and why she had driven it. She mentioned leaving her mother's table at the hardware store for repairs; she didn't mention Helga's home, delivery service the next day.

"Where were my keys?"

"Under a towel by the dishes at the sink. They must have gotten buried in the chaos that day." He seemed to buy the lie, nodding and scratching his crotch then frowning and blushing, when he saw that she'd noticed. She looked away. "How was the trip?"

"You didn't pack enough underwear!"

"I got tied up with the food and forgot about the clothes in the washing machine."

"Five days with two pairs of briefs. Thanks to you, I've a terrible case of jock itch."

"Didn't they have a washing machine?"

"It was a cabin in the woods! No phones, poor heat; we were lucky to have running water."

"Couldn't you rinse out a pair each night?"

He looked as if he could rip out her eyes. "And where was I to hang them – on the antlers over the door? Knowing those idiots, I'd be the laughing stock of the campus. I thought about lifting boxers from Marty's bag. He'd never have noticed, boozed as he was."

"I don't know much about cabins, my family always stayed in tents, but most of our campsites had a laundromat nearby. Did anyone look into that?"

"Your stupidity is amazing. Professional men don't 'look into' laundromats." He scoured the refrigerator, slamming the door shut. "It's a Friday in Lent. Where's the fish?"

"I made a meatless casserole for dinner. I thought you'd be tired of eating fish."

"We never went fishing. The lakes up there are still frozen this time of year."

"Didn't the Dean know that?"

"Of course he did. Everyone knew but *Stevie.*"

"If you weren't fishing, what did you do all week?"

He sighed. His shoulders slumped. "You would think at some point people would grow up and leave that stuff behind. I swear, I didn't touch her! I'm not about to dishonor my seed discharging it in local swine. But they have no morals. The marriage vow means nothing to them. You think you know someone, then you live with them and realize you've made a mistake."

"But Archie invited you back. He must think you enjoyed yourself."

"Of course he thinks that, what else could I do? My job is still in his hands."

He scratched himself then abruptly stopped. "I'm taking a hot shower and then a long soak in the tub. Draw the bath then run to the pharmacy for something to kill this plague. And put on something decent. You smell like a peasant. You don't have to look like one."

CHAPTER 21

The Saints

STEVE WALTZED IN FOR DINNER like a teacher after recess eager to re-appropriate dominance over his brood. The "Deliver us from Evil" lecture came first when Katie brought up The Lord's Prayer assignment. "Know your values," he said, pointing his fork at her face, "and when evil approaches, always choose morality."

"What's *morality*?"

"Doing what God wants, like running away from the wicked." Pinch nodded.

Then came his edict on Confirmation names when Katie asked him which saint he had chosen. "Patrick, of course, just like my father before me."

"Did you like St. Patrick because he chased the snakes out of Ireland, Dad?"

"'Like' had nothing to do with it. The decision was pre-ordained." He turned to Pinch. "Do you recall my mother's Confirmation name?" She shrugged, wondering why he thought she'd know, since Kathryn O'Malley always avoided conversation with her. He smiled at Katie. "We'll ask her next week. As her namesake, you'll take the saint that she chose."

Katie stuck out her chin. "Sister CeCe said to find a saint that we *liked*."

"Find 40 saints you like, but your name will honor your grandmother – like it, or not!"

Pinch disagreed but didn't argue; his edicts would mean nothing in eleven days. But Katie didn't know that and was near tears clearing the table for dessert. Pinch passed her a note at the sink. *Maybe Grandma O'Malley chose St. Joan. They both rode horses growing up!* Her spirits revived, Katie proudly served the blueberry pie and politely asked Steve how his trip had been.

"It sucked," he said then sneezed into his napkin. Pinch blinked. Katie's jaw dropped. *Suck* was not a word commonly used by medieval orators. Pinch asked if the weather had been spotty. "A lot of things were spotty. The roof leaked, our bedding was damp, and the place smelled like a cave. The shower was like a phone booth. I could barely turn around, and the first one in got all the hot water." He sneezed three times in succession then threw his napkin on the table. "I'm going to bed. Put the kettle on and bring up some chamomile tea."

"What about dessert, Dad?" He waved her off and plodded up the stairs.

He was sidelined in bed with the flu, the next few days, and when he missed Palm Sunday Mass, Pinch used the opportunity to update Cecelia…the two women sketching how, and when, to tell Katie she'd be flying to Chicago without Pinch. By Tuesday he was well enough to realize Katie was gone all day. "She's working with Cecelia at the daycare center during Spring Break." Pinch said.

"Why wasn't I consulted? I don't like her hanging around with that woman."

"She's not hanging around. She's learning how to care for children, something that will help her if she has some of her own."

He managed an abbreviated jog on Wednesday and reviewed her "new" research for his book before parking in the recliner, dozing off in front of the TV. Pinch packed both their bags while he napped and was wheeling them into the foyer when Katie burst in from her daycare chores. She gave Pinch a tremendous hug then ran upstairs to start packing her things for the trip. Dinner was a quiet act of social solitude...Steve too tired to pontificate, Katie bright-eyed and humming quietly, Pinch mentally rehearsing how – and when – to tell Steve they'd be flying without her tomorrow morning.

Katie closed her bedroom door when Pinch came to kiss her goodnight. "Sister CeCe told me you're staying, Mom. She said you're a hero like Joan of Arc but without a horse!"

Pinch smiled. Cecelia knew how to sell a story. "I'm glad you're not upset, Honey."

"I'll listen to my tapes, so I don't have to listen to Dad."

Steve was already up and out, getting in his jog before leaving for the airport. Pinch was helping Katie bring her things down to the foyer when he stormed into the house and phoned the police to report a dog beating. "Can you believe it?" he said after hanging up the phone. "The idiot's kicking his dog for chasing a cat! People like that should be shot."

"Did you ever have a dog, Dad?"

"An Irish setter. My mother named her *Gilda* which is Celtic for, Servant of God."

Katie cringed. "Was the real Gilda a saint?"

"She may have been. My mother would know. A hit-and-run driver killed our Gilda when I was nine, and I've never wanted a dog since. Where is the respect for man's best friend?" He showered then joined them for breakfast. "I'm so looking forward to this trip, my dear. I've made some calls to Northwestern – they're looking for a Classics Professor. I'd start in the fall, only part-time, but we can stay with my parents until something permanent appears."

Katie gasped. "*We're moving?*"

"Perhaps," Steve said.

"I don't want to move, Dad."

"You don't have a vote."

"*Mommy....*"

"Don't bother her, Katie. Your mother can vote when she brings home the bacon. Suffice to say I've a problem with certain standards out here."

Pinch felt as if she'd been tripped, then stomped upon. First for not having a say in the matter and second for his plan to move back to Chicago while she wanted to leave him in New York. When he left to pull up the car for the drive to the airport, she wheeled her suitcase from the foyer to the parlor and cautioned Katie not to argue about moving. "He's getting a grant to finish his book. He won't leave that money on the table." Or, would he…?

Steve left the car double-parked at the curb coming back in the house, all smiles. He grabbed his luggage, looked around then asked Pinch where her bag had gone. She rubbed her hands together as if kindling courage, wringing out the fear. "I'm taking a later flight to attend a hearing for a woman I found beaten, and lying in the curb, on my way to the library."

His mouth dropped, followed by his suitcase. "And this is the first I hear about it!"

"You've been sick—"

"I'm fine now, and I will not pay to change your flight."

"Her defense team is covering all of my costs."

"Who beat her up, Mom?"

"Her husband, Honey, and just like Dad did with the dog down the street, it's important to help when we can."

"That's a different story. What happens between man and wife is nobody's business. Maybe she deserved it – have you thought about that? Come. *Now!* You're holding us up."

She crossed her arms. "I'll only be a few hours later."

He stared at her, a sick grin growing on her face. "I don't like surprises, my dear. You stay, you'll pay."

Pinch walked Katie to the door and kissed her goodbye. "I'll see you tonight at Uncle Bryan's, Honey, and when Dad gets back from the hockey game, we'll all go to Grandma O'Malley's."

She watched them leave from the living room window and sank into the sofa once the car was out of sight. She rubbed her rumbling stomach; her insides were ripping apart. His crippling hold on her life would soon end, but nobody said that expelling the dead would still hurt.

The plan was to meet the posse at The Market and go to the courthouse en masse. She met up with Gertie beforehand to tour her new living quarters and cried at the sparse efficiency suite she and Katie would soon call home. Gertie gave her a hug. "It's just for a blink in time, Pinch. The Market's like one of them farm incubators, a safe place to hold us Chickies til we're up to fending on our own."

The posse had gathered curbside. Pinch knew them all, Big Earl and Helga's presence a surprise. "Jody. Who's missing?" Lydia asked, a *Sheriff* badge pinned to her jacket.

"Marlena is out of town. Isabel's on duty at the hospital. Cecelia's at the daycare."

"And the Saints…?"

Big Earl raised her hand. "They'll be there, Chili Mama. I put in the call myself."

They piled into two vehicles. Joe took Lydia, Helga and Paul. Pinch rode with Big Earl, Gertie, Feather and Jody. "Hear tell we're bringing you in, come Tuesday," Big Earl said to Pinch who nodded then looked away. "You'll be fine, Chile, take it one day at a time. Chili Mama said she's met your man. Don't think she's ever known one of the pimps before."

"He's not a pimp, he's my husband."

"Sorry, Pinch," Jody chimed, "some of us don't see the distinction."

Big Earl apologized. "We'll call him 'the man that you married' until further notice."

Until further notice, Pinch muttered.

The courtroom's paneled walls and ancient pews were bathed in a hallowed patina. Pinch had an urge to genuflect; it passed when the posse high-fived the contingent of gaily dressed women already seated – former domestic violence plaintiffs affectionately called, the Saints. "They know how hard this is," Paul explained. "They came for Gertie, to prove life will go on."

Gertie's husband came in wearing restraints and a defiant look; it was the first time Gertie had seen him since the attack, and she folded under his gaze. Jody whispered something to her. She turned around, and the Saints began to cheer followed by a harmonica note that cued the singing of the song, "I Will Survive." Gertie straightened in her chair. The singing stopped – on a dime – when the door to the judge's chambers opened, and the bailiff said, "All Rise."

The judge was tall, his face severe. He had an air of Abe Lincoln to him. He scanned the room and tersely said, "I trust the audience knows that musical displays will result in Contempt of Court."

"Yes, Your Honor," the Saints said in unison, their tone and body language now free of frivolity.

The hearing lasted less than an hour, Jody producing enough viable witnesses for the case to proceed to a trial. "You got nothing without me, farm girl," the defendant shouted as he left the proceedings.

"I reckon prison ain't helped yer eyes," Gertie said. "I'm

walking free with a posse of pals, and yer on a leash with a pad in the pokey!"

Pinch hadn't expected the confrontation; the tension left her stomach in knots. Joe drove her to the airport. She asked if he was coming on Tuesday to help her move out.

"I will if they need me," he said. "We each have a role to play."

"You're all so organized. And those Saints! I thought the judge would kick them out."

"He's a no-nonsense guy who's presided over some of their cases. They know him well and know his rules, and they're careful not to push him. It's too important for the Gerties of the world not to face their abusers alone." He looked over at Pinch and smiled. "A crusty, wise woman once told me that, 'being there' is 50% of caring."

"What did she say was the other half?"

"Judiciously kicking butt."

CHAPTER 22

Making Home

THE FEISTY SKY OF THE WINDY CITY welcomed its daughter with a turbulent entry. Seeing long ribbons of tail lights on the access roads, Pinch stopped for a ginger ale to settle her stomach before catching a cab. She was plucking change from her purse when an airport announcement gave her cause to pause. "What did that say?" she asked the fast food cashier.

"It's all noise to me, Lady, here's your drink."

People swarmed by the gates. She wheeled her bag off to the side for a place to sit and drink, but the shoeshine stand had the only empty seat. She glanced at her shoes. They looked as tired as she felt. En route to the stand, she heard the message peal again. *Paging Sparkle O'Malley. Sparkle O'Malley, proceed to the nearest courtesy phone.* Two teenagers by the courtesy phone giggled when she identified herself. Seconds later, a familiar voice spoke into the phone. "Hey, Sparkle. Sorry I'm late. Traffic was a bear. Where are you?"

"Kevin, what a surprise!" She gave him the gate number

by the shoeshine stand and was barely seated when she saw him approach – arms stretched out like Christ of the Andes, waving at her from his wrists, then blowing her a kiss. He looked broader than at Christmas, and his hair was longer, pulled back in a ponytail. He ambled to the chair, looked up at her and grinned. "How did you survive the seminary, Kev, with such a flair for the dramatic?"

"Since when does a priest have to be catatonic?"

"Catatonic, brother dear, would be an improvement over some."

He jerked back playfully. "Sounds like Sparkle has locked horns with a fire-and-brimstone sort. What's the matter…have a problem with salvation stories?"

"That depends on who's being saved, and who's getting nailed to the cross."

"Ah, selective sympathy. Perhaps we could discuss this later."

"Perhaps…."

The shine took forever. Kevin didn't seem to mind, scanning the crowd, getting a pulse on the people; his people. He was a street priest, a shelter shaman, spiritual equivalent of a cop on the beat, polar fleece and blue jeans softening the crisp white collar at his neck. He gathered her in when she alit from the stand, his chest blocking out the indifferent crowd, his arms doing for her soul what a stranger just did for her shoes. "Thanks. I needed that."

"Me too," he said, grabbing her bag. "C'mon, let's make home."

Home used to evoke comfort and joy, but she didn't

know where home was anymore. Certainly not in New York with Steve. And even though she agreed to pass their child-hood home to Bryan, she'd felt displaced when she returned at Christmas time – the downstairs decked in *his* family's décor, her bedroom belonging to *his* daughter.

They wove through the crowds at the baggage carousels. She was glad she decided not to check her bag, wanting to get to Bryan's before Steve got back from the hockey game. "How come you didn't go to the game, Kev?"

"I gave my ticket to Katie. She wanted to go. And this gives us time to catch up."

She patted his arm. "Thanks for thinking of us. If you ever decide to leave the priesthood, I know another sensitive, *practicing* Catholic who'd make someone a great wife."

She left out Cecelia's age and occupation.

He held the door open to the parking lot, a mischievous smirk plastered on his face. "Why do married people always want the rest of the world to get hitched?"

"I just wish you had a more permanent place to call home."

"Home is more than brick and mortar. It's a place deep inside that you build with special memories, a place you can visit when you need to feel loved. We're making home right now. And we're lucky, Pinch. We grew up safe and loved. Most of the kids at the shelter have been hurt so bad that they've sealed off their hearts so their old wounds won't hemorrhage. Don't worry about me. I'm in a good place."

A stiff wind scuttled conversation on the walk to his car, a junkyard heap that screeched when he pried the doors open and trembled when he turned the key. She snapped on her seatbelt. "Is this the best the Church can do given what Rome pulls in every Sunday?"

"My other car was stolen, and I'd rather put the money toward the kids. These screaming doors work as an alarm. I wouldn't have gotten here sooner with leather seats."

They cruised out of the parking lot. A cold breeze licked her ankles via a rusted-out hole by her feet. Traffic stalled well before the service road met the highway. "Are you sorry you're not at the game, Kev, instead of sitting here going nowhere?"

He reached for her hand. "I've only seen you and Katie once since Mama died. I've missed you both, so no regrets. Is Katie okay? She started crying when Steve suggested she spend the evening with his mother instead of going to the game with the guys. I thought she'd be thrilled. Remember the fun we had with Grandma Rose, her *what-if* possibilities, and how, after we decided what to do, we brainstormed 20 minutes on how we might do it differently!"

"Remember that Sunday night when Mama came home from work, and we were sitting in the kitchen eating home-made, hot fudge sundaes," Pinch said. "The ice cream was warm, the fudge was frozen, and Mama rolls her eyes and says, 'That's not a hot fudge sundae!'"

Kevin laughed. "Then Grandma says, 'You must be wrong, Maggie dear...we have the *hot*, we have the *fudge* and look at the clock – it's still Sunday.' The best part was Mama's face when Grandma asked her to brainstorm with us on how to make a hot fudge *Monday!*"

"But Steve's mom isn't like that, Kev. How did he react to Katie going to the game?"

"That was weird. He seemed annoyed."

"Probably worried his pious image will take a hit, cursing the Ref with beer breath."

Kevin shook his head. "It might be too late for that. I was up in the attic, with Katie, looking through Mama's old photos, and out of the blue, she asked if I knew Steve's friend, Fanny-the-Finger, and why did wearing *orange* nail polish make a lady a whore? She left with the guys for the game before I could probe. What's that all about?"

A gust of wind shook the car. Pinch pulled her coat tightly to her chest and filled him in on the nail polish sermon and finding *Lola's Passion* in her sink. "Please don't mention any of this to Steve. I don't want trouble this weekend, and I know you don't care much for him."

"When did I ever say that?"

"Some things don't need to be said."

He raised his right hand and shrugged. "I was doing mission work in Brazil when the two of you were dating. When I got home, eh? It was enough that you and Mama loved him."

"And now…?"

"He wouldn't be my first choice for my sister's life mate. Want to tell me what's going on?"

Not yet, she thought…his term *life mate* an ominous reminder she was talking to a priest, and why risk his rejection when they'd just started making home. "It's a long story."

"Give me the edited version."

"It doesn't condense well."

He pulled a black and white photo from his chest pocket. She held it up in the headlights of the cars stalled behind them. "Wow," she said, smiling at the girl in makeshift hockey gear, crouched in front of a goal cage on a spit of ice in a field.

"How old are you there?" he said.

"Maybe, seven. That equipment was way too big, but still I was a darn good goalie."

"Too good. That's why we built a bigger cage."

"I thought you guys built the new one because the frame on the old one broke."

"It did. After we stomped on it with our skates."

"How pathetic! First you make me play goalie – a first grader fending off guys in their teens – and when I rise to the task, you come up with a scheme to make it easier to score."

"It was Bryan's idea! I just did what I was told."

"Do you always do what you're told?"

He laughed. "Not anymore, and apparently, neither do you. I opened the safe-deposit box in our names. The signature card is in the glove compartment. Since we're crawling along, I'll pull the car over and you can sign it, now." He veered out of traffic then held a flashlight as she penned her name to the card. It started to snow. The stalled drivers honked their horns in frustration. He suggested they stop at a nearby church. "I know the priest. We can sit things out in the rectory. At least it will be quiet and warm." He called ahead on his portable phone telling 'Father Pete' they'd be at his door in 15 minutes.

The blowing snow on the narrow side streets consumed all of Kevin's attention. Pinch used the flashlight to study the photo. She wanted to touch that little girl, so brazen in her big equipment, wanted to be that sprite with a dazzling smile rivaled only by the brightness in her eyes. It was a time when her fantasies were rapidly fading; when Santa had died and the Easter Bunny had hopped away for good; when she'd fallen in love with the moon and the stars; when she'd asked next of kin to call her *Sparkle*. Bryan refused. Mama obliged. Kevin and her grandmother delighted in delighting her. "Can I keep this, Kev?"

"Yep. What do you see in that kid?"

"Energy. *Sass!* Confidence. Grit. Partly in my body language, mostly in my eyes."

"Even behind that hockey mask it's hard to miss all the life percolating in your eyes."

"You sound surprised, but Mama always said I am the spitfire in the family!"

"You were, Pinch, but you've lost your fire. I could hear it in your voice when we talked, last week, and I read it in your eyes, tonight."

She flicked off the flashlight. "I thought men of the cloth only read spiritual things."

"The language of sorrow is spiritual."

He glanced at her. She shifted in her seat. "You're suddenly sounding very priestly. Somehow I missed the move."

"Mama always said I'm the fastest in the family."

He was too perceptive, this street-smart priest. "What did you read in my eyes tonight, Kev? The condensed version, please. No sermons."

"Five words, Sweetheart. *Sparkle doesn't live here anymore.*"

She wanted to shout, "Does to…." but her voice got lost in her throat.

He rode with her silence, now and then looking in her direction. They reached the rectory at ten o'clock; she wished she were hugging Katie instead of greeting another priest. Father Pete led them to his sitting room. A healthy fire lit up the space; Gregorian chants sanctified the air. He left them with wine, finger food and a pair of blankets, the latter in case the fire went out before they did. "Is this typical fare for a drop-in priest," Pinch muttered, "or does every stranded fool get this kind of service?"

Kevin winced. "Sparkle may have lost her shine but not her edge – mind if I hold your sword for the weekend?" She apologized for the snit she was in and lay an imaginary weapon at his feet. He promised to put it in the safe-deposit box, along with her other things.

She borrowed his portable phone and called Bryan's house to tell his wife, Amy, they were staying put til the snow stopped. "If Steve wants to leave for his parents' house, before we show up, tell him not to wait for me, and I'll hitch a ride over in the morning."

Kevin took the phone. "I've still got my house key, Amy, so don't wait up for us. *Of course we'll be quiet!* Bryan is the oaf in the family." He pocketed his phone with a smile. "Didn't want to tell her I could sneak into that house wearing blindfolds. Nothing's changed there since we were kids."

"Like avoiding that noisy porch step?" Pinch said.

"And leaning hard on the door so it doesn't creak when it opens."

"Didn't Bryan know that? He always woke me up when he came home late."

"The subtleties of stealth fade after a few beers. Does Steve like to drink?"

"Not at home or alone. But he will have a few beers tonight at the rink, with Bryan."

"He was ticked that you stayed in New York. Katie said you were helping a friend."

She poured a glass of wine and settled on the sofa then told him how she'd come across Gertie while working behind Steve's back. "That was four weeks ago, but he thinks it happened last week when he was gone. He's mad I stayed and mad I didn't *tell him* I was staying, til this morning. But if I told him sooner, he'd have looked up the case and asked what I was doing in that neighborhood."

"Won't he check when you get home next week?"

"Probably…. But I'm moving out on Tuesday."

His face froze.

She put down her wine and scooched forward on the sofa. "Don't hate me for doing this, Kev. The Monsignor thinks if I play nice with Steve, he'll play nice with me, but I've already taken a swat in the face, and I'm sorry – my other cheek is off-limits. He's already sucked all joy from my life. I can't let him do that to Katie."

Kevin started stoking the fire, smacking and stabbing the logs til they broke into chunky, smoldering lumps. Then he sat beside her and took her hand; his skin was street-worn, like his car. She turned her head. Couldn't bear to see disapproval on his face. "*Look at me, Pinch!*" He squeezed her hand til their eyes locked. "I am so proud of you for not breaking under that kind of pressure. Do what you have to do to get out. I'll back you all the way."

She didn't realize how rigid her shoulders had been til they fell into his chest when she burst into tears. "I thought you'd agree with the Monsignor."

"I'm out on the streets and know from my kids that home isn't always a haven. Marriage is society's ideal. I'd get less flack leaving the priesthood than you'll get leaving Steve, and I won't have to watch my back, in the process. So tell me, *now*, what the heck is going on?"

She began with the slam to her face, how she thought of giving up, but the Stranger wouldn't fold which lead to the memoir job and Lydia's Friday morning chili-fests. Then there was Gertie and the trip to The Market, the lure of orange lipstick, *Lola* in the sink, and countering Fanny's lurid repute with Monet's innocent petals. He stared at the floor as she spoke, kneading his fist in his palm but looked her way when she fluttered her hands, as if petals graced her nails. "That's pretty cool," he said. "Sounds like some of Grandma rubbed off on Mama, after all. No wonder Katie was confused – Steve painting morals, by color." He looked at his fingers then started *thwacking* his palm again. "What if I wear orange polish to Easter brunch?"

She threw a grape at him. It missed wide, but his hand flew out snagging it on the fly. He popped it in his mouth and winked; she was glad he stopped the punching motion. He asked her to finish her story. "Okay, but keep the jokes to yourself."

He flashed a grin. "I wasn't joking. Grandma would approve!" She stared him down. "Or not...." He shrugged. "Please continue."

"Only if you listen as if you're hearing my Confession. Everything stays in this room."

She described Steve's visit to Lydia's and Katie's *Judas* performance. "When he overreacted to Katie's trip, I knew staying was suicidal. I've got some money, a place to stay, a job and local support. But nothing comes up when I try visualizing the future. How do you move forward, Kev, when you don't know where you're going?"

"Rebuilding your life is a process not a miracle. It takes time and courage and is harder still after losing trust in people and things that were supposed to be fail-proof. Don't look too far ahead. Envision being safe and mentally sound. Where are your copies of the papers you sent me last week?"

"In Mama's little table. The pedestal opens – look at this!" She took the baseball card, orange feather and letter from her purse and extended the letter, but he reached for the card.

His eyes narrowed, then widened. "I was counting my tooth-fairy money one day, when Bryan hits me up to buy Mama a birthday gift and comes home, instead, with this baseball card he bought from the kid across the street." He looked at the card and smiled. "A *Ted Williams* card was a hot commodity – he was a baseball star *and* a war hero flying with our air force in Korea. Well Bryan couldn't stop gloating, waving the card in front of my envious eyes til I snatched it from his hand and took off running." He furrowed his brow, then nodded. "I was at Mama's table when he ran upstairs to make a pit stop. I was going to hide it under the doily. Then I saw a gap in the tabletop that looked like a piggybank slot... inviting me to drop in my treasure. But the card got stuck. I tried pushing it down with something else and that thing fell through the crack, so I ended up jamming it down with the butt end of that feather which also took the dive." He reached for the letter. "What's this?"

"It was in the table with the card and feather. It was sealed. I opened it last week."

"Grandma used to leave Mama's mail on that table. This must have been my prod before I used the feather." He read the envelope, looked at her face, shook his head and covered his eyes. *"Aw jeez,* she never read it. I wish—"

"Stop wishing, Kev, just read it."

CHAPTER 23

A Penetrating Chill

KEVIN LEANED FORWARD reading the letter, as if pouring his body into his father's words. Pinch fingered an antique Bible on a desk wondering which contradictory directive today's faithful were counseled to follow. *An eye for an eye,* or *turn the other cheek?*

The snow had stopped falling. She was anxious to leave. Kevin stood up and folded the letter then wiped his eyes on his sleeve. "I was seven when Dad died. I never realized how much I wanted his approval at being the man I am today. But I think we were cut from the same cloth." He handed her the letter. "Thanks for bringing this."

It was after midnight when they ventured out dodging snowplows and salters casting a safety net on the slippery streets. She wasn't aware she'd fallen asleep til the car did a shimmy dance when Kevin cut the engine. The windows had fogged up, the defroster on par with the car's bodywork. She wiped a spot clear and looked at the house. All was still and dark. "Wait," she said, when he turned to open his door, "I want to enjoy peace and quiet a little longer." When she gave the okay he finessed his door open, spacing the creaks to minimize the noise. She left from his side. "Nice going, Buster. You could moonlight cracking safes." Her voice sounded louder than it should have.

The trek to the porch was short, but her leather soles made it treacherous. She held the railing and waited below while he deftly cleared the noisy step, hoisting her luggage up to the landing and leaving it by the front door. He extended his hand to help her over the ornery stair, but her balance shifted each time she reached up threatening to take her for a spill. He came back down and held her steady from behind. "Grab the rail," he whispered, "then flick your leg up to the quiet step." She started to giggle. "Knock it off, Sparkle. I'll never hear the end of it if we wake them up."

She grasped the rail. Her glove lost its grip, her feet slid forward, and she fell back hard into his chest. They tumbled together, head first to the curb, into a mound of snow from a previous storm. They started laughing – their feet high enough above their heads to make getting up a chore. She grabbed the branch of a bush and pulled herself up before falling, face first, on his chest. She couldn't stop laughing. "I think you're trying to kill me," he said. "Don't move. I've got an idea." He wrapped his arms around her waist, and on the count of three, they rolled sideways into the street.

He was up in a flash and extended his hand. Her clothes were soaked, ankles cold, shoes compacted with snow; but she hadn't had this much fun in years and didn't move, taking in the peaceful surroundings. "Jeez, Pinch, what's the matter now?"

"I'm thinking...."

"You can think inside. C'mon, take my hand."

"That's what you said ten minutes ago on the porch, and we're further from the door."

He pulled her up. They gingerly walked, arm in arm, toward the porch. Rather than risk another fall, she stepped on the noisy stair. The porch light came on.

Someone inside was tugging at the door. "I'll get it," Kevin said. He leaned on the handle and pushed hard knocking Steve into tomorrow when the door flew open. "Sorry about that, Buddy," Kevin said when Steve wobbled into view.

Pinch asked Steve if was he was okay. He grabbed his jacket and yawned. "Come on, Lolita. Get your daughter. Let's get out of here."

Katie was sleeping on a love seat; a blanket lay crumpled on the sofa. "Why don't you stay for the night, Steve? The sofa bed sleeps two," Kevin said, "and I'll grab the recliner in the den." Steve started shaking Katie. Kevin tapped his arm. "At least let her stay."

Steve pushed him aside and tottered to porch. "Get her up, my dear. I'll be in the car."

"You can't go with him, he's drunk," Kevin whispered.

"He's just groggy. Help me with her." Katie wrapped her arms around Kevin's neck; he carefully descended the porch steps with his cargo. Pinch grabbed her luggage. She side-stepped to the rental car, tossing her stuff in the back then returning for Katie's things…finally sliding next to Steve whose forehead now rested on the steering wheel.

"You okay, Buddy?" Kevin asked, securing Katie's seat belt. Steve picked up his head and turned on the engine. The car jerked forward while Kevin was backing out. *Hey...!*" He jumped out, shut the door and rapped his fist on the roof.

The car pulled away. Steve burped. The smell of stale beer choked the air. Pinch turned around and looked at Kevin standing alone in the middle of the road, hands on hips beneath the streetlamp.

"Don't ever pull that crap again," Steve said. He had taken a shower while Pinch settled Katie in a bedroom down the hall and was sprawled on the sumptuous four-poster bed in his parents' guest suite, snacking on figs and sipping on brandy, naked beneath a blue silk robe – a welcome home gift from his mother. Kathryn O'Malley wasn't happy when her only begotten son had moved to New York last year, this lush retreat, no doubt, a reminder of what he had left behind. It was 2 am, and he was on his second brandy; he should have been courting sleep, not confrontation. She pretended not to hear him, unpacking her suitcase, not looking toward the bed. It was an elegant bed, high off the floor and crowned in a purple canopy – its four corner posts flanked with wispy, white sheers, and tied in place with burgundy colored rope-cords. The suite included a circular garret; its leaded glass windows and wide window seat lent the alcove a medieval air. Steve pushed her arm with his foot when she slid her suitcase under the bed. "I said I do NOT appreciate being put off for some *husshy* who was roughed up by her man."

"She's not a hussy. He beat her because she refused to have sex with a friend."

"Good God, you mock our marriage for that ilk?"

"I didn't mock us by supporting her. She's his wife...but it is *her* body."

"And what do you make of a wife engaging in sexual forays with others than her *spouth,* including beasts of the animal kingdom?"

She lay her purse on the floor by her nightstand. "I told you, that was a dream."

He refilled his brandy and sat down on her side of the bed. "And was tonight a dream made incarnate?"

"What are you talking about?"

He waved his glass in the air. "Your little tryst with the Celibate, out making merry all night, who knows where, with a man this time – not a beast. I heard you pull up. What took so long to get out the car? Disengaging another tentacle?"

His inference turned her stomach. She'd have left to sleep elsewhere, but where could she go in this house without raising questions? "I asked Kevin to take my confession."

It was sort of the truth. She'd been confessing all night.

"And who will take his confession?"

"For what?"

"Don't play me for a fool. I saw the whole thing. He couldn't keep his hands off you. If you don't feel shame getting felt-up under my nose, I can only wonder what happened when the two of you were alone."

"Are you crazy! He's my brother – a priest, for God's sake!"

He slurped down his brandy. "He's a man, 'horny' like the rest of us. With all the noise you made, I *woouldn't* be surprised the whole family *winnessed* your *tit* - tillating exhibition." He laughed at his joke. "Puts another spin on brotherly love, don't you *shink?*"

She would have shot him if she had a gun. "Are you saying that kinship will never deter a man, alone in the dark, with a member of the opposite sex?"

"Indeed."

"Then should I worry that you and Katie slept alone in Bryan's living room tonight?"

His face contorted. "How dare you! *That's disguthing.*"

"And so is your suggestion about me and Kevin. Now if you don't mind, I'm tired and would like to go to sleep."

His head dropped. He handed her his empty glass. Was he done or did he want a refill? She stared at his feet awaiting his instruction; despite the imposing height of the bed, his toes were touching the floor. When no directive came, she suggested he close his eyes and lie down. "I'll get the lights after I do my teeth and brush my hair."

He slowly raised his head and eyed her chest and hips. His breath quickened. He scanned her face, eyes wide with expectation. She backed away. "Not tonight, I'm beat."

She washed out his glass and brushed her teeth. When she returned, he was still sitting on her side of the bed – eyes shut, body leaning, primed to keel over on the mattress. Good, she thought, once he's down I'll grab a blanket and sleep up in the garret. She tiptoed passed his feet and bent over to grab her brush from her purse. The bed creaked. Her legs stiffened – his hands clutching her hips from behind. He stood up and pulled her toward him then tossed her face down on the bed. "I'll bet you're beat, you've been putting out all night."

She crawled to the other side of the bed. He pulled her back, straddled her thighs, his legs tightening around her like a vice. His hand swept under her body, groping then ripping the button off the waistband on her slacks. "Stay still," he said. When she didn't comply, he shoved her head into the downy bedding pinching her air supply. "*Stay still, I said!*"

She stopped resisting. He eased his hold on her head. She turned her face and exhaled in spits, like a hot rod revving in idle. Her body went limp. "'At's a good girl." Sliding both hands under her body, he grabbed each side of her zipper, wrenching it apart in a violent jerk, tearing her trousers to the knees. She started to cry. He tugged the tatters from her legs and in another swift move ripped off her panties. He sighed and kissed her bare bottom. "God you have a lovely *assh,* the forbidden fruit in my Garden of Eden tempting to be plucked – and fucked – by someone willing to take the plunge." He tickled her ear with his nose. "Poor Archie and the boys, debasing themselves with a whore…. But good ol' *Stevie* has the last laugh, playing out their *fansisses* without the burden of adultery." He tied her wrists from behind with the belt of his robe, pulling it like a rein to see if it held. "Foreplay was never my forte. But we both lucked out, The Celibate *woomed* up your engine!" She tossed and kicked. He giggled and called her his feral filly, reining her up from the bed til her feet touched the floor. He parted her thighs with his knee and pulled her tightly against his groin; his robe licked the back of her legs when it slithered to the floor. Her body shook violent shivers. "Don't worry, my dear, you'll be hotter than hell in a minute."

She choked on her breath when he raised her hips. "Please. Don't. I'm sorry. Steve."

"Not now, Princess. We're going for a ride." He slapped her thigh, pulled the rein, and violently jerked forward. The coverlet on the elegant bed muffled her cries as he rammed her from behind – alternating his points of entry chanting *whore* with each penetrating thrust.

She didn't know how long it lasted. The room was dark when she opened her eyes, and the air reeked of brandy and body fluids.

Her hand grazed her leg. She was wearing a nightgown. He let out a snore. She didn't move, trapped between two nightmares – the body beside her and the theater in her head playing and replaying the violent skit each time she closed her eyes. Her soul was lost, her body misplaced. She needed a toehold into something real, something beautiful, something to grab onto. *Toe*…hold. She wiggled her toes, imagined them painted, ten orange petals in fields of Monet. She called them by name. Tangerine, Coral, Peach. When that color faded, she pictured them yellow, then purple, then green. Red, pink, and blue, then finally white! A shimmering white, studded with sparkles like stars that morphed into snowflakes, that melted to opals, that spilled from her eyes, salting her cheeks, then ascending to heaven – twinkling like stars that morphed into snowflakes, that melted to opals that spilled from her eyes, salting, ascending, twinkling, morphing, melting, spilling on the elegant sheets.

When she awoke a few hours later, her only bedmate was the sun.

She cringed stepping down from the bed. The pain

heightened with every step. Her torn clothing was gone. Her bra and blouse were folded on the bottom garret step. She locked the bedroom and bathroom doors, filled the tub and slunk low til the water lapped her chin. It helped not to see her skin; it felt as if it was smeared with feces. She soaked. She sponged. She cried. She dried. She crept toward a three way mirror, eyes closed, hoping to find a piece of Pinch there, praying she wasn't dead. Three Pinches looked back! She tilted the mirrors. The threesome merged into a single redhead with eyes the color of life and a chin set in grit.

Steve smiled when she came into the kitchen. He was reading the paper, a bottle of aspirins next to his coffee cup. "Good morning, my dear, I should have slept in too. I can't remember when I had my last hangover. Take a plate – there's Danish in the breadbox."

"I'm not hungry," she said to the breadbox. "Where is everyone?"

"Grocery shopping."

"Have you seen Katie?" She needed to hug Katie.

"Yes. She slept well, and I'm not surprised, the beds in this house are like clouds. We'll be leaving for Church soon after they return. Have you finished unpacking?"

"Yes."

She poured herself a cup of coffee trying to reconcile his idle chatter with what had happened six hours before. He put out his cup. "Can I get a head on this?" It took some doing to fill his request without emptying the pot down his neck. She brought the aspirins to the sink and spilled a handful in her palm, downing two, pocketing the rest. Ointment from the medicine cabinet eased her topical pain. But the sanitary napkin she'd found in the bathroom was chaffing her skin while catching the secretions seeping between her legs. She declined joining him on a "jaunt" around the block. And she tightened when he stopped behind her chair, and kissed her on the cheek, precisely when his father burst in bearing groceries and a smile.

"Hey, you lovebirds, that's why there's a guest bedroom!" After putting down the bags, he welcomed Pinch to his home with a kiss on the other cheek.

Steven Sr. was a third-generation, Irish-American. He had a carefree nature and an easy smile and was heir to a small, meatpacking plant when he met Kathryn Cleary in Ireland. Kathryn was beautiful and barely 16. The only child of an Irish rancher, she was put on a horse before she could walk, her equestrian prowess unequalled. Steven was smitten on the spot proposing marriage two weeks later. When Kathryn's father withheld his blessing, the couple eloped, Steve born within a year – a fair-haired boy with his father's charm and mother's astounding looks. Pinch warmed to Steven Sr. on the day that they had met, but she hadn't yet thawed Madam Mother-in-law.

Kathryn gave Pinch a nod, entering the kitchen, Katie followed behind her toting a bag of candy. "We bought a white chocolate bunny for my Easter basket, Mom. Grandmother said it's better because it won't stain things. Remember those *M & M's*?"

Pinch nodded and was eager to change the subject – it was the night Vanessa had slept over, when her wedding ring had fallen down the drain. She complimented Kathryn's decision and quickly reminded Katie they had to get ready for church. "There's Mass today and The Stations of the Cross. We'll probably leave early to get our seats." Steve agreed. Then he left with his father for the jaunt around the block.

Pinch staggered getting up from the table. When Katie asked what was wrong with her leg, she said she pulled something, slipping last night on the snow. "What took you so long? Dad was having a hissy fit!"

Kathryn was at the sink counting out potatoes for dinner. She suddenly veered around. *"Katie O'Malley! Don't ever talk about your father that way!"* She glared at Pinch. "Hasn't she been schooled in the Fourth Commandment?" Katie blushed and apologized then excused herself and ran upstairs.

Pinch reddened, but not from shame. "I beg your pardon, Kathryn, but how did you square – *Honor Thy Father and Thy Mother* – with marrying against your father's wishes?"

"How dare you question my faith!"

"I'm not questioning your faith. I'm trying to understand how you interpret, 'Honor thy Father,' in the context of the Fourth Commandment."

"I wasn't a child when I married Steven!" Her words came out like bullets.

"You were barely 16. It's family lore how Steven robbed the cradle."

Kathryn pursed her lips. Though still attractive, her classic features grew gnarly when she was annoyed. "Insolence may run in the Duffy family, but we honor our elders here."

"And what about daughters? Are they honored here?"

Festering was the only way to describe Kathryn's expression. But festering was no match for Mt. Etna ripping to spew. "I've tried to please you for 15 years, and I've yet to be honored with a kind word or a hug."

Kathryn arched her back. "I believe an apology is in order."

"Yes, but I don't expect one."

The Stations of the Cross was an Eastertide ritual, a walking meditation on Christ's torture and death commonly performed in church from noon to three on Good Friday…the purported day and time of the actual occurrence. With so many people to accommodate, pictures of the 14 Stations were provided in the pews for those who would like to meditate in their seats versus up and down the aisles, in front of each Station. Despite Steve's urgings to walk with the family, Pinch stayed in the pew, kneeling more comfortable than jostling in the aisles. Later that afternoon, with Kathryn ruling the roost in the kitchen and father and son in front of the TV, Pinch sought Katie's company finding her reading *The Lives of the Saints* in Steven's well-stocked library. "Do you want to do our nails before dinner, Honey?"

Katie jumped up, and in the quiet of the her room, they talked about hockey, boys and Confirmation names, plying two coats of *Ashes* to their fingernails…Katie also doing her toes.

Steve's father, always the engaging host, drew Katie into the dinner conversation, asking her to regale them with a Joan of Arc anecdote. She had kept a low profile since Kathryn's scolding, but her face lit up when asked to talk on a subject dear to her heart. She barely got going when Steve interrupted and asked his mother her Confirmation name.

"Margaret."

Steve grinned and looked at Pinch. "Your mother's name!" Then he turned to Katie. "*Kathryn Margaret O'Malley*. It has a nice ring, doesn't it?"

Katie looked at Pinch and shrugged. Kathryn appeared not to care. "More mashed potatoes, dear?" she said, passing the bowl to Steve.

He ladled two dollops onto his dish and told Pinch to get his mother's recipe. Kathryn raised her wineglass, twirled it gently, took a long sip and announced, "Clearys don't share family recipes with non-blood relatives."

"Then give it to Katie. She's blood," Steve said, "and just about ready to tackle my pots and pans."

Katie looked up; Pinch couldn't tell if she was pleased by the cooking prospect. Not that it mattered. Kathryn wouldn't share a favorite anything of Steve's with anybody.

Katie pulled *The Lives of the Saints* from beneath her pillow. "Grandpa gave it to me, Mom! He wants me to take one of his books home every time I visit. He's so cool." Pinch hoped leaving Steve would not ruin their relationship. Everyone loves feeling heard, and Steven always made time to listen, especially to his granddaughter. Katie slid the book back under her pillow. "Aunt Amy is coloring Easter eggs tomorrow. Can I stay there instead of going to the cemetery with you and your brothers?" If Mama were still alive, Katie would be coloring eggs with her tomorrow – Pinch offering the cemetery trip to fill Katie's Easter Saturday void.

"I'm sure Grandma Duffy would like that. Will you make an orange egg for me?"

"Okay. Tell Grandma I miss her and I love her…. And I'll color an egg for her, too"

Pinch kissed her goodnight then went downstairs. Steve's parents were watching *The Ten Commandments* on TV, Steve in the kitchen brewing the three of them a pot of chamomile tea. "Care to join us for a nightcap, my dear?"

"No, I'm nauseous. I'll sleep in the garret so I don't disturb you in bed."

His eyes lit up. "Are you pregnant?"

She shrugged.

"How soon will we know?"

She believed her condition was stress, not hormone related…and if she were pregnant, she didn't want him to know before she was safely settled in The Market. "I'll take a pregnancy test next week. But til we know for sure, let's keep any talk about babies to ourselves."

"Okay, but I'll tell the Celibate." He kissed the back of her hand. "Take the bed. I'll sleep in the garret. It's too drafty up there for someone in your condition."

CHAPTER 24

The Wild Card

BRYAN PICKED HER UP at 10am, Kevin already in the car for the drive to the cemetery. They stopped at their parents' and grandparents' graves leaving a flower and saying a prayer. "Isn't it funny that Pops wanted me to be the priest in the family?" Bryan said.

"And I planned to join the police force after my stint in Vietnam," Kevin said.

Bryan smiled. "War tends to give one religion."

"And a better appreciation for life. That's why that letter meant so much to me."

"What letter?" Bryan asked.

"Sorry. I thought…" Kevin looked sheepishly at Pinch.

She handed Bryan the letter. "Kev saw it last night. Reading it here feels appropriate."

They left Bryan alone and retreated to a nearby bench. Pinch eased herself down beside Kevin, their backs to their brother who was sitting on their father's headstone, his baseball cap propped on his knee, the letter held taut between his legs. Kevin turned hearing Bryan blow his nose. "He was devastated when Dad died."

"And you weren't...?" She was tired of hearing how bad it'd been for Bryan.

"It was different with him. They both loved baseball, and when Dad came home from Korea, he spent lots of time teaching Bryan how to pitch. The winter he died, while I was out practicing how to ice skate with my first-grader friends, Bryan was perfecting his pitching delivery throwing snowballs to Dad in the yard. We both lost a father, but Bryan lost a buddy."

A blue jay snatched a piece of straw from the ground and flew off to a stand of fir trees. Kevin tapped her knee. "So when are you moving back?"

"The plan was this summer. But Steve just announced that he's looking for a job out here, and I'd rather be where he isn't."

"How long have you been grading his papers?"

"Since we've been married. I usually don't mind, I miss teaching. And I don't do all his tests, but this thing with the Dean really riled me."

"Talk about ethics violation. This guy makes Steve look like a novice!"

"Who makes Stevie look like a novice?" Bryan patted her shoulder from behind and came around the bench. "Thanks for the letter – how'd you get it?"

"The base of Mama's little table opens. I found it in there last week."

"Along with this!" Kevin handed him the baseball card.

"Is that my *Ted Williams* from Mickey O'Keefe? I paid 20 cents for this prize!"

"No," Kevin chimed, "*I* paid 20 cents for it. You were supposed to buy Mama a gift and sold her out for a cardboard slugger…there's a proud moment to share with your kids."

Bryan ignored the twit and asked a bundle of questions about the letter, the card and the table which Kevin addressed, Pinch lost in thought over what he may have overheard. But she jumped up when he tucked the letter in his jacket. "I'll take that back, Bryan, thank you."

"I'll make you both a copy." He turned to Kevin. "Wasn't that great? I felt like Dad was talking to me. And *Ted* is back where he belongs."

He was about to pocket the baseball card when Kevin snatched it out of his hand. "Yes he is…and the letter belongs to Pinch."

Bryan put his hands up. "Hey, man, keep the card, but Pinch got the cufflinks so the letter is staying with me."

"What cufflinks?"

"The one's Dad wore on their wedding day. Mama gave them to her."

"And you put the table out with the trash after Mama died. If Pinch hadn't rescued it, no one would've seen the letter."

They started shoving each other. Pinch wormed her way between. "Stop it, *idiots*! Look where you are. Is this how you honor our parents, our grandparents? Let him have it, Kev." She turned and wiped a tear. "Just make sure I get a copy, Bryan."

He put his arm around her. "I said I would. Don't you

239

trust your big brother?" She stiffly accepted the embrace, annoyed at herself for not bringing them copies.

Bryan broke the silence on the car ride from the cemetery. "So who made Steve look like a novice? I'd love to throw that in his face. He told a cute usherette last night that I'd like to meet her after the game."

"Isn't that a bit childish on both of your parts?" Kevin said, staring out his window.

Bryan shrugged. He looked at Pinch through the rear view mirror. "Want to clue me in, Sis?"

"It's personal," she said.

"Too personal for me, but not for Kevin?"

This time Kevin looked directly at his brother. "I think you'd better stay out of it."

"Fine. Who wants to be dropped off first?" Pinch and Kevin pointed toward the other. When the car made a turn in the direction of the O'Malley's house, Pinch asked him to stop at a coffee shop claiming she needed a pick-me-up. Kevin concurred. Bryan said he'd wait in the car. He sounded indifferent but looked hurt.

"Please join us," Pinch said. "We need to talk." They ordered three lattes and took a table in the corner. Kevin left for the restroom. "I didn't mean to insult you, Bryan. What you overheard relates to something I've asked Kevin to help me with." She fiddled with her napkin. "I'm leaving Steve."

"Jesus Christ, Pinch! How can you take Katie's father away at such a crucial time in her life? I thought I could do anything at her age, but my confidence dried up when Dad died."

Pinch put her elbows on the table and covered her face with her hands.

"What's going on?" Kevin said, sitting down. Pinch looked at him and shook her head.

"Remember the thing about me being a priest? Here's the rest of that story," Bryan said. "Pops was always calling me, 'my grandson the priest.' Then one day Dad says, 'Hush, Pop. Let the boy decide. It's not up to you, or me, what he does with his life.'" Bryan's eyes glistened. He leaned over the table and took her hand. "It's been forty-something years, Pinch, and I'm still in awe at the faith Dad had in me. That's what fathers do. You never knew him, so you can't feel the loss, but don't deny Katie a strong hand to support her choices. Tell her Kevin. Tell her she can't leave Steve."

She pushed his hand away. "How dare you make assumptions about my feelings? I may not have your paternal sound bites, but that doesn't give you the right to impose your past upon my present. And do not debate me on voids, Bryan Duffy. I've missed him, too. *I've missed him my whole fucking life, a void that can never be filled!*"

People glanced their way. "You're proving my point exactly," Bryan whispered. "A father fills a huge space in a kid's life. Don't you owe that to Katie?"

"Hey, Bro," Kevin said, "that's not your call. You overheard something and wanted an explanation. You got it, now forgot it."

"Why should I condone something I don't believe in?"

Pinch warmed her hands on her coffee cup. "What about me? Should I be condemned to a life I don't believe in?"

Bryan leaned back in his chair. "I've known Steve longer than you. How bad can it be? Has he hit you yet?"

"*Yet…?*" She lunged at him across the table knocking over her cup. The pain in her pelvis, and Kevin's quick hands, all that kept her from reaching him. She winced sitting back in her chair then wiped the spilled coffee and tossed the wads in Bryan direction. "I must have missed the 'hitting' clause in my marriage contract. But tell me, Bryan, as the expert on 'bad" – *how many whacks must a woman take before earning a Get out of Jail Free card?*"

A man loudly cleared his throat. "Take it easy," Bryan murmured. "I only meant that leaving doesn't look so bad if you've been knocked around."

Kevin tapped Pinch. "C'mon, let's go." Bryan gulped down his drink. Kevin put up his hand. "Take your time, Bro, we'll grab a cab. And by the way, you'll answer to me if Steve finds out she's going before she's gone."

Bryan smirked. "You mean as a priest or as my younger brother?"

"Take your pick. You won't like the penance either way."

The fresh air outside felt good on her face. "Let's walk a bit, Kev, before catching a cab." While waiting at the corner, a car trying to beat the red light hit a pothole spewing sheets of water their way. A quick pivot kept her from getting doused. The jerky motion, however, skewed the position of her sanitary napkin. She hunkered to the nearest building and turning toward the wall, slipped her hand beneath her coat righting the wayward pad. Kevin was staring when she turned around, his clear eyes a milky blue. "Sorry," she said forcing a smile. He didn't speak. He didn't move. His eyes got wider and wetter.

"You've been walking funny all day, what's up?"

"I think I wrenched my back when we fell in the snow."

"Then why aren't you holding your back? Did Steve hurt you the other night?"

"Don't be silly."

"I'm not laughing, Pinch. What happened – did he rape you?"

"*Kevin!* I'm married…not dating."

"And you signed a marriage license, not a license to be raped."

She wondered what a shelter priest knew about marital sex and slowly walked ahead stopping in front of a clothing store, pretending to scour the display. He came and stood beside her. "There are laws against marital rape. We can go to the cops."

"That would complicate my plans to leave him next week."

"Not if he got arrested."

"We were alone in the bedroom. Who would believe me?"

"Your wounds are your witnesses."

She shook her head.

"At least let me take you to a doctor."

"No, I'm okay. I'm just sore." They were talking to each other's reflection in the window. It was better that way. It hurt too much to see the sorrow in his eyes. His words made her wonder if she should have done things differently. But what could she have done…at that hour…in his parents' house… with Katie down the hall? She turned and spoke softly to his starched white collar. "There are no easy answers. Each time I take a step forward, something pulls me back. I feel like I'm dancing in quicksand. God's punishing me for being a bad wife."

"Steve's punishing you, Sweetheart, not God. And you're doing a good number on yourself as well. I'll go with you to the O'Malleys. We can crash in that pool house they've got in the back yard and figure out how to keep Bryan from howling to Steve." She nixed meeting alone in the pool house. "Then come with me to the shelter. Call the house on my phone here. Tell them you'll be back by dinner."

"I can't, Kev, I'll explain later. But being alone with you poses problems, for me, with Steve. Let's start back. I need you to make some calls to New York."

She rattled off names and instructions in the cab. "And tell them at The Market that I need to move out this Monday morning, not Tuesday. If you hit a wall there, call Lydia Wright directly. If that doesn't work, try her ex-husband, Joe. He owns a pawn sh—"

"Hold on!" He pulled out a mini tape recorder used to note what he saw on the street; she recorded her to-do list emphasizing someone tell Cecelia that the moving date was changed. Then they brainstormed how to keep Bryan quiet. "Tell him about your black eye. He gives brownie points for getting decked."

She shook her head. "He wants to keep Steve in the family. One black eye may not be enough. I never told him *when* I plan to leave. We might buy enough time if he thinks you've convinced me to stay."

"He'll never believe I changed your mind."

"Tell him I saw the merit in what he'd said, once I cooled down. It's not a stretch. I really have struggled with the father thing, but the theory doesn't hold in Steve's case."

The vein in his neck was pulsing. "Why would Bryan believe that I saw the light?"

She cocked her head. "Because seeing the light is what you do for a living, and if he thinks he's saved my marriage, his ego may keep him from doubting you."

He turned off the recorder and put it in his pocket; the *Ted Williams* card slipped out in the process. *"Shit."* Pinch said, scowling at the slugger. "Even if Bryan doesn't rat, he's sure to tell Steve where I found the card and the letter. I'm dead if Steve opens that table." Her mind began spinning "what-if" resolutions. "Okay, I've got it. Take out your recorder." She pulled Helga's card from the lining of her purse and recorded the contact information. "She's one of the posse. She knows about Steve, knows about the table, and knows where it is. Tell her there's a house key taped behind the light at the door. She'll love stealing the goods on him so he doesn't get the goods on me." Her levity lasted less than ten seconds. "But what if someone calls the police after seeing her snooping for the key?" She slumped forward and started to cry. "Kev, I can't take this anymore."

They were one block from the O'Malleys. He told the cabby to drive past the house and buried her head in his shoulder. "Don't worry. She'll get the papers out. And if she doesn't, one of the gazillion folks on my tape will. This posse of yours are my soul mates – we may not be pretty, but we get the job done."

"I don't want anyone getting hurt. I just want to leave him – is that so bad?"

"No, it's not."

"But the Monsignor thinks I'm a bad wife, and Bryan thinks I'm a bad mother, and Steve thinks I'm doing bad—"

"Stop it, Pinch! Who cares what they think. You weren't born to be abused – *period.* And no ifs, buts, maybes or bads will ever change that fact, so stop defeating yourself."

She wiped her eyes. "You sound like Lydia Wright. But she backs up her beliefs with pithy rhymes, riddles and quotes."

"Ecclesiastics, Chapter 6 – Verse 13: *Separate thyself from thy enemies and take heed of thy friends.*"

"Impressive, Kev. Which camp is Bryan in?"

"I don't know, Sweetheart. We'll find out soon enough."

CHAPTER 25

The Kiss

THE O'MALLEY HOUSE WAS EMPTY when Kevin dropped her off. The planning done, all she could do now was wait. She took a dose of aspirins and settled on the library sofa intending to read, but fell asleep, roused when the back door slammed. She hoped it was anyone but Steve, then smelled the tobacco and heard the familiar footfall. "I bought myself a gift," he said waving a pipe in the air; two shopping bags from a downtown boutique hung from his other hand. He sat beside her. Their thighs touched. Her body constricted but had nowhere to go. "I've decided not to pursue the teaching position out here. My contacts indicate the job is below me. Just as well. With Archie approving my fellowship, we can make haste on *The Horses of Camelot*." He patted her leg when she nodded then clasped his hands behind his head. "I've done some reflecting since church yesterday. I've been neglecting you my dear, but that's about to change. I've arranged to renew our marriage vows. We'll do it in May on our anniversary and christen a new chapter in our lives." She nodded again, knowing that he'd expect that. "I feel reborn, and I think you'll like the more adventuresome me." His face was bright. He reached for her hand. "I bought you something as well. Let's go upstairs."

His gift, no doubt, was compensation for his drunken assault; if things went as planned, she'd be gone before he tore up her body again. He gave no indication he'd spoken to Bryan, and needing to appease him for a few more days, she warily followed, freezing when, after shutting the bedroom door, he told her to close her eyes and face the wall. She stared at the shopping bags wondering if they were part of a ploy for another *adventuresome* attack. She wiped her brow. "Are you okay, my dear? Don't overdo until we know about the baby."

She fled to the bathroom corralling her fear; a cool wet cloth helped reduce the simmering heat within. Her gifts were on the bed when she returned – a black woolen sheath with a yawning neckline, smoky black stockings, and patent leather heels. A black push-up bra was positioned above a black garter-belt; the belt's spread-eagle straps rekindled her fear. He poured himself a brandy. "I want you to wear it tomorrow."

She picked up the dress, ignoring the rest. "It's too sexy for Easter Sunday."

"I don't think Christ had a problem with sexy, Mary Magdalene being part of his coterie. And why shouldn't my wife turn a few heads? The only good thing about my trip with the boys was seeing you through another man's eyes. You wouldn't believe how those rogue scholars fantasized bedding you."

"*What…?*"

248

"Indeed. And I must admit, I'm smitten by the notion of watching men drool over what is mine." He waved his pipe toward the garret. "Go up and try on the dress and the shoes, and then do a little strut coming down and passing my chair."

She'd been promoted from a horse to a vamp, in one day, in yet another role to play for his amusement. "It's too saucy for the occasion. I'll try it all on when we're home next week."

"No. Try them on now. If they don't fit, I can return them today."

He whistled "My Wild Irish Rose" as she carted the dress and shoes to the garret. She tried not to scowl descending the steps and couldn't strut, even if she wanted, needing the bedposts to steady her walk. He said she looked ravishing but her posture was weak.

"These heels are too high. I'm afraid I might fall."

"Then, wear your own pumps. You'll still be the envy at brunch."

She covered her cleavage with her palm. "Can I borrow a scarf from your mother to wear during Mass, out of respect?" He went down the hall and returned with a 'silk' the color of Kathryn's stone cold eyes. When she strategically draped it across her chest, Steve called it a match made in heaven.

"I saw you in town today. I didn't see Bryan, just you and the Celibate."

"Bryan left shortly after we stopped for coffee. I wanted to stretch my legs before cabbing back." Given his mellow demeanor, she asked him to stop calling Kevin, the Celibate. "There's nothing going on between us, Steve. We've a typical sibling relationship."

"No, my dear, he lights up whenever you come in the room. Were your thesis correct, Bryan would do the same."

Kathryn pouted seeing her scarf on Pinch when they left for the church the next morning. Steve assured her it was only for during Mass. Pinch tamped down the scarf and kept her raincoat buttoned during the service and didn't dally near Kathryn, afterward, when mother and son bid a tearful good-bye. Steve scowled seeing the scarf when Pinch took off her coat at the brunch, but he brightened when Bryan announced the meal was delayed because Kevin had forgotten to pick up the bacon.

Five adults and five children cavorted at the dining room table when the family finally sat to eat. The din in the room made it easy for Pinch to watch Steve watch Kevin, whispering and giggling with Katie. When she noticed Bryan was watching her, she grabbed her cup and scanned the table asking, "Anyone want more coffee?"

Steve and Kevin held up their cups. She filled Steve's first, draining the pot. "I'll go make a refill," she said.

"Let me," Kevin said, "I'm not used to being served anyway."

"It's a shame you boys in the Church can't marry. My cup always runneth over," Steve said. "And you don't have to stop for the bacon when you already bring it home!"

Kevin's face was tight when Pinch joined him in the kitchen, an empty teapot in her hand. "Stay calm, Kev, I've only one more day." Her lips barely moved as she spoke, her eyes peeled on the door. "How'd you do with the posse?"

"Calls made…no confirmations," he whispered.

"What about Bryan? He's watching me like a hawk."

"Can't say but I don't think he'll squeal. He thinks you need counseling and liked that I agreed." She glared at him. He smiled. "Call me after you leave, we'll set up a session."

They were busy with their respective pots when Amy walked in with a stack of dirty dishes. She asked Pinch and Katie to join them at the Easter parade. "It's just down the street. My boys are going – all the neighborhood girls will be there!"

"Sounds great. I think Katie will love it."

"Love what, Mom?" Katie said, walking to the sink with more plates.

"The Easter Parade!" Kevin shouted.

"Are you going, Uncle Kevin?"

"No. But let's see if there's anything to wear in the hat trunk up in the attic."

Katie returned a few minutes later with a leopard skin pill-box hat on her head. "Check it out, Mom, it was Grandma Duffy's! C'mon up. We found something for you, too."

The attic was cool and musty; Pinch couldn't remember the last time she was there. Kevin was sitting by an open trunk, a fireman's helmet on his head. Bryan's four-year-old son sat on his knee, the brim of an old policeman's cap resting on the bridge of his tiny nose. Kevin handed her a tall faded hatbox. Inside was a copper-colored cloche, a bright green feather in its band. "It was Grandma Rose's favorite hat," he said. "I used to fiddle with the feathers. The orange one you found in the table goes next to that green one."

She tried on the hat at a pitted mirror hanging from a nail in the rafter. Its form-fitting shape nestled nicely on her head and felt like a warm embrace. Katie handed her a photo from an album she was viewing. "Is this Grandma Rose, she's wearing that hat?" It was a black and white glossy of a smiling woman holding a baby in a long white dress. She was standing in front of a church, two bored-looking boys beside her.

"This must be when I was baptized. How come I've never seen it?" Pinch said.

"How come a lot of things…?" Kevin said, slipping his nephew off his lap. He returned the fire helmet and cop's cap to the trunk, nodding when Katie asked to keep the leopard skin.

They all turned toward the door, someone mounting the attic stairs. Steve walked in and gave a quick look around. "How do you like my new hat, Dad?" Katie asked doing a pirouette. Then she pointed to Pinch. "Me and Mom are wearing them in the Easter parade."

"It's, *Mom and I,*" he said staring at Kevin, "and you're not going to the parade."

"But we already told Aunt Amy we'd go."

"And now you can tell her you won't. We need to return to your grandmother's house for a copy of their updated will."

Katie stomped her feet. "No way!!"

Steve raised his arm and cocked his wrist, poised to backhand the pillbox off her head, but Kevin caught his arm midair and pulled it down to his side. Katie had fallen backwards trying to avoid the anticipated blow and was cowering in a dormer, face lined in fear. Steve shook off Kevin's grip. The two men glared at each other. "Take your cousin downstairs, Kathryn," Steve said, "then get your stuff together and wait for us at the door."

Pinch tucked the two hats in the hatbox and started for the steps, but neither man moved. She grabbed Steve's hand. He looked at her and smiled. "My mother wants her scarf back, my dear." When he lifted it off, her pop-up breasts looked like hot cross buns ready to spring from their pan. She crossed her arms over her chest and looked sheepishly at Kevin. His eyes were huge. She was slipping behind Steve when Bryan walked in.

"There you are," Bryan said to Kevin and gave him a copy of the letter. Kevin, in return, handed over the *Ted Williams* baseball card. Pinch watched the exchange peering around Steve. Kevin winked at her when Bryan showed the card to Steve – she assumed the swap was part of the pay-off to keep Bryan happily quiet. When she didn't see another letter, she stepped around Steve and asked Bryan for her copy.

"Jesus Christ, Pinch! Cover yourself up!" Bryan said, shielding his eyes. "It's Easter Sunday, for God's sake, and I've teenage boys in the house!" Steve tossed her the scarf and waved her away as if he was also appalled. "We're heading out for the parade," Bryan said, shaking hands with Steve and asking Kevin to lock up when he left. He stared long at Pinch, now wrapped in the scarf, then shaking his head turned and took off down the stairs.

"Bryan…wait! *Where's my copy of the letter…?"*

"Your husband has it," he shouted back, "so behave your-self little one."

She stole a glance at Kevin. The vein on his neck was throbbing, his lips moving silently. She thought he was pray-ing for restraint and didn't want to be there if his plea was denied. She took Steve's hand and tried leading him to the stairs. But he stood pat, then smiling at Kevin pulled Pinch's hand to the front of his trousers and slowly dragged it across his fly. "Patience, and celibacy, must be heavy crosses to bear, Father Duffy, so I'll remove this tempting morsel before one of your heads courts trouble."

She heard Kevin's portable phone ringing when she and Steve descended the attic. They were settling in the rental car when Kevin ran out on the porch waving a small piece of paper. Katie bolted from the back seat. Pinch had the hat-box on her lap and was fumbling to open her door, when Steve grabbed her wrist, tucking it tightly under his arm, then leaned on the horn til Katie returned.

"It's your baby picture with Grandma Rose, Mom."

Steve snatched the photo. "Good grief, those feathers. It looks like a cockatoo is sitting on her head." He tossed it to Pinch. She stashed it in the hatbox before he could take it back for safekeeping...his reason for withholding the letter. He grabbed the scarf when they reached his parents' house and told them to wait in the car.

Katie asked for her hat, as soon as he left, and after plac-ing it above her headphones, leaned back and got lost in her tunes. Pinch used the photo as a guide to reinsert the orange feather in the headband of the cloche. Katie lifted her head-phones. "What's a cockatoo, Mom?"

"A pretty bird, Honey. Did Uncle Kevin say anything when he gave you the picture?"

"Just to read it," she said, her voice trembling. "Do you have a boyfriend, Mommy?"

Pinch swung around in her seat. "No! Who said that?"

Katie shrugged. "Uncle Kevin said to tell you that Big Earl was coming to the house tomorrow for some hot fudge Monday, and not to tell Dad cause he'd have a hissy fit."

"Big Earl is a very tall woman whose name is *Earlene*. Uncle Kevin say anything else…?" She wondered if Helga had emptied the table.

"No. What's a hot fudge Monday?"

"There's no recipe, you make it up as you go along."

"Can the fudge be white chocolate?"

"Sure, and it can be hot or cold. Would you add some-thing in for color?"

Katie thought a minute. "Jellybeans melting in white chocolate would be cool!"

"Sounds pretty and delicious. But Uncle Kevin is right… let's keep this to ourselves."

Katie put her headphones back on. Pinch put away the cloche. She thought she'd wear it tomorrow, a fitting head-dress for a woman about to take flight. She picked up her baby photo. What did Kevin want her to read there? Unlike Sparkle in her hockey gear, nothing screamed out in this early portait of her life. She shrugged and flipped it over. The script looked new and hastily scrawled. *P. R. Duffy's Rite of Passage! 9:00am. H.F.M.*

She threw the photo back in the hat box, Steve approaching with a large envelope.

He snapped on his seatbelt and looked at his watch; it was far too early to go to the airport. Katie asked to go back to the Easter parade. "No," he said, backing out of the driveway. "I have a surprise for your mother."

Pinch's stomach tightened, but before she could dwell on the possibilities, he pulled into the lot of the park where he'd asked her to marry him.

The ground was soggy from Thursday night's snow, and none of them were wearing boots. Yet he lead them through an overgrown path to a secret grotto telling Katie how he had wooed his princess with a champagne picnic and a diamond ring tucked in the petals of a rose. "It was a joyous day, my dear, when you ceded your life to me. And in a few short weeks we'll renew our vows here in this glorious setting."

"What does ceded mean?" Katie asked.

"Yielding. Surrendering. Giving control to another," Steve said.

"Why'd you do that, Mom?"

"She was a frisky little thing needing a strong hand to rein her in. And Archie is right," he whispered to Pinch, "I'm lucky you've still got some kick left to tame."

Their shoes were wet and smeared in mud when they reached the secret grotto – his pristine "chapel" strewn with glass, its stream afoul with foil wrappers, used condoms, and crushed metal cans. He was not Prince Charming on the drive to the airport, scowling at every red light and barking at Katie to "take that God-awful hat off your head" when he saw her in the rearview mirror. She did as she was told though a few minutes later, Pinch spied the hat perched on her shoulder. Grandma Rose would have been proud.

It was after nine at night when they pulled up to the house. Steve dropped them at the curb with the luggage, then left for a parking spot. Pinch felt behind the outdoor light; the spare key was there. She saw no sign of entry in the foyer. Nothing looked moved in the parlor. But the slight disarray of the cloth on the pedestal table told her what could not be seen.

Katie was in bed before Steve came in. She was unduly quiet, nodding more than talking. Not that Pinch minded, being physically strained, emotionally drained, mentally challenged to get through this last night unscathed. When Katie wouldn't let go after kissing her good night, Pinch drew her close and stroked her hair. "What's the matter, Honey?"

"I'm sorry for being a bad daughter, Mommy, and for getting Daddy mad cause I wanted to go to the parade and hockey game. And for making Grandmother O'Malley yell cause I broke the Fourth Commandment. And I'm sorry for liking St. Joan more than St. Margaret; and for loving my new hat even though Daddy really hates it. But I can't help it, Mommy cause it smells like Grandma Duffy.

"I'm going to ask Sister Cece to help me stop making Daddy mad cause if you have a baby boy, he's not going to want me anymore, and send me away. But I'll show him that I *can* be good, and I promise to help you with the baby. And I'll share all my stuff so he'll see that *I am* a good daughter, and

Grandmother O'Malley will see that *I am* a good Catholic girl who honors her father and her mother."

Pinch pried Katie's hands from around her neck, wiped her eyes, and gently touched her cheek. "Oh Katie, Honey, listen to me. You are all any parent could ask for in a daughter – just the way you are – and do you really think I would let him send you away?"

"But you don't have a vote…remember, Mom? So I'll be real good, you'll see." She gritted her teeth. "He'll see."

Pinch felt like a child, helpless to relieve a beloved's concern, paralyzed knowing, hoping, things would be better tomorrow yet unable to say why. "Who said I was having a baby?"

"I heard Dad say that he wanted a boy, after Uncle Bryan showed him a letter, and that maybe he'd get one cause it looked like you were having a baby. He said you were taking a test for it when we got home – is Big Earl helping with the test?"

"No, she's helping me move some things around." Pinch yawned twice in rapid succession. "I'm just tired, not pregnant, Honey, so forget all this talk about a baby, okay?"

Pinch had hoped to be sleeping, or pretending to be, before Steve came up for the night, but her extra time with Katie had foiled that idea. He was whistling Irish ballads on the bed, pipe in hand, and smiled when she entered the room. He still had the letter, and she only had tonight – what would it take to ease it out of his grip? She knelt by the bed. "May I have my father's letter now, Steve?"

The whistling stopped. He patted her head. "It's special, isn't it? But come off the floor, there's no need to grovel; you're my wife not a chambermaid." She sat on the bed, hands folded in her lap while he puffed perfect smoke rings in the air. Then he nodded and spoke to the ceiling. "When I was a lad, I pretended I had siblings. It was all in my head, mind you... boys don't have dolls to replace real people. I wonder, would you indulge me in a little role-playing, my dear? We'd keep it within these four walls of course – I'd feel foolish if others knew how lonely I was. And I'll give you the letter for your efforts when we are done."

She nodded and he thanked her profusely. She felt as bright eyed as he looked and asked him if he'd wanted a sister. "And a brother," he said. "What nicknames did you have?"

"Bryan didn't have one, Kevin was *Kev,* and I was just *Pinch,* though sometimes Kevin called me *Sparkle* and in tender moments, Mama and Grandma called me *Pinchey.*"

He kissed her softly on the mouth; his lips tasted like cherry tobacco. "Then 'Sparkle' it is! Did you play many indoor games together?"

"The guys did. I was much younger, and their games were usually over my head."

"I heard about a game where age doesn't hinder participation." He told her to lie on the bed and knelt beside her.

Her heart began to race. "You're not going to hurt me, are you?"

"Of course not, we're just kids! So I'm your older brother, and after watching Dr. Kildare on TV, I've decided I'd like to become a physician." He put on a serious face. "I'm sorry you're not feeling well, Sparkle, let me check your heart." He lay the bowl of his pipe on the front of her nightgown and leaned in close as if listening. "Sounds fine, now please sit up, and take a deep breath while I check your lungs." He put the pipe against her back and rested his chin on her shoulder. "Breathe deeply. Again. Good!" Then he faced her and put the pipe stem on her lips. "Now open wide and say *aaah*."

The whole thing was bizarre... But innocent enough and a small price to pay to recover what Bryan had stolen. She closed her eyes and opened her mouth. When he filled it with his tongue, she pushed him away. "You're supposed to be my brother! Let me be the doctor."

He pushed her down and started tickling her. "Don't be silly, only boys are the doctor – now lay still, Sparkle, so *Kev* can finish your exam."

His hand was suddenly between her legs. She bolted up. "Stop it, Steve. The game's over!"

He tickled her with the stem of the pipe, her protests sandwiched between broken bits of laughter. "Now I know what I've missed growing up without a sister. Isn't this fun? You're laughing so hard you're crying. Oh, you *are* crying. Sorry, my dear." He wrapped her in his arms from behind and held her in place. There was a timid knock on the door. "Come in," he said.

Katie stood by the door, rubbing her eyes, staring at Pinch. "What's wrong, Mom?"

"Nothing, Honey, I had another bad dream."

Katie kept staring at her. "Want to sleep with my tiger?"

"Hey," Steve said, "I'm the only tiger in this room. Come give us a kiss then go back to sleep. I won't tolerate tardiness the first day back at school." Katie did as she was told. He grabbed her foot as she slid from the bed. "What's that on your toes?"

"It's just a dab of nail polish, Steve…." Pinch nodded for Katie to leave the room.

Steve peered at her foot then smacked her ankle. "I want that off by breakfast. We'll discuss your punishment tomorrow night at dinner."

Katie ran from the room. Steve glanced at Pinch's feet when he rose to close the door. "May I have my copy of the letter now?"

He admitted that she'd earned something for playing his sibling game and left the room, returning with the letter. She started to cry seeing the crinkly paper and thin envelope. Bryan had given him the original! But Steve only handed her the first two pages. "Page three will cost a kiss," he said, "a passionate kiss to seal our born-again marriage."

A kiss was a cheap exchange for the page where her father had acknowledged his desire for a daughter. She closed her eyes and channeled Scarlet kissing Rhett, in *Gone With the Wind,* leaning, kissing, sighing – leaving Steve solidly satisfied. She pulled back and reached for page three, but he held it above her head. "One more time, *Sparkle*, with the same accoutrements, but this time in the heat of the moment, say that you love me…and call me *Kev*."

She turned away, a terrible taste rising in her mouth. "I can't."

He petted her head. "Of course you can, *Pinchey*. Mama wouldn't mind. It's only a game." He waved page three in front of her face. "And we're playing for Daddy's letter."

"Why should I trust you when you keep upping the ante?"

"Power has its privilege, but your assessment is fair." He put page three in the Bible, placed his right hand on the cover and swore to relinquish the entire letter if she gave him the same kiss, "with the added sweeteners."

It was a kiss the devil knew. *God, forgive me.*

CHAPTER 26

Hot Fudge Monday

KATIE REMOVED HER SOCKS at the breakfast table per Steve's instructions. After finding a tinge of nail polish on a toe, he sent her upstairs to finish the job. "She needs to learn the devil is in the details," he told Pinch. "Look how salient details last night turned a kiss into a tour de force." Her stomach turned on the memory. It was still in knots when he left for school. She held Katie in a long goodbye at the door, holding back tears spying the leopard skin hat in her book bag. *Take care of her Mama. It's going to be a rough day.*

She started the sorting in Katie's room slapping things they were taking to The Market with a rainbow sticker from Katie's arts and craft box and haphazardly tossing the stuff on the bed – her teddy bear and tiger the only toys. She tied an orange bandana, from a long forgotten cowgirl doll, loosely around her own neck; its fiery color help brightened her mood finishing the heart-wrenching process. The bed was covered with pillowcases stuffed with Katie's things. Her bedside lamp topped the heap, lying on its side as if sleeping. The room looked disheveled. But by looking for rainbows the posse would know exactly what to grab. She was leaving to "rainbow" her bedroom when she heard the front door lock *click*. Grabbing the edge of the comforter, she quickly rolled it over the pile and was dusting the re-erected lamp with the bandana when Steve burst into the room.

He eyed the mess saying something about spring cleaning. She was glad he didn't notice the lamp was unplugged or ask about the sticker on its shade. She wiped her sweaty upper lip with the back of her hand. "Shouldn't you be at school?"

"Yes, but this won't take long."

He grabbed her arm, led her downstairs, and shooed her into the powder room pointing to a bag on the sink. "Hurry, I'll wait out here on the bench," he said and shut the door.

The bag contained a pregnancy test kit, urine sample required. Whatever the outcome, one of them would be devastated. She sat on the toilet lid, counted to 100 and came out shaking her head, but the foyer was empty. She heard him upstairs. *Please God, not in Katie's room.* The phone rang. She picked it up on the third ring in the kitchen.

"Mrs. O'Malley...? I'm calling from the hardware store about the table we repaired last week. That new spring lock needs to be replaced. Will you— or is that Mr. O'Malley on the other line— will either of you be home later this week?"

"The table worked fine when I opened it last night," Steve said.

"I know, sir. But these things are unpredictable. One never knows when they'll go off."

Pinch heard a click on the line then Steve descended the stairs. "Hold on," Pinch said, putting down the phone then meeting him in the hall. He nodded expectantly toward the powder room. She shrugged. "I couldn't produce the sample. I'll try again during the day."

"Call me at work when it's ready to be mailed." He kissed her forehead than left.

She returned to the phone. *"Phew!* That was close, Helga. Good thing you heard him pick up the other line."

"I didn't. But we never know if the pimp– sorry, 'the man that you married,' is home."

"*Man that I married.* Word gets around quickly with you people."

"Important stuff does. Now listen up, Pinch. The first contingent will soon be on your street. Hang something on your doorknob when it's okay to come in. It's 8:30 now. How much time do we have?"

"His morning class ends at 10:30."

"Is there a lot to take out?"

"A few small pieces of furniture but mostly portable things."

"How are you feeling?"

"Tired. Scared. Depressed. Other than that, just ducky."

"Hold on for two more hours. You can nap at The Market before CeCe brings Katie."

"I can't thank you enough for emptying that table. What if he'd found the stuff?"

"But he didn't, Pinch, so forget the *what ifs* and focus on what is."

Pinch rapidly rainbowed the rest of the house – it helped that she'd mentally sorted the stuff over the last two weeks. She secured her pearl hatpin to her grandmother's cloche, perching it on the hall tree. Then she slipped her suede jacket from under the mink, its shallow pockets swelling with Lydia's gifts of *Sass* and *Passion*. She hung the jacket on a hook below the hat; "Mt. Etna" would soon be dressed for success! After tagging Mama's table and the billowing fern, she opened the blinds overlooking the street. That's when she saw the balloons.

There were seven of them, in lollipop colors, tethered to the door of a black panel truck. Gertie was bending under the hood poking a stick at the engine. Feather was leaning against its back door twirling a yellow flower and eyeing the oncoming traffic. A middle-aged woman to Gertie's left was pacing the sidewalk, a hand-held device pressed to her lips. Approaching from the left was Jody's sister, Dr. Vasquez. She was walking a Doberman Pinscher and smiled at two women swinging hand weights, walking briskly in the cool morning air. Were the walkers part of the posse? Or maybe Saints eager to belt out a song on the sidewalks of New York. A lump rose in her throat. She was humbled and grateful, felt loved and blessed watching strangers take time and mark space for her needs. She wanted to remember this moment forever but needed something to etch the memory. Despite her growing estrangement from God… *The Word was made flesh and dwelt amongst us,* said it all.

She gathered the day-to-day items Steve would've missed had she stowed them too soon and tagged the bundle with a rainbow sticker, leaving it on the little table. "Done!" she shouted to the billowing fern, raising her hands in an alleluia gesture. But her arms reluctantly fell to her sides, too tired to celebrate. Her brow was dripping; she wiped it in the kitchen then snatched Katie's mirror from it's haunt on the sill above the sink. No battered eye of an ugly Stranger peered back as it had seven weeks ago. Today's eye was clear and the color of newborn grass. Before nestling the mirror upstairs in the hope chest, she tied a purple ribbon onto the front door knob.

Like a pebble tossed in a quiet puddle, the ribbon sent ripples through the street. Feather rapped her hand on the panel truck. Gertie dropped the hood. Big Earl pulled up in her white plumber's van. Helga jumped from her vehicle across the street. Paul strode toward the house, "billystick" in hand, nodding at the power walkers trekking up the street again. Gertie came in first with the balloons, followed by Feather who pinned the flower to Pinch's sweater. Paul stayed outside with the Doberman while the posse filed in giving Pinch silent hugs in the hall. Then a multitude of Saints voiced support via Jody's walkie-talkie. "You go, Girl! Chin up, Kid. Don't worry, Doll, we got the front line covered!"

The situation called for a quick strike and rapid retreat so the heartfelt support was brief. Dr. Vasquez resumed walking the dog; Paul scaled the stoop to watch the street from the door. Jodie placed a balloon outside the door of each room needing attention. The buoyant markers and rainbow stickers lent order to what could've been chaotic. Gertie and Feather started moving out the light stuff, Helga and Big Earl tackled the bulk, and Jody kept track of the crew on the street passing data thru their multiple walkie-talkies. Things moved apace. Pinch went to slip the mirror in the hope chest but got called to Katie's room to verify some bundles whose rainbows had fallen off in the frenzy when Steve had come home. Once her room was cleared, her door was shut and her balloon brought to the foyer – a visual sign to everyone that one room had been done. A message blared over Jody's walkie-talkie before Pinch made it to the hope chest. "Possible Mr. P. sighting. Car's the right color and make."

"Where are you, Marlena?"

"End of the block, south corner…he just turned up the street."

"*Have you got that, Paul?*" Jody yelled from the upstairs hall. "*We've a Mr. P. alert! Shut the front door. He may just be driving by.* Listen up everyone. Our mission is getting her out. The *stuff* is a bonus."

Pinch followed Jody down the stairs. "*Mr. P?*"

"We call the abusers pimps. In deference to you, we're calling Steve, Mr. P."

"But it can't be Steve, he's teaching a class."

"Maybe he let them out early. Do you think he suspects you're leaving today?"

"He'd have stayed home if he thought I was leaving."

"*Mr. P sighting!*" It was a different voice.

"Go ahead, Flo."

"He just passed the house and turned my corner. Seems we tied up all the parking."

Jody looked at Pinch. "Are you sure there's no reason he'd leave early today?"

"Maybe to mail in my pregnancy test. I need to get rid of that kit."

Jody's jaw dropped. "You think you're pregnant!"

"No, but he wants to believe I am, and I'm not going down that road right now." She snatched the kit from the powder room and stuffed it in a bag waiting transport out the door.

"What about a gun, does he have one?"

"Of course not!"

"May day! May day!" Flo burst through again. *"He must've found a spot around the corner because he's walking toward me…. Yep, it's Mr. P!* Got the pock mark to the right of his nose, another above his lip."

Pinch looked quizzically at Jody.

"CeCe gave us a detailed description, down to the size of his horns. *Joe, are you there?* We may need interference."

"I'm on it, Jody. I'll meet him at the stoop."

With Steve now bearing in, Paul reopened the door, standing behind it so the posse had room to pass. They heard Steve yelling from two doors away. *"Hey, hey! What's going on, here?"*

Joe stopped him on the steps. Pinch did a double take. He was wearing a brown bomber jacket and a lime green baseball cap – gray strands from his wig hung like swamp moss from the cap. He was holding the base of an old brass, table lamp and asked Steve if he knew how much longer the garage sale was going on. Steve pushed him aside, ran up the stoop and shoved the door wide open knocking Paul into the wall. He raced toward Pinch, his face twisted and red. Feather slid between them, eyes steady, body steeled in a martial arts crouch. When Steve tried pushing her aside, she deflected his

269

touch with a flick of her wrist, rearing him back on his heels. He tried with both his hands, but her leg flew up knocking him into the hall tree. On his third attempt, she took out his legs felling him onto his rear. He rose to his feet wiping his mouth with the back of his hand. "What the hell is going on here, my dear?"

"I'm leaving, Steve."

"Says who...?" He raised his shoulders and expanded his chest. With his hands on his hips and a smirk on his lips, he looked like a man with an edge.

"Officer, please explain to my husband what we're doing, and why you are here."

"Mrs. O'Malley is moving out, sir, and I'm here to make sure no one gets in her way." His edge was the club in his hand and the gun on his hip.

Steve glared at Pinch. "You're making a big mistake."

"No, I'm correcting one."

Big Earl and Helga descended the stairs with the hope chest and proceeded toward the door. Steve's demand to see what was in it was met with a "get-out-of-my-face" look from Big Earl. When the women kept walking, he leaned on the chest with his forearms forcing them to stop, though they held the chest in place. He raised the lid and using both hands, violently rummaged the contents. Pinch's eyes widened; the cash-filled tampon box looked poised to pop open from the jostling. "Time's up, bottom feeder," Big Earl said. When he didn't stop, she pushed the lid down with her chin, smashing his elbows.

He extricated his arms and bristled to the kitchen, Paul tagging closely behind him.

By now, all but the master bedroom balloon were hanging in the foyer. Jody ran upstairs for a walk-through. Joe dawdled by the front door – Paul now shadowing Steve. Pinch put the yellow flower in the headband of the cloche, slipped into her suede jacket and was pinning on the hat when Joe skittered out the door and helped Lydia up the stoop.

She was wearing the same getup she'd worn when Steve came to her apartment. Pinch checked for Steve then whispered, "What are you doing here?"

"Thought I'd lend ya a hand."

"You might have asked first."

"Ya might've said, *no.* She tottered to the mirror with her canes and patted the sides of her wig.

"My dear! Where are my book notes?" Steve was slamming the desk drawers in the kitchen.

Pinch motioned to Joe. "Please get Lydia out of here before Steve sees her."

"I demand to know where you've put my *Horses of Camelot* research!" Steve said. He rounded the corner then stopped short seeing Lydia poking the balloons with a cane.

"Lordy me! That you, Tex?" She sashayed toward him, smiling. "Hey, Clem, looky see. It's the fella I told ya about… the one who showed up at sister Stella's when me, Clarissa, and Trudy Crystal was looking to study some asses."

Steve looked confused. "What are you doing here?"

"Come for the garage sale. Helping my brother, Clem here, find a nifty shade for his new old lamp." She pointed

271

at the base in Joe's hand then covering her mouth whispered aloud, "He's a bit style impaired." She smiled a gappy grin. "Hey Clem. Fetch me ya lamp so's I can show it to my friend, Tex."

It was comic opera time again, and Pinch couldn't resist. "You know her, Steve?"

"Land sakes! That ya bride, Tex?" She looked Pinch up and down carefully avoiding eye contact. "Nope. Never had such a skinny thing in our study group. By the way, Tex. Been ripping through the *dic*-tionary since ya barged in that day. Already in the *C's*. Checking out the 'courts' this time. Clarissa's working with ya court*house*; Trudy Crystal's got ya basic court *order*; I'm wrestling with ya basic court*ship*. Last one hit the skids when my sweetie come to choking on a turkey bone in my home-brewed Thanksgiving tea. Say...! How 'bout me doing a courtship interview with you and ya bride right here?" She fluttered her eyes at him.

"You're nuts." He looked around the room. "I've never seen this woman before."

Lydia jabbed him in the ribs. "Course ya have, silly cowboy. Ya brought me flowers and a chocolate shake looking to surprise ya bride but she never showed." She pointed a bony finger at his face. "And how ya howled when them pussies fell on ya head. Poor dears...thinking they was getting some mints for the effort."

"I'd like this woman removed from my house at once," Steve said to Paul.

Lydia fanned her face with her hand. "Getting hot in here, Clem. Let's mosey on. Looks like they're plum out of

272

lampshades." She stopped at the mirror and adjusted the collar on her coat. Then she pulled a pipe from her pocket and plucked it in her mouth.

"Hey! That's my pipe!" He went to grab it, but she swatted him away with her cane.

"Swipe my pipe, Tex, I'll have this here officer arrest ya."

"But that's my pipe. The briarwood, my dear."

Lydia shrugged and started for the door. "Thought it was a gift for services rendered."

Steve twitched. "Services? First you try to poison me, and then I get attacked by your cats."

"You *were* there, Steve?" Pinch said.

Lydia nodded. "And sister Stella's thinking on pressing charges, busting in like ya did."

"Go for it, gimp. No one will believe a nutcase over a man with my credentials."

"*Cre*-dentials? Hey Clem…that like them tapes Stella has of when Tex came to call?"

"Reckon," Joe said. He looped his arm under Lydia's and guided her down the stoop.

"Isn't it illegal to tape someone without prior notification?" Steve asked Paul.

"Not if it's security surveillance on private property," Paul said.

Lydia had occupied Steve long enough for everything to get in the vans. Pinch pulled the lipstick from her jacket and applied it. "Good God. What's that blasphemy called – *whore-ange?*" Steve sneered.

She blotted her lips. *"Kiss My Sass!"*

"Don't get cocky. There's still Katie. What judge would grant custody to an unemployed woman, living who knows where, over a Professor living in the family home?"

"And how long do you think you'll be employed once the college finds out I was grading your papers, *and* the Dean's, so the two of you could go on an orgy in the woods?"

Steve looked at Paul and laughed. "Who'd believe that story?"

"Copies of class rosters and tests are being held in Chicago if I need them."

"So you've consummated a contract with the Celibate." He passed his tongue slowly over his lips. "A clever way for him to secure your unorthodox taste for brotherly love."

"You really are disgusting, Steve."

"And what about you? Is stealing a sign of virtue? I stop at the bank to deposit my father's will and discover you've lifted jewelry from the safe-deposit box."

"I only took what was mine before we met and the gifts I've received since we married."

Jody came downstairs and caught the end of the conversation. "Let him discuss it with your lawyer." She guided Pinch toward the door.

Feather followed them out, walking backwards behind Pinch. Paul stayed on the stoop, the front door open – Steve somewhere inside. The movers were standing beside their vehicles. The rest of the posse and Saints lined the curb across the street. Gertie released the balloons when Pinch step onto the sidewalk. There was a smattering of applause. Jody led her

274

up the block to where her sister was waiting to drive to them to The Market. "Why is everyone still here?" Pinch asked.

"Rule #1 – no one leaves the site before you do," Jody said.

They had just passed the house with the barking dog when Steve opened the upstairs window. He called down to Pinch waving an item that gleamed in the sun. Paul drew his gun. Feather pushed Pinch to the nearest stoop, the three women crouching behind it. "Did you forget something, my dear?"

Pinch poked up her head. "Katie's mirror…!"

She darted for the house, but Jody pulled her back. "Stay here with Feather, I'll get it."

Steve smiled when he flicked his wrist. *"No!"* Pinch screamed watching the mirror plummet and shatter on impact in the gutter.

She ran passed Jody and knelt in the street, bawling at the sight, picking up the pieces. Gertie came over to help. Lydia shuffled beside them and peered in the gutter as if curious about the commotion. She tapped Pinch gently on the arm with her cane. "Get a grip, Pinch. Don't let the pimp see ya pain."

"It was my birthday gift from Katie. She made it herself. He's smashed what I love into nothing."

Lydia leaned in closer. "Be grateful it ain't her bones he smashed." But her heart had no room for gratitude, filled as it was with anger and grief, and she couldn't stop crying – the weight of the past seven weeks pouring out in a free fall. "C'mon, Pinchey, suck it up. Show the fucker ya hurting, he'll piss on ya wounds."

"I'll pick up the rest Pinch," Gertie said. "It's time you were heading on home. Didn't get to tell you, but I met Miss Katie at the daycare last week. Gal's got more spunk than a newborn colt, so I reckon she's got the goods to make her Mama another mirror."

Sometimes it takes a stranger to say what you already know but are too hurt to see. Pinch smiled through her tears...then her eyes picked up the agitation on the faces across the street. How long had the harmonica been playing? How long had the Saints been glaring at Steve? How long had they been singing, "Hound Dog?"

Steve shouted over the chorus from his second floor perch when Pinch got up and turned to leave. "One more thing, *Sparkle*. What shall I tell the Celibate if he calls?"

She looked up at his pitiful face. "Tell him Sparkle doesn't live here anymore."

~

THE DOOR CREAKED OPEN. By the *swish* and *swosh* of cloth on cloth she knew two of them approached. There was rustling at the nightstand. "Can we wake her up, Sister?"

Pinch rolled over in her bed. "I'm awake, Honey. What time is it?"

"Four o'clock," Cecelia said.

"And the day...?" Why couldn't she remember the day?

"It's hot fudge Monday, and we brought you some!" Katie said.

Pinch sat up in bed and reached for a tissue nearly toppling the plastic tray on the stand between the twin beds. She started to cry. Katie nestled in her arms. "What's wrong with her, Sister CeCe?"

"She's just tired, Katie. It's okay Mrs. O'Malley – your season of sacrifice is over."

Katie scooped a gooey concoction into three paper cups. "I made it up myself, Mom. Uncle Kevin said to send him the recipe."

"You talked to him!"

Katie nodded. "He said not to wake you up and to call him when you get a chance. He's bringing some kids to New York in the summer and wants us to show them the Statue. How long are we staying here?"

"At least til school is out in June. We can work on what comes next between now and then."

After Cecelia left, Katie plopped on her bed and sat cross-legged, facing Pinch. "The people are nice here, Mom. Check this out!" She motioned three times with her hands.

"I see you've met Feather. Now let me try." She signed *I Love You* back to Katie. "Thanks for the delicious surprise. Your Great-grandma Rose would be proud. Now I have a surprise for you. If we're going to start talking with our hands, let's make Grandma Duffy proud too." She plucked *Lola's Passion* from her suede jacket pocket, tossing it to Katie.

"Cool! But what about Dad?"

"Your father doesn't have a vote."

"What about St. Joan...?"

"He doesn't have a vote."

Katie grinned. *"Way cool!* Can we do our nails after we eat? This menu says that dinner is six o'clock."

Pinch nodded. "Does it say what they're serving tonight?"

"Pest-oh bors—"

"Pesto-borscht Chili?"

"No," Katie giggled, "what's an omelet blanket? Don't they know omelets are for breakfast?"

"I'm sure they do. But sometimes it's good to forget what you know."~

ACKNOWLEGEMENTS

Much thanks goes to Mary Webb – for her writing wisdom and unflinching respect for writers at all stages in their development, for teaching her Three Stage Method of critiques, for her bountiful energy, generous heart and infectious passionate spirit.

To my first readers, Mike Payne and Nancy Fajman – for their early support and sustained interest in the book.

To my "Piatti" proofreaders: Maggie Bafalon, Gail Baumgarten, Sue Beasley, Judy Benedict, Jeanmarie Bergin, Nadine Blanchie, Kay Briggs, Barbara Cappa, Carol Carillo, Barbara Critchlow, Carmen Curtis, Jan deUrioste, Betty Eubanks, Pat Jeans, Vibs Lichtman, Pat Madsen, Marsha McElroy, Mary Ann Osborne, Meg Pauletich, Leslie Pfeifer, Linda Quandt, Marge Reading, Edith Rubanyi, Lise Sage, Jill Starr, Dianne Tinnis, Patty Topkis, Marian Worrall, Sandi Worthington, Bobbi Zane – for their help and heartfelt friendship.

To the Rehoboth Beach Writers Guild – for their nurturing environment, writing classes and social venues. Particular thanks to Maribeth Fisher and Steve Robison for their writing and e-publishing classes, respectively.

To Jane Knaus for her friendship, design and marketing wisdom.

To early readers: Kris Aker, Lyn Burleson, Helen Flood, Jess Gordon, Sharon Werner, Jane Knaus, Joe McCann, Blanche Messick, Libby Owen, Pam Smith, Peggy Smith, Kathryn Teller, Ray Vomero, Trudi Vomero – for their feedback on story and characters.

To Sarah Cypher, whose detailed critque helped clarify my vision, and to Linda Palmer who helped polish the manuscript.

To Damon, Alisha and Ben at *Damonza.com* – for designing a book that exceeded my expectations.

And most importantly to Dan...for his unwavering support and relentless belief in this story.

AUTHOR BIO

Lucille [Ceil] Payne was born and raised in New York City. Her interest in writing was fed in Mary H. Webb's writing workshops, Berkeley, CA, and further fueled at Writers Conferences from New York to Hawaii. While living in Northern California, she was newsletter editor at the local chapter of the National Organization for Women and wrote gender equity articles for the Danville–Alamo Branch of the American Association of University Women. A long–standing advocate against domestic violence, she took volunteer training with Battered Women's Alternatives and actively fundraised for STAND! Against Domestic Violence.

After living on the West Coast for 25 years, Ceil and her husband, Dan, retired back East and live in Southern Delaware. She is a member of the Rehoboth Beach Writer's Guild, and Lancaster Literary Guild. Dancing in Quicksand *is her first novel.*

Proof

Made in the USA
Charleston, SC
12 November 2014